I0594572

SENTINELS OF TZURAC

TERRA MAJOR UNDER THREAT

JAMES RAVEN

All rights reserved. No part of this book may be reproduced or transmitted in any form or by any means, electronic or mechanical, including photocopying, recording, or by any information storage and retrieval system, without permission in writing from the publisher.

First published in 2012 by
CreateSpace Independent
Publishing Platform

2nd edition published in 2013
by James Raven
www.jamesraven.com.au

This edition (3rd) published in 2020
by James Raven
www.jamesraven.com.au

Interior layout by
Publicious Book Publishing
www.publicious.com.au

Prepublication Data Services details available
from the National Library of Australia

ISBN: 978-0-9871243-5-7 (pbk)

Also available in ebook:
ISBN: 978-1-62345-165-3 (ebk)

Also available as an Audio Book.

Copyright © James Raven 2012

All characters and events in this publication are fictitious, any resemblance to real persons, living or dead, or any events past or present are purely coincidental.

To Julie
For her support and
encouragement

PROLOGUE

AFTER two hundred years of bloody war between the civilisations of the planets Tzurac, Kyronis, Armonus, Diunon, Treldar and Urgellan, peace now reigned in the Grekadian Domain. An alliance known as the Federation of Planets had been formed, governed by a Council of Elders comprising two of the most revered and respected representatives from each of the six planets. The alliance provided welcome relief from protracted inter-planetary battles in which the planets had struggled to gain access to and control of an extremely valuable energy resource known as Xytrinium.

A deep-blue crystalline substance, Xytrinium had been formed in some of the planets and stars when they were first created. Subjected initially to extreme heat and then compressed under immense pressure as the planets cooled, Xytrinium had the density of diamond and an atomic weight heavier than gold. The energy trapped within Xytrinium was so potent that one-tenth of an ounce could power a large city for a year, without the potentially devastating side-effects of other energy sources such as uranium and plutonium.

The Tzuracians – a race reasonably tall in stature, with fair hair and blue eyes, and bearing a close physiological resemblance to Terranians (Earthlings) – had been the first to discover the substance and its unique benefits. They had used Xytrinium for more than a hundred years before the inhabitants of the other planets became aware of its existence.

Tzuracian alchemists had developed different methods of processing and using the blue crystal. In medicine, Xytrinium was used as a pharmaceutical with incredible healing properties. When liquefied and blended with different alloys, Xytrinium dramatically increased the strength and resistance of manufactured products by increasing their capacity to withstand heavy impacts and extreme temperatures. It was ideal for the hull structures of spacecraft and for weaponry such as broad blades and daggers. It was also used as a fuel, replacing conventional propulsion methods and allowing space vessels to travel at hyper-speeds over far greater distances than previously imagined.

One of the most significant medical discoveries, the details of which were kept top secret and restricted to only three of the leading Tzuracian alchemists, was the successful assimilation of purified Xytrinium with the Tzuracian DNA structure. The effects were miraculous. It amplified the senses, increasing hearing and magnifying sight, especially night vision; increased bone density and muscular strength; gave rapid healing to injury; developed telepathic abilities; and increased the one-hundred-year life span to an amazing four hundred years.

In closed chambers, the Tzuracian Senate had agreed this particular use of Xytrinium for DNA infusion would not be of benefit to the entire population. They reasoned it might cause chaos and undermine the whole structure of their well-ordered and peaceful society. However, the Senate recognised that, by introducing this substance into the DNA of their Sentinel armies, they could equip their soldiers to provide superior protection for the citizens of Tzurac. And, through successive generations, the Tzuracian armed forces would be replenished with soldiers of exceptional qualities who could protect the planet and its citizens into the future. If both parents were Sentinels, their offspring would inherit Sentinel DNA; if only one were a Sentinel, there was an even chance that their offspring would too. So, the six-thousand-strong army of Sentinels, who lived by a code of honour to serve and protect their citizens and to dedicate themselves to a life of service in the army, accepted this decree and underwent treatment with Xytrinium, turning them into a superior fighting force.

Following the adoption of the Xytrinium–DNA technology the Sentinels were held in very high regard by the citizens of Tzurac.

Their families were well catered for and led very comfortable lives and most Tzuracian children dreamed of becoming a Sentinel. But only those with Sentinel parentage and the necessary DNA structure were given the opportunity to lead a soldier's life. Then, even with their exceptional abilities, Sentinels went through years of military and technical training. It was a life that started at age fifteen and involved disciplined training in martial arts, weaponry and survival techniques, as well as in the values of servitude and obedience.

The Tzuracians were a peaceful race with a strong belief in the preservation of nature and the proliferation of all life. Fearing that more aggressive races might try to use Xytrinium as a weapon of destruction, the Tzuracians had chosen not to share their knowledge of the substance and their secret had lasted for more than a century. But when the other planets finally became aware of Xytrinium and its use in creating powerful armies of Sentinels, a two-hundred-year war had ensued over control of the resource. The Tzuracians were not warmongers but they had been quick to take up arms in defence of Xytrinium.

During the inter-planetary battles over Xytrinium, the secret process of DNA enhancement had been destroyed. An explosion in the Tzuracian city of Kharmar had obliterated the special instruments and equipment used for this process and killed the three alchemists who knew of the complex modification process. It had been a devastating blow for the Tzuracians, preventing new recruits from being DNA-modified and forcing the Tzuracians to rely solely on existing Sentinels to pass on their DNA to their offspring. But it had ensured that the secret of DNA enhancement would not fall into enemy hands.

Through the use of their powerful Sentinel armies the Tzuracians had finally been victorious in ending the war. As a concession to the other planets, and to maintain long-lasting peace, the Tzuracians signed a binding treaty with the tribes of the other planets, agreeing to share some of their Xytrinium as an energy source under specific conditions. Tzurac would only supply Xytrinium in exchange for primary produce from other planets and Tzuracians would share in any Xytrinium resources discovered by other Federation members in the future. Xytrinium was to be used only for the good of the races and never for weapons of war. Tzurac, on behalf of the Federation, would maintain surveillance of planets throughout the universe and prevent any potential disaster if this precious crystalline substance was discovered elsewhere. When in transit, Xytrinium would be escorted under guard by Tzuracian Sentinels to protect the cargo against black market pirates, known as Bladers, who might attempt to steal the Xytrinium and sell it to other renegades. Although peace had been restored between the planets in the Grekadian Domain, rogue elements opposed the call for peace and sought to seek power and control for themselves. The Sentinel escorts needed to be vigilant.

PART 1

UNDER SIEGE

LESS than a day into its scheduled consignment voyage, the craft's thrusters suddenly went into a high-pitched scream and the hull began to vibrate uncontrollably. Within seconds the thrusters cut out and the craft stopped dead in its tracks. It had been hit.

Captain Ahrmon Tyros, the officer in charge of the consignment, was immediately disoriented. He had been standing in the main cabin in the centre of the craft monitoring the visual scanner that displayed the perimeter of the transporter. Suddenly, a renegade Treldar battle ship had materialised from nowhere at the rear of the ship, deactivating its cloaking device just before the transporter was assaulted. There had been no time to avoid the ambush.

The craft attacked by directing a high-powered magnetic reverse-polarising beam on the craft's propulsion system. This over-excited the super-magma energy flow of the transporter, disabling the power source and rendering the defence shields and weaponry useless. The reverse polarisation also interfered with the crew members' nervous systems and the distortion was amplified in the Sentinels' highly sensitised neurological circuitry. It severely affected their motor skills and their highly attuned senses.

To steady himself, Ahrmon clutched onto one of the headrests of the metal seats that were bolted to the floor. He shook his head, trying to shrug off the distortion, but it had no effect. He pressed his communicator on his earpiece and spoke as clearly as he could.

"Lieutenant Dakhar, report!"

At first Ahrmon heard only white noise of interference on the open line. Then a zapping sound, like the noise of a laser pistol, cut into the interference. There was another blast and another again. Then dead silence.

Ahrmon tried his communicator once more. He called to the other members of his unit stationed at different locations throughout the craft. Lieutenant Dakhar was on the starboard deck guarding the armoury with Corporal Pella. Sergeant Caden and Private Morell were in the cargo hold and Private Strax was monitoring the crew's sleeping quarters on the port deck.

"Caden, Morell, Pella, Strax, report in!"

Sergeant Caden responded instantly. Amid the interference on the line, Caden sounded desperate. Even though his speech was slightly slurred his message was clear.

"We're under attack Captain! There appears to be half a dozen or more... they look like Bladers..."

Again the communication was interrupted by static. Then Morell interrupted.

"We're surrounded, but still holding them off. It's hard focussing with this damn dizziness. Can you get here as fast as you can, sir?"

Suddenly the line went dead.

Ahrmon realised that his troops were also affected by the pulsating vibration that was echoing throughout the ship. It was creating weird sensations similar to alcohol intoxication, with blurred vision, loss of balance, slurred speech, and slowed reflexes. Trying with all his mental strength to combat these effects Ahrmon instinctively dived for the intercom panel on the wall and waved his hand across the switch. He could hear an interfering static on the open channel, but he needed answers. Ahrmon yelled into the intercom.

"What, in the name of the Ancients is happening, Captain?"

There was no answer. He spoke again with urgency.

"Come in Captain Gharrok. This is Captain Tyros. Can you hear me?"

There was a faint response above the static.

"Yes, I can just hear you," the pilot responded. "Sorry Captain Tyros. There was no warning. They just appeared from nowhere and opened fire. The shields are inoperative and so is the weaponry. My head is spinning, I..."

"Thank you Captain," Ahrmon interrupted. "Arm yourselves immediately and stay alert! Can you send a distress signal to Tzurac Command?"

"I've already tried, sir, but the attackers are jamming all external communications. I'll keep trying Captain. Over and out!"

On the screen Ahrmon could now see the plunderers, wearing protective headbands to shield them from the distorting frequency, and boarding the craft through the cargo hold with little resistance. These marauders were cold-blooded killers who would stop at nothing to steal their bounty. Ahrmon knew that the pilots, who only had basic weapons training with laser pistols, wouldn't stand a chance against the attackers if they reached flight control. Time was of the essence. The attackers had to be contained in the cargo hold.

Ahrmon tapped his earpiece and started calling his unit.

"Dakhar, Pella, Strax, can you hear me?"

There was no response.

"Answer me!" he called again.

There was static on the line when Dakhar responded.

"Yeah here, Captain."

Then Pella: "Here sir."

Strax responded seconds later.

"I know you're all affected by this pulsating frequency," Ahrmon continued, "but I need all of you in the cargo hold immediately! The Bladers have Caden and Morell pinned down. There are about half a dozen of them. I'll see you there. Out!"

"There's one less to worry about, Captain," Dakhar responded. "I took care of him at the armoury. Over, and out!"

The cargo hold was one deck below Ahrmon. Ahrmon moved as fast as he could but, being disoriented, he occasionally slammed into and bounced off the internal walls. He was experiencing everything in slow motion and his impaired vision made the passageway appear twisted and distorted.

On each side of the passageway hot vaporised super-magma was gushing from ruptured pipes. Ahrmon knew that coming into contact with the super-magma would instantly char his body. His main thought was to reach the cargo hold before his men were annihilated. He knew that the slide pole to the deck below was about one hundred yards ahead. Once there, it was an easy slide to the deck of the cargo hold and then a fifty-yard span to his right to the automatic metal sliding doors that provided the only other access.

He was nearly out of breath by the time he reached the slide pole and he was still shaky on his feet. Ahrmon channelled his thinking: *Focus, concentrate, just like you did in training.* His hands were sweating inside his leather gloves and the annoying pulsating frequency was still interfering with his concentration.

Ahrmon quickly removed his gloves, tucked them into his leather belt and wiped the palms of his hands on the outside of his drill uniform pants. Leaning over the hole in the grilled metal deck floor he glanced down at the deck below. It was a drop of approximately ten yards. Below that was a fifty-yard fall onto the hot, metallic-silver pipes that traversed the craft from the thrusters. Under normal circumstances he could easily leap to the deck below, but now it was a real challenge.

Ahrmon leant back to his upright position while raising his head, wiped his now-beaded brow with the sleeve of his right arm, focused on the slide pole in front of him, licked his dry lips, took a deep breath, then jumped out to the slide pole which was approximately ten feet away. At full stretch he just managed to grab the pole with his left hand and slide rapidly to the metal grid floor below, landing with a heavy thud.

Still standing, he shook his head, refocused, grabbed the pistol handle with his right hand and pulled it from its holster. He knew that in his present condition he would be incapable of wielding his staff sword and that his laser pistol would be the best weapon of choice. Laser fire would be safe in the cargo hold where the Xytrinium was stored in heavily shielded containers and there were no fuel pipes.

Ahrmon staggered as quickly as he could to the metal sliding doors and waved his hand across the electronic switch to the left of the door frame. The doors parted from the centre, retracting instantly to each side. Ahrmon was surprised to see that the shooting had ceased, but he was extremely apprehensive and ready for anything unexpected. His eyes, moving from left to right, quickly scanned across the large expanse.

His apprehension suddenly changed to shock and heartfelt pain when he spied his elite Sentinels scattered across the breadth of the floor, lying motionless with laser wounds to their torsos. All appeared fatally wounded.

Then his eyes fell on Lieutenant Dakhar. Dakhar was standing in the centre of the room and a Blader flanking his left side was aiming a laser pistol directly at his head.

"Glad you could join us, Ahrmon. Don't be shy, come on in."

He was addressed by the grinning Blader in a guttural, Treldarian voice. The Blader continued.

"You can drop the act now Ahrmon, the game is up. Bring him here to me!"

Before Ahrmon could raise his laser pistol, two burly Bladers who had been concealed on either side of the doorway lunged forward, grabbing both his arms whilst tugging the weapon from his hand and the staff from his belt. Ahrmon struggled but he was too weak and still disoriented. Lacking his normally powerful strength he was no match for his captors. He felt like a helpless rag doll as he was dragged roughly towards their leader, who was still pointing his laser pistol at Dakhar.

Ahrmon recognised the insignia of crossed daggers on his attackers' well-worn uniforms. This identified them as a splinter group of guerrilla freedom fighters or Bladers from the planet Treldar – a band of renegades who had opposed the peace treaty from the outset.

During the two-hundred-year war Bladers had worked alongside the Treldarian army. But, after the war, they had deserted and adopted a life of piracy, preying on vulnerable space travellers and defenceless cargo ships, taking no prisoners (except for the women they fancied) and confiscating the bounty for trade or personal use. They would lay in wait along known flight paths in their invisible cloaked ships to ambush unsuspecting foes. The Bladers were a law unto themselves and extremely hard to apprehend, since those with whom they traded gave them sanctuary.

The leader of the Bladers had long, thick, straight black hair, swept back in a pony tail, dark sunken eyes and overgrown stubble around his mouth and chin. The look on his hard, pitted face was one of proud satisfaction, like a predator that had just swallowed its prey. He wore dark-brown, tight-fitting leather pants tucked into suede-leather knee-high boots, with a matching battle jacket over a red shirt. The epaulets on the jacket identified his rank as an officer. Judging by their condition, his leather clothes had seen many battles; they were well worn and creased with stale sweat and faded blood stains.

The Blader leader spoke to Ahrmon as if he was a known acquaintance.

"Hello Ahrmon, remember me? Captain Cronaz. Your plan went well," he said in a friendly voice.

Lieutenant Dakhar gave a puzzled look in Ahrmon's direction.

"Who are you and how do you know my name?" responded Ahrmon, defensively. He had never seen this man before.

Cronaz was unfazed.

"Stop pretending Ahrmon," he said showing signs of mild impatience. "Just give me the code to release the cargo. Don't worry; you'll get your share as we agreed when we sell the stuff."

"Listen!" exclaimed Ahrmon angrily in a louder voice, "I don't know who you think I am, but I have no idea what you're talking about and I'm not about to give a thieving murderous rogue the code to a valuable cargo."

"Okay, Ahrmon, have it your way," replied Cronaz, casually. As he spoke, Cronaz slowly and forcibly placed the barrel of his antique laser pistol onto the temple of Dakhar's head. "But if you do not give me what I ask for, I will have to kill your Lieutenant!"

In that instant, Dakhar lunged at the weapon, trying to wrest it from his captor. The weapon discharged and Lieutenant Dakhar slumped to the floor, lifeless, blood seeping from a nasty gash on his forehead. The Bladers standing beside Ahrmon grabbed him more tightly, one of them thrusting the sharp edge of a dagger against his throat as he struggled to break free to tend to his friend.

"No use worrying about him, he's dead," Cronaz spoke coldly.

Ahrmon was incensed. His wide eyes glared into the eyes of the Blader leader and his pulse was racing. Struggling against the grip of his captors he called out in a rage.

"You murdering swine! I'll see you executed for this and I'll be there personally to give the order."

"They'll have to catch me first," Cronaz retorted. "Besides, they won't be looking for *me;* they'll already have their killer when they board this craft and find the weapon that killed the Lieutenant in *your* hand. We've been told not to kill you, so, adieu Captain Ahrmon Tyros."

Before Ahrmon could respond, he was struck heavily from behind and everything went black.

***

It was a little over six hours after the assault on the transporter when the Tzuracian Security Force or TSF boarded the spacecraft. Their tracking system had shown no movement of the craft for some time and there had been no response to their attempts at communications, prompting them to investigate. Security guards were now busily searching the craft for survivors and any clues that might assist in the capture of the attackers.

"Captain Tyros, can you hear me? Captain?"

Ahrmon was still dazed and not sure where he was or who was calling his name in a raspy voice. He was sitting upright on a metal bench in the cargo hold of the transporter. His head was still pounding from the blow he had received. His vision was partially blurred and he was trying hard to focus on the large, shadowy figure standing in front of him. Suddenly his memory flashed back to the moment before everything had gone black and he lashed out violently at what he thought was the Blader leader.

"Hold onto the Captain and cuff his hands behind his back," ordered the now visible figure to the two Sentinel guards standing either side of Ahrmon.

Ahrmon could now discern that the officer in charge was dressed in the imperial red and black colours of the Security Force and he felt the vice-like grip of Sentinels tighten painfully on his arms as they followed orders. And there, just a few feet away, lying motionless on the floor was the body of his closest friend, Lieutenant Rhyk Dakhar, a pool of congealed blood underneath his head from the fatal laser wound.

One of the security guards approached the officer who Ahrmon now clearly recognised as the Chief of Security, Khane Zarkwin.

"What is it Lieutenant Brantz?" asked Zarkwin.

"Sir, the Xytrinium consignment was removed using an electronic tampering device."

"Thank you officer, record that in your report. That will be all."

The officer saluted rigidly with a right hand snap to his forehead, replaced his arm to his side, reversed on the spot, snapped his heels together and marched off to resume his search of the transporter.

Using his black-leather gloved hand, Zarkwin carefully picked the offending laser pistol up by the barrel. He stood silently, his piercing dark eyes staring directly at Ahrmon for quite some time. Then, with conviction in his gravelly voice, he decreed:

"Captain Tyros, I'm arresting you on suspicion of conspiracy against the Federation and for the murder of Lieutenant Dakhar. Sentinels, take him to the holding cell and secure him."

Ahrmon struggled as the two Sentinels forcibly marched him away and, looking back over his shoulder, he tried desperately to explain to Zarkwin the events that had taken place.

"Listen, Zarkwin, I didn't do this. It was the Bladers. Listen to me!"

His pleas fell on deaf ears.

***

During the voyage back to Tzurac, secured within the boundaries of his small cell by a force field, Ahrmon's mind, now fully recovered from the side-effects of the attack, could not rest. He had mixed feelings of grief and guilt for the loss of his loyal comrades, combined with anger for the senseless murder of his lifelong friend. He paced back and forth, trying to reason with his inner voice.

How did the Blader leader, Cronaz, know his name? How could he prove his innocence when none of his company of escort Sentinels were alive to bear witness to his innocence? Was there an insider trying to frame him and for what purpose? Who gave the orders to leave him alive? Was there some sort of conspiracy? How would he be able to console Lieutenant Dakhar's family now that he had been accused of murdering their son? Would his reputation and his unblemished army record attest to his innocence? Or could the accusations of the highly respected Chief Zarkwin convince the Senate of his guilt?

Ahrmon reflected on his childhood when he and Dakhar had played and fought together like brothers; sparred with their staffs and blades; laughed and cried together; protected each other; kept each other's secrets and talked out their fears until they were old enough and strong enough to become cadets and, eventually, fearless Sentinel warriors. Ahrmon wrestled with his mixed emotions, torn apart by the loss of his friend and filled with anger and hatred for the Blader leader whose face he would never forget.

THE TRIAL

SIX hours later the Security Force craft carrying Ahrmon arrived back at Tzurac, a planet about the same size as Saturn. Tzurac rotated slowly on its axis, giving it longer days and longer nights than Earth, with only two equinoxes. The atmosphere created two seasons: a mild summer and a very cold winter.

The surface of the planet was covered with an abundance of rivers and creeks filled with melting snows in summer from the high-peaked mountains. Waterways ran into huge lakes which supplied fresh drinking water and irrigation for those farming in the rural areas. The Tzuracians were vegetarians and although their physiology required protein, all their essential nutrients could be obtained through an abundant variety of exotic plants. Lush, natural vegetation thrived in the open land between the many satellite-cities dotted all over the surface. Satellite-cities were connected by underground networks of vacuumed tubes, allowing capsules of commuters to travel at very high speed and low noise by means of magnetic propulsion.

Many of the cities that had been devastated during the wars had been either restored to their original design or demolished and rebuilt over the buried remains. Other cities, like Kharmar, which had once been a magnificent science centre for the elite scholars, remained in a deserted ruined state, slowly eroding over time.

The Tzuracians were highly evolved in technology and the arts. They had harnessed the natural elements, working in harmony to preserve the planet's natural resources and life forms. On the surface of the planet there were no visible signs of industry or advanced technology, only simplistic structures. Since the wars, the automated machinery and communications had been housed deep beneath the surface for security from potential enemy attacks.

Tzurac's capital city, Khazor, was one of those cities that had been partially demolished and rebuilt into a citadel. It was the seat of power for the Federation where the Council of Elders resided and where the Tzuracian Senate administered the sacred laws and justice system for its citizens. The city also contained the elite military academy of the Sentinels. High walls surrounded and encompassed the many domed sandstone buildings with their arched windows and doorways. The roads and laneways were paved with smooth cobblestones cut with laser precision and built to resist the wear and tear of the citizens' daily activities as well as the pounding boots of the regular Sentinel patrols.

Ahrmon was placed in one of the high-security cells located within the Senate Chambers in the confines of the citadel. Over the next few days he wrestled with his thoughts and emotions, contemplating his unknown future and reliving his past.

He thought of his parents who had also been Sentinels and how close they had been as a family. Ahrmon had loved his mother and father and he missed them so much, even though fifty years had passed since their death. Ahrmon's parents had also loved him dearly and they had been very proud of his achievements, not only when he was a small boy with an inquisitive mind and an adventurous nature, but also when he graduated as a Sentinel cadet and when he reached the rank of lieutenant, first class.

Ahrmon unclipped a fine gold chain from around his neck to which was attached a thin, small gold alloy medallion about the size of a Tzuracian coin. Holding it in the palm of his hand, he pressed the centre, causing the two sides to spring apart. On the inside of each half was a coloured portrait, one of his young father and the other of his mother, both smiling. Focussed on their portraits, Ahrmon's mind drifted to past memories. He recalled how his father, Zandhar, had first taught him how to ride a horse using gentle words instead of harsh commands to gain the animal's respect. His father's advice echoed in his mind:

"If you treat your horse like a friend, the horse will be your friend for life. If you treat an animal with disrespect they will show the same response towards you. The same principle applies to others that you meet in life."

Ahrmon admired the wisdom of his father and his father's strength of character. Zandhar had a gentle heart that showed compassion, but his mind was very strong and quick. Ahrmon's mother, Velura, was of a similar nature and, together, they had raised Ahrmon in the same vein.

Unfortunately, as an only child, Ahrmon had no brothers and sisters with whom to share his grief when his parents passed away. But he had been consoled by his best friend, Rhyk Dakhar, strengthening the bond between the two men that had started in their childhood. Ahrmon had been accepted by Rhyk's parents almost as a second son and he had shared in most of their family's special occasions and social engagements. But now, following the murder of their son, Rhyk's parents appeared to have alienated him. They had not even come to visit him in his cell to hear what had taken place. He realised they would be mourning the loss of their son and he knew how great their pain would be. *Surely they could not blame him for the death of his closest friend?*

During Ahrmon's time in confinement, soldiers from his regiment paid regular visits, reassuring him of their belief in his innocence and giving him confidence that the charges against him would be dismissed and his position reinstated. But Ahrmon was anxious.

Four days passed before he was eventually brought before the Senate in the Senate Chambers to answer for his accused crimes. Ahrmon was very familiar with the Senate Chambers. He had visited them on several occasions in the past when escorting offenders. But now he was appearing before the Senators as the accused, something that in his worst nightmares he never imagined could happen to him.

As he entered the Chambers, escorted by two Sentinels, Ahrmon was overwhelmed with sounds from the crowd in the public gallery. The Chambers were crowded with citizens mainly from Khazor and with Sentinels that Ahrmon recognised from his own regiment.

Casting his eyes over the noisy throng, Ahrmon immediately recognised Rhyk's mother and father. They were staring coldly at him as if they had already condemned him. Ahrmon's heart sank. Obviously they believed the false charges that had been brought against him. He pleaded desperately to them with his eyes, trying to say sorry for the loss of their much loved son and hoping to convince them of his innocence. They were unmoved.

Ahrmon's gaze was suddenly broken by the Master of the Chambers' shrill voice. To quell the noise in the gallery he had to shout loudly while stamping the stone floor heavily with his gold-coloured metal staff. The sounds reverberated under the huge domed ceiling that covered the great stone hall.

"Silence!" he yelled. "Silence in the Chambers!"

Instantly the crowd quietened and the room hushed. The atmosphere was charged with apprehension.

The five Chamber Senators who had been selected from the legal fraternity of the Senate were seated in a close semi-circle along a bench overlooking the gallery. Their bench was elevated considerably higher than the citizens seated below in the gallery. Sulkhram, who was the most senior of the Senators, raised his hand and motioned to the Sentinels guarding Ahrmon to come forward and place him in front of the Chamber members. The guards instantly responded to the command and then stood at attention either side of Ahrmon, weapons at the ready. Sulkhram began.

"Captain Tyros, you have been charged by Chief Zarkwin with treason and with the murder of Lieutenant Rhyk Dakhar. You have been summoned here to answer to these charges. How do you plead?"

There was dead silence in the Chambers. The air was still and the crowd motionless. Ahrmon felt as if he were in a bad dream from which he might suddenly awaken. But the sudden realisation that his life hung in the balance brought him back to cold reality. He could hardly speak. His throat was parched, his palms sweating, his heart racing and he was still in shock from the whole experience.

Somehow he managed to force the words out in a clearly defiant tone.

"I am innocent, sir!"

The senior Chamber member spoke again.

"Do you have anyone on whom you can call to testify in your defence?"

Ahrmon knew that all his unit members who had been on board the escort transporter, those who could verify his account, had been killed. There was no-one to vouch for his innocence.

"No sir, there is no-one alive from the incident that I can call upon. They were all murdered by the Bladers who stormed our craft. If Chief Zarkwin captures the cut-throat killers I am sure the truth will be revealed."

Ahrmon slowly and carefully related to the Senate members the events that had taken place aboard the ill-fated craft, explaining as clearly as he could his surprise with what had happened.

"Is there anything else you would like to say in your defence, Captain?" asked Sulkhram when Ahrmon had finished.

Ahrmon thought carefully for several moments before he answered.

"Only that I ask for a reprieve, at least for the time it takes me to hunt down and bring to trial the marauders that killed my unit of Sentinels and Lieutenant Dakhar!"

"Thank you Captain," Senator Sulkhram intervened. "Sentinels, please escort Captain Tyros back to his place. I now call upon Chief Zarkwin to make his case."

Zarkwin rose from his seat on the other side of the Chambers and took several paces across the floor. His heavy footsteps on the stone surface echoed loudly in the still silence. Reaching his mark in front of the Senators, he began his address to the gallery. Speaking confidently and deliberately in his raspy voice, he related his account of the events.

"Members of the Senate, five days ago I received a distress signal from the cargo transporter 'Kargnaus 23'. It was carrying a consignment of Xytrinium and Captain Tyros and his company of Sentinels were charged with escorting it. When the Security Forces finally reached and boarded the craft, we found that most of the party on board had been killed and Captain Tyros was lying unconscious on the floor with this laser pistol in his hand."

Zarkwin displayed the offending weapon to the Senators, before continuing.

"Examination of both this weapon and the laser traces found on Lieutenant Dakhar's person revealed a match, and the only skin residues found on the weapon were those of Captain Tyros. I would add that this weapon is an old Treldar military-issue laser pistol that hasn't been in use since the peace treaty was signed. I believe that this pistol actually belongs to Captain Tyros. It was a souvenir from the war, handed down to him by his father, Zandhar. It was missing from

Captain Tyros's weapons display when we searched his quarters two days ago looking for evidence of his conspiracy."

Ahrmon couldn't believe what he was hearing! *How could this weapon have been in the hands of the Blader leader when it was secured in his personal living quarters?* Before he could fathom this, his thoughts were brought back to Zarkwin's continuing account.

"Furthermore, I have here a coded transmission to an unknown spacecraft sent from Khazor two days before Captain Tyros's scheduled transporter flight."

Zarkwin paused momentarily, reached into the side pocket of his jacket and pulled out a small opaque disc which he held up to the Senators.

"Communications captured the transmission, but initially paid little attention to the scrambled signal. However, having now deciphered the coded message, it is clear that the sender possessed Captain Tyros's security access key code and applied ancient Treldarian symbols. These symbols translate to the flight time and path of the Kargnaus 23 transporter. The consignment of Xytrinium that Captain Tyros was escorting had also been forcibly removed using the same techniques that Bladers have used in similar crimes.

"On the basis of my investigations, I believe that Captain Tyros conspired with these plunderers, informing them of the scheduled movements of his spacecraft. I believe that Captain Tyros killed Lieutenant Dakhar to stop him from interfering and reporting the Captain's treachery and that he used this Treldarian laser pistol to make it look like the Bladers were to blame."

The crowd, amazed at Zarkwin's evidence, was becoming restless, muttering and talking amongst themselves. And Ahrmon was feeling defeated. *With this fabricated evidence, it would be hard for the Senate not to believe Zarkwin's testimony.*

Ahrmon was now resigned to the realisation that Zarkwin was trying to frame him for the crime. He knew that Zarkwin had been harbouring a grudge against him for many years. This was obviously part of a premeditated plan for Zarkwin to take his revenge.

***

Zarkwin had once been a Sentinel cadet with Ahrmon and Dakhar. In their youthful days at the Military Academy, the strongly built Zarkwin had been the bully, always threatening and intimidating those smaller than him.

Ahrmon had managed to avoid an encounter with Zarkwin for a couple of years, ignoring Zarkwin's abusive verbal attacks and school-yard tactics. However, one day in the weapons hall, while practising their sword techniques, Zarkwin had provoked Ahrmon into a fight in the presence of all the other students. The Master-at-Arms had momentarily left the hall, allowing Zarkwin to make his move.

"Hey Tyros, let's see how good you really are against a live opponent, instead of practising on a defenceless wooden dummy and a hologram," Zarkwin called, grinning arrogantly.

Thinking that Zarkwin needed to be taught a lesson in humility in front of the whole class, Ahrmon had retaliated confidently.

"Alright Zarkwin, I accept your challenge."

Then, Ahrmon had turned to his friend, Rhyk Dakhar, as the referee.

"Rhyk, would you be the referee and scorer?"

The other thirty or so cadets had suddenly stopped what they were doing and taken their vantage points. Moving quickly, and with little disturbance in the now electric atmosphere, they had surrounded the two contenders in a wide circle. This was the first time one of the cadets had stood their ground against Zarkwin and there was an air of anticipation amongst the group.

"Yes, of course Ahrmon," said Rhyk. "Cadets, take your places."

The opponents stood facing each other, their eyes fixed in a glazed stare. Zarkwin grinned over-confidently, while Ahrmon had a more reserved expression. Then, unexpectedly, Zarkwin did something which was strictly prohibited in fencing class. He wrenched the protective cover from his razor-sharp, double-edged blade. The crowd drew breath and the tension was obvious: Zarkwin was intending to inflict serious damage. Ahrmon had no option. He followed Zarkwin's lead and pulled the protective cover from his own blade.

Zarkwin cut the air rapidly with sweeping blows in the shape of an 'X' and flicked his sword to the raised starting position at chest height between him and Ahrmon, his left arm resting with his hand on his hip in the classical stance to commence play. Ahrmon slowly raised his sword to cross Zarkwin's and placed his left hand on the back of his lower torso. Zarkwin and Ahrmon stood motionless, waiting for the signal.

"Commence!" shouted Rhyk.

Zarkwin instantly made the first thrust, straight towards Ahrmon's head. But Ahrmon was too quick and counter-blocked, stepping back and nicking Zarkwin's glove holding the handle of his sword.

Zarkwin slashed at the right side of Ahrmon's body. Again Ahrmon deflected the blade, spun around to his left and sliced across the back of Zarkwin's fencing jacket. Ahrmon was careful not to draw blood, just marking Zarkwin's protective uniform to score points. The overconfident smirk on Zarkwin's face changed to anger.

"Two points to Ahrmon," called the adjudicator. "Cadets, please take your starting positions again."

Zarkwin snapped back in a raised, irritated voice.

"We don't need to start again! I just need to finish this right now."

With that, Zarkwin lunged at Ahrmon's chest in a death strike. But Ahrmon was too fast, stepping to the right and at the same time deflecting the thrusting blade by sweeping his sword in a downward strike and slicing through two of the buckles on the side of Zarkwin's jacket. Realising that Zarkwin had turned this test of skill into a life or death duel, Ahrmon withdrew his blade to his right side and stood upright, appealing to his opponent.

"It's time to end this fight before one of us is badly injured. We can continue at another time, under supervision, in a more controlled manner. Thank you for the challenge Zarkwin, I look forward to the next bout."

But Zarkwin ignored the call, determined to humiliate Ahrmon and show the class that he was the better swordsman.

"You're dead, Tyros!" Zarkwin suddenly yelled out, charging at Ahrmon like a madman, weaving his sword rapidly in circular sweeps from side to side. The power and speed behind these movements created a whistling sound as Zarkwin's sword cut through the air.

Ahrmon blocked Zarkwin's thrusting blade defensively and, with a deliberate, swift, and accurate strike, completely severed Zarkwin's right hand. Zarkwin's sword fell to the floor with his gloved hand still clenching the hilt. As blood poured from his dismembered limb, Zarkwin screamed out in agony and collapsed to his knees in pain, the cadets stunned by the scene.

Turning his head towards Ahrmon with hate etched in his face, Zarkwin cried out in a chilling voice.

"You'll regret this, Tyros! One day I will have my revenge. This is not finished."

One of the cadets rushed to Zarkwin with a towel, trying to wrap his arm where it had been severed, but Zarkwin pushed the cadet aside and stormed out of the hall publicly humiliated, and physically and psychologically scarred for life. Ahrmon stood motionless without uttering a word as the cadets cheered for Ahrmon's victory over the bully they all despised.

The injury had ended Zarkwin's future as a Sentinel, relegating him to service in the less elite ranks of the Security Force. Over time, Zarkwin had been promoted to the rank of chief, but he still harboured deep hatred for Ahrmon and was now seizing the opportunity to avenge him. The words of revenge that Zarkwin had threatened on the day of the ill-fated fencing match reverberated in Ahrmon's memory.

***

Ahrmon suddenly became aware of his current surroundings and could not contain himself.

"That's a lie Zarkwin! You've fabricated the whole thing!" he yelled.

The two Sentinels guarding Ahrmon restrained him and the Master of the Chambers stamped his metal rod on the floor several times, calling loudly to the now excited noisy crowd in the gallery.

"Quiet down! And you, Captain Tyros, another outburst like that and you will be escorted back to your cell."

The gallery crowd fell silent while Senator Sulkhram directed his next question to Chief Zarkwin.

"The evidence that you have produced so far appears to be valid, but we only have *your* word for this account of events and *your* assumptions of the conspiracy. Chief Zarkwin, is there anyone who can substantiate this?"

Zarkwin looked confidently at the Senator with a wry smile on his face and responded in a loud and clear voice.

"I would like to call on Private Morell as a witness."

Ahrmon gasped. His mind flooded with questions. *Surely Morell had died in the attack? If Morell was actually alive, why would Zarkwin call him as a witness for his prosecution?* Gasps of disbelief also came from the gallery.

"Silence!" called the Master of the Chambers once more and the crowd immediately fell quiet.

The sound of slow footsteps echoed from the back of the Chambers, drawing closer with each step to where Chief Zarkwin was standing. Ahrmon immediately recognised Morell in spite of a large blue bandage wrapped around his head. Morell stood beside Zarkwin and gave a respectful Sentinel salute to the Senate. He then about-faced and stood silent while Zarkwin addressed the Senate once more.

"Members, as you can see Private Morell was badly injured, but survived the attack. Just before he passed out he heard the conversation between the Blader leader and Captain Tyros. If you please Private Morell, could you tell the Senate members exactly what you overheard?"

"Yes sir," said Morell. "The words of the Blader leader will remain in my head forever because I felt at that time that our Captain had betrayed us. The Blader leader sounded quite friendly when he said, 'Hello Ahrmon, remember me, Captain Cronaz. Your plan went well.' Then something inaudible was said by Captain Tyros. I recognised his voice although his response was muffled. Then the Blader leader spoke again saying, 'Don't worry, you'll get your share as we agreed, when we sell the stuff.' Then everything went black."

Zarkwin cut in before the senior Senate member could speak.

"Sirs, I believe that Lieutenant Rhyk Dakhar, on hearing the Blader leader's words, tried to prevent Captain Tyros from joining forces with the rebels. In the ensuing struggle I believe that Captain Tyros was struck on the head by Lieutenant Dakhar but, just before he fell unconscious, Tyros was able to shoot Lieutenant Dakhar with the Treldar pistol he had smuggled on board. That way, the blame could be placed on the Bladers after they had left the cargo transporter. I also think that the rebels then decided to double-cross Captain Tyros rather than share their bounty. The only skin residues found on the laser pistol belonged to Captain Ahrmon Tyros, as you can see in the evidence folder before you."

Sulkhram spoke abruptly.

"Thank you Chief Zarkwin and Private Morell. I think we have heard enough. Please return to your places."

Sulkhram then cleared his voice before addressing the gallery.

"Citizens, we have heard the testimonies of the accused, the accuser and the witness. The Senators will now retire for one hour from the Chambers to make a decision based on these testimonies and the supporting evidence. Sentinels, please escort the accused back to his security cell — we will reconvene in one hour." Both Sentinels saluted before marching Ahrmon away and the crowd erupted, some waving their hands angrily towards Ahrmon, and others gesturing in disbelief.

Ahrmon was overcome with anger mixed with fear. He replayed in his mind the events that had just taken place in the Chambers. *How could Morell testify in favour of Zarkwin's accusations?* Ahrmon felt thankful that the Sentinel had survived the ordeal, but he couldn't help thinking that his case would have been stronger had Morell not lived. In relating only part of the conversation with the Blader leader, Morell had effectively sealed Ahrmon's fate.

Fear was now starting to take over and a thousand memories were starting to flood Ahrmon's mind. *As a Sentinel at the age of only one-hundred-and-thirty years, he was too young to die.* Ahrmon wished he had told the Senators about his impeccable service record, a factor that might have swayed their decision in his favour.

The hour in his cell seemed to be the longest hour he had ever experienced in his entire life. Then he heard the sound of the force field shut down and the Sentinel guards reappear to escort him back to the Chambers. As Ahrmon entered the Chambers, the Master of the Chambers thumped his staff on the floor and called out "Silence!" to the unsettled crowd that had now returned to the gallery.

The senior Senate member commanded the Sentinels to bring Ahrmon forward to face the Senate and the gallery. A deathly silence hung over the Chambers as the crowd waited in anticipation for the verdict to be announced. Ahrmon's heart was racing, pulsating loudly in his throat, his anxiety making it hard for him to breathe. Sulkhram spoke in a slow, articulate voice.

"Citizens, the Senate has reached its decision concerning the charges that Captain Tyros conspired against the Federation and murdered Lieutenant Rhyk Dakhar. After reviewing the testimonies, the evidence and the statement by the witness, the Senate has found Captain Ahrmon Tyros *guilty* of these crimes. In accordance with our system of justice, Captain Tyros is sentenced to death. He will be executed in two days' time."

There was an immediate roar from the citizens who were now standing on their feet in the gallery. Some cheered in support of the verdict and others yelled curses against the decision. Once more, the Master of the Chambers pounded his metal rod on the floor.

"Silence! Contain yourselves!" he called.

While the noisy throng in the gallery composed themselves, Ahrmon struggled to recover from the shock. The blood had drained from his face and his eyes had turned into an icy stare. He could feel his heart working under stress and his chest tightening. He was perspiring all over his now-trembling body. He had never experienced these sensations before, not even in battle facing his enemies.

"Captain Tyros, do you have anything to say, before the guards escort you back to the security cell?" enquired Senator Sulkhram in a condescending manner.

Ahrmon was trying to find his voice and, after what seemed like a long pause, he finally regained his senses. He picked up a small vessel of water from the bench at the side of him, gulped several mouthfuls, and replaced it. In accepting his fate, his mind was now calmed and his pulse had almost returned to normal. Ahrmon proceeded to speak slowly and precisely.

"Sirs, you have made a gross error in your judgement at the expense of an innocent life. Your verdict has been reached with very little evidence and speculation based on fabrication and lies. A thorough investigation has not even been undertaken to identify who sent the message on the disc to inform the Bladers of our scheduled consignment and how they knew my given name. There are others who have access to security codes for communications and to the living quarters of the Sentinels. I have been a dedicated, loyal soldier

31

who has always upheld the Code of the Sentinels with great respect for the Federation and our justice system. I'm extremely disappointed in your lack of compassion."

With a searching glance towards Rhyk's parents, he continued.

"Lieutenant Dakhar and I were the closest of friends for all of our lives, both in the Service, and outside the Service. Without question, we would have given our own life to save each other. When you capture the rebel leader and his band of merciless cut-throats, you will learn the truth of what really happened. Then, you will all have on your conscience, for the rest of your lives, the guilt and burden of taking an innocent life."

"Enough, Captain Tyros!" said the senior Senator, with authority. "You have disgraced your Regiment and dishonoured the Code of the Sentinels. You have murdered one of your own men and left his family in mourning. You have also brought shame to your family name. You are not fit to wear that uniform. For this, you will pay the ultimate price. Sentinels, take the prisoner to his cell. Citizens of Tzurac, the Senate hearing is now adjourned."

There was a surge from the crowd in the gallery as the Senate filed out of the Chambers. Those who believed Ahrmon was innocent were calling out, angrily. Others were cheering. Lieutenant Dakhar's parents were nodding quietly in agreement with the sentence. And there was one person standing apart from the crowd, hands on his hips, gloating with a wry smile on his face; Chief Khane Zarkwin.

PROVIDENCE

ALONE in his cell on the first night awaiting his execution, Ahrmon tried to console himself and savour his final moments of life, even though he felt sick to his stomach. As a Sentinel he was prepared for death. But this was not going to be a proud warrior's death, dying in a battle for glory; it was going to be a shameful and wrongful execution.

Reflecting on his life, his only regret was that he had not married and fathered a son to continue in the service as a Sentinel. He had always imagined that one day he would enjoy the feeling of bonding with a life he had helped to create, playing with and instructing his son while his son grew and developed. But now it seemed that he had been too dedicated with his career and with his efforts to better the quality of life for the inhabitants of Tzurac, so they could live without fear in a safe world. The one thing he could feel good about was that he would be joining his parents as well as his best friend in the afterlife.

Ahrmon's thoughts were abruptly interrupted by the sounds of several loud blasts outside his security cell. He saw the guard turn to face the entrance and brace himself by taking a rigid defensive stance.

"Identify yourself!" the guard demanded.

But before he could be answered, a beam of red light struck the guard on the chest. The guard reeled back several paces and slumped to the ground, unconscious. Then two familiar faces materialized at the cell barrier. It was Staff Sergeant Gadden and Lance Corporal Vardez, loyal Sentinels from Ahrmon's regiment. Ahrmon sighed with relief.

The Sergeant was a tall, burly character, ruddy-faced with a contoured beard and moustache that matched his thick, short-cropped fair hair. The Lance Corporal was quite a contrast, rather short in comparison to the Sergeant, with gaunt features and a pale complexion. Both were veterans of the wars and had fought several battles in Ahrmon's regiment. They respected and trusted their leader, knowing that it wasn't in his character to do the things of which he'd been accused. They were determined not to let their Captain be executed for someone else's crimes.

"What are you doing?" exclaimed Ahrmon, half glad to see them and half surprised at their dramatic entrance. "He's not dead is he, Sergeant?"

"No Captain, only stunned him," replied the Sergeant in his distinctive deep Diunon voice. "No time to lose, sir. We've got to get you out of here before he comes to."

By now the Sergeant had disabled the force field and began handing items to Ahrmon.

"Take your staff and robe sir, and conceal your staff beneath your robe. Just let me do the talking if we run into anyone." The staff was easily concealed as a Sentinel's staff could be collapsed into one third its original size.

"Wait up Sergeant!" said Ahrmon. "There's nowhere to run, and this citadel is heavily fortified with security guards stationed everywhere. We'll be caught for sure before we even reach the main entrance to the city wall. Besides, I don't want any harm to come to you two. You could both be thrown into confinement and dishonourably discharged for assisting in the escape of a condemned prisoner. I order you, Sergeant, right now to desist in this mad caper!"

The Sergeant was not to be deterred.

"Begging your pardon sir, and sorry to go against your orders, but we've made up our minds, and there's no turning back. You can dishonourably discharge us later sir for disobeying orders. We have a plan. Just follow us, and we'll all get out of here safely."

It was pointless arguing and wasting valuable time. Ahrmon reasoned that he had nothing to lose, so he followed their lead without another word.

Within seconds they were pacing quickly along the passageway.

Ahrmon noticed that the security surveillance cameras on the walls and ceiling had been blasted out of commission and he felt proud that his comrades had prepared so well for the escape.

But when they reached a small metal plaque on the passage wall they instantly froze, glancing apprehensively at each other. They could hear the cries of guards on the warpath. The escape attempt had obviously been discovered and there was commotion outside the security cells.

Frantically, Sergeant Gadden began pressing in a sequence the five ancient symbols engraved on the plaque until suddenly a panel on the wall started to slide sideways, leaving an opening wide enough for the trio to enter. No sooner had they passed through the opening than the sliding panel slammed shut behind them. It was pitch black and completely silent.

"Don't make any noises," whispered Gadden, while reaching for the staff hanging on the side of his belt. He released his staff from its holster and pressed a button at one end activating a strong blue glow from the tip of the staff. He signalled the others to do likewise.

"Follow me and watch your step," the Sergeant whispered again.

In the blue light, they weaved their way through hallways of huge sculptured stone pillars engraved with carved ancient symbols, pillars that had once supported the ruins of a past civilisation. Ahrmon marvelled at what he saw. He had no knowledge of these catacombs and was overwhelmed.

"How did you know about these ruins Sergeant?" Ahrmon asked, curious to learn more.

The Sergeant was obviously proud to have inside knowledge.

"My great grandfather was an architectural engineer and he discovered the blueprints in the library archives when they were rebuilding the citadel. He kept them a closely guarded family secret so that he could come here and study the ancient writings. That's how I knew about the secret passage and the code to open the hidden sliding door."

After walking at a fast pace for about twenty minutes, the trio reached the tunnel's exit, which opened into a small cave in a rocky outcrop concealed by dense forest. It was nightfall and the three moons of Tzurac shone so brightly in the clear star-studded heavens that they illuminated the countryside as if it was half daylight. There was a chill in the air, but the regimental robe Ahrmon was wearing served one of its many purposes, insulating him against the cold.

"Well, so far so good," came a half-excited high-pitched voice from behind Ahrmon. It was the first time the Lance Corporal had spoken since their escape.

"We're not there yet, Corporal," said Gadden.

"No Sarge," Vardez acknowledged.

"Where are we going Sergeant?" enquired Ahrmon.

"Well Captain, the spacecraft hangars are just over the other side of that hill. One of your old loyal cadet pilots, now in the position of flight commander in charge of Operations, has arranged for a deep-space fighter to be unsecured and primed for a night test flight. It should be just on the outskirts of the airfield. It's equipped with provisions for six months and all the navigation charts you'll need to find one of the habitable planets that the Federation has not yet incorporated into their treaty of alliance," said the Sergeant. "This way, you'll have a long life of freedom to enjoy. Unfortunately sir, we'll not be joining you as we have our families to take care of."

Ahrmon pondered the implications.

"I appreciate what you've both done for me in risking your lives and your careers, but I fear for your safety in the event you are caught."

"Don't worry about that Captain," the Corporal's high voice resounded. "No-one has seen us and we both have solid alibis."

The Sergeant motioned them to follow as if leading them into battle.

"Come on you lot, we can't stand here wasting precious time! And keep the noise down in case of patrols lurking about."

Arriving at the airfield, Ahrmon was surprised at how well the craft was camouflaged, especially considering its size. It was hard to distinguish the black fighter against the backdrop of the tall silhouetted trees. Ahrmon recognised this model of craft as he had flown ships of this class when he was a cadet officer, training at the Academy. To attain his commissioned rank of Captain he had to master the piloting of various types of craft. This model was a Class Ten Destroyer, fully-armed and designed for deep space flight at hyper-speed and for rapid assaults. It could mute the sound of its thrusters when needed to avoid detection and change colours like a chameleon to blend into the environment. It was a perfect escape vessel.

"Best climb aboard Captain, as time is of the utmost and may the Ancient spirits protect you for a long and peaceful life."

There was sadness in the Sergeant's voice, knowing he may never see his great Captain again. And Lance Corporal Vardez echoed the sentiment.

"That goes double for me sir."

"Thank you both for my life and for the honourable service you have given me over the years," Ahrmon replied with deep sincerity. "I'll never again meet such fine and loyal soldiers. I'll always wear my Sentinel's pledge ring with honour as a reminder of the great comradeship we have formed. Farewell, my friends."

With a respectful Sentinel's salute, Ahrmon disappeared into the craft and its hatch closed behind him. Once inside, he paused momentarily, realising that he was about to leave Tzurac and his close companions behind forever. But he had no choice and no time to lose – he had to attend to the task at hand.

Ahrmon identified the provisions mentioned by Sergeant Gadden and the navigational charts on the electronic tracking monitor. He checked and found a spare regimental robe and staff and a laser pistol in the storage compartment. Ahrmon activated the mute mode then powered up the thrusters. The craft suddenly came to life. It rose off the ground, hovered temporarily, and then at lightning speed silently disappeared into the night sky.

At first Ahrmon was unsure which course to plot. He thought the best strategy to avoid detection was to head for an area least frequented by the Federation. The Sideros-Hudor system on the far side of the universe had several habitable planets that could sustain his life form and the provisions would definitely last the journey. So he set the co-ordinates on the tracking monitor for planet Nebularis and the navigation panel to 'auto'.

Next Ahrmon interrogated the computer to gain a current update on the planet. The information flashed onto the blue fluorescent screen.

» PLANET NEBULARIS IN THE SIDEROS-HUDOR SYSTEM
  - CURRENT STATUS
» SIMILAR ATMOSPHERIC CONDITIONS TO TZURAC
» INHABITED BY LARGE EXTREMELY DANGEROUS CARNIVOROUS
  ANIMAL LIFE FORMS
» LUSH VEGETATION, FRESH WATER, SUPPORTS ECOSYSTEM
  OF CARBON PLANTS AND MICRO - ORGANISMS
» DISTANCE 200 LIGHT YEARS
» EST. TIME TO REACH TARGET AT HYPER SPEED - 2 MONTHS

Ahrmon also checked the energy graphics on the screen to confirm that he had an adequate supply. The last control that required deactivating was the tracking device, operated by a switch that was hidden discreetly underneath the control panel. Ahrmon set the switch to 'off'. This would give him the advantage, preventing the Security Forces detecting his flight path. Now tracking would only reactivate if his ship was attacked or failed to land safely.

There were two systems used for deep space travel. One method was to place the craft in 'sleep mode' and the pilot in a hibernation capsule that suspended all body functions for the duration of the trip. This conserved energy resources for extended space/time travel. The alternative was to remain in the normal 'live' system and maintain usual daily activities. Ahrmon decided that he needed to be on guard for any unexpected activity by Bladers or for Federation scouting patrols. He needed to remain on full alert.

As his flight progressed, Ahrmon kept active, maintaining his martial art skills honed with the aid of programmed holograms for unarmed combat, weaponry, laser target practice and exercise forms with the staff and blade. He needed to be prepared for any unexpected events during the long voyage as well as for the unexpected on Nebularis.

The Sentinel staff was a unique piece of equipment. When contracted to the length of approximately eighteen inches, it could be used as a short-stick defence and attack weapon for close hand-to-hand combat with an opponent. When extended to the length of a five-foot staff, it could be used against other weapons such as lances, spears or swords. Further, with a press of a concealed switch on top of the staff it could also unfold from the hilt down the centre into a double-edged, razor-sharp blade.

The metal blade, like the rest of the staff material, was tempered using Xytrinium and could not be broken unless struck with extreme force at an acute angle by another Xytrinium blade. When a Sentinel was wielding this weapon, an unusual experience occurred. The sword would resonate and harmonise with the Sentinel's whole body due to the Xytrinium contained within both the Sentinel's DNA and the staff. To a Sentinel, the weapon felt very light but to anyone else trying to use it, the sword felt like a lead weight making it sluggish and difficult to manoeuvre.

The Sentinel's regimental robe was also unique. It looked like woven velvet and was midnight-blue in colour with a maroon lining. Sentinels used it as a wearable lightweight shield. Each Sentinel's robe had their personal insignias of six encircled symbols woven with gold thread into the sleeve. The symbols were the same as those engraved on the Sentinel's pledge ring worn on their index finger. These symbols represented the insignia of the ancient clans to whom the Sentinel's family belonged and contained the date of their pledged allegiance to the service as well as their own given names.

Ahrmon reconciled himself to the fact that he would be unable to wear his uniform with pride amongst the Tzuracians again. But while on this mission piloting a Federation craft, Ahrmon decided to maintain his Sentinel appearance in case he encountered a Federation patrol that was unaware of his fugitive status. He could attempt to bluff his way through these encounters, but if that failed, his craft was well equipped to fend off an attack.

The two-month voyage in deep space was relatively uneventful, although Ahrmon managed to avoid a close encounter with a meteor shower and the distant passing of a Federation patrol craft. The voyage allowed him time to reflect on the life that he had left behind. At various times he thought of his regiment of loyal soldiers who had become close companions, remembering how he had fought with them and laughed with them. Ahrmon's thoughts also turned to his close friend Rhyk, to Rhyk's parents and to his own mother and father.

Ahrmon's father, Zandhar, had been the epitome of a true Sentinel. Reaching the rank of General he was an exceptional strategist and a strong leader, commanding the respect of all who served under him. But Ahrmon knew the other side of this military officer. The mind skills Ahrmon had learnt from his father were reinforced through mind-linking and daily meditation in which thoughts were exchanged without the need of spoken words, forming a strong bond between father and son. These were the moments that Ahrmon missed so much after his father had reached his four-hundred-year lifespan. From time to time, Ahrmon could still hear his father talking to him through his mind, reassuring him that he was there in spirit watching over him.

The voyage also provided a good opportunity for Ahrmon to contemplate what he would do with the new life that had been thrust upon him. *Would he maintain his regimented life as a Sentinel and serve the Federation by hunting down the marauders and bringing them back to Tzurac to confirm his innocence? To undertake that mission he would need to contact his soldiers back at Tzurac and that may undo the freedom that he had been so lucky to acquire. Or would he just put all that behind him and find peace within while living the rest of his life in obscurity?* Ahrmon could not decide. He would wait until he reached Nebularis before making a final decision.

***

One day, while deep in thought, Ahrmon was informed by the craft's navigator that he was within orbit range of Nebularis. On the computer screen Nebularis appeared as a phosphorescent green planet with two red moons. Ahrmon slowed the craft to cruising speed, activating the outer force field just in case of 'unfriendlies' lurking near the planet. A safe place was needed to land his vessel but he had heard that some of these uninhabited planets were used as havens for hunted fugitives and pirates trading in stolen merchandise.

Ahrmon was interrogating the planet's surface contours on the computer to configure the trajectory of the craft when suddenly, without warning, he was thrown to the floor by a massive impact battering his vessel.

"What in the name of the Ancients was that?" he yelled instinctively.

He quickly jumped to his feet, scrambled to the pilot's seat and scanned the peripherals of the craft. There appeared to be no damage as the craft's force field had already been activated. But tailing him, at a distance of some five hundred yards, he recognised a spacecraft similar to the Blader craft that had attacked the fateful Xytrinium transporter, Kargnaus 23. The Destroyer's sensors had not detected the craft which had obviously been laying in wait using its cloaking device.

Ahrmon's mind was racing and his adrenalin rushing. As a counter-measure he immediately launched several flares in the direction of the attacking alien craft, causing a huge blinding explosion. While creating this distraction, he hit the camouflage switch and set the thrusters on full.

Swerving instantly to the right, he manoeuvred his Destroyer behind the Blader's ship. Within a split second, he set the craft's laser sights on the other ship's power source and fired several laser rounds. A direct hit immediately disabled the Blader's ship sending it crashing downwards in a smoking spiral under the gravitational pull of the planet beneath. The rogue craft's pilots wouldn't have known what hit them.

Relieved, but still shaking from the surprise attack, Ahrmon reactivated the auto pilot. Reducing the power of the thrusters, he began the Destroyer's slow, controlled descent to Nebularis.

NEBULARIS

AHRMON approached the planet's surface apprehensively. Fortunately there were no more hostile spacecraft and he was able to land the vessel safely on the grassy plains of a wide valley shadowed by tall, tree-covered mountains. He activated the craft's apparatus to sample the atmosphere of the planet and then the navigation equipment to survey the surface and locate the Bladers' crashed vessel. Ahrmon was anxious to find out if there were survivors and whether there was a remote possibility that the Blader leader responsible for Dakhar's death was on board.

The heat source of the Bladers' craft was about five hundred yards away in a north-westerly direction. Ahrmon switched the craft's camouflage mode to 'auto' and shut down the main power. He donned his robe, picked up his staff and the laser pistol from the storage compartment, as well as a water capsule, and opened the craft's side hatch to disembark.

Just as he stepped out of the craft, an unexpected laser beam flashed close to the left side of his face. It was immediately followed by another flash above his head. Instinctively, Ahrmon dived from the craft, hitting the ground hard and rolling behind a large outcrop of rocks nearby.

From the angle of the laser blasts he pin-pointed the source coming from several large trees about one hundred yards away. Ahrmon reached on his belt for the miniature remote-control device that operated the instruments on the pilot console. He guided the craft's lasers to target the trees and fired two blasts that partially ignited the foliage. This provided the distraction he needed to work his way around through the cover of the forest trees to where his attacker was located. He arrived within minutes, but to his surprise, there was no sign of anyone.

Then, peering back in the direction of his craft, Ahrmon spotted a Blader limping hurriedly towards the hatch which Ahrmon had inadvertently left open as he dived to escape the laser blasts. Ahrmon realised immediately that if the Blader managed to enter the craft he could steal it, leaving Ahrmon stranded on the planet. Or the Blader, unfamiliar with the controls, could accidentally destroy the craft. Either way, the Blader had to be stopped.

Realising that he was too far out of range for the craft's remote control to respond, Ahrmon bolted at full speed to the craft, reaching the open hatch just as the Blader disappeared into the hull.

With his short-staff in hand, he cautiously stepped inside. As he did so, a downward thrusting sword blade slashed past the left side of his head. Ahrmon's quick reflexes helped him narrowly avoid contact by diving forward into the hull and simultaneously deflecting the blade with his short-staff. He activated his double-edged blade just in time to counter another strike aimed at the right side of his torso.

Spinning around with his sword defensively clasped in both hands, Ahrmon faced his attacker directly. The Blader was wielding a barbed wide-bladed sword. His singed clothing was tattered from the laser blast, his right leg bleeding and his face partially blackened and bloodied from several abrasions. Although the Blader was weakened from his wounds, he was fighting wildly in a desperate struggle to survive.

The Blader charged at Ahrmon, aiming his blade at Ahrmon's chest, but Ahrmon was more than his match. Without hesitation, Ahrmon countered by stepping to one side. The blade just missed Ahrmon, puncturing one of the craft's main energy transference lines. The rapidly escaping hot super-magma fluid set off a chain reaction through the hull of the craft, igniting everything on contact.

In a split second, acting on instinct alone, Ahrmon dived out through the hatch and rolled behind the same clump of rocks that he had previously used for protection, this time shielding himself with his robe. Seconds later, there was a deafening explosion from the

Destroyer, showering metal fragments in all directions. Luckily, the rock formation Ahrmon had crouched behind, together with his robe, insulated him from the repercussions of the huge radiated blast and the extreme heat from the fireball which followed. Ahrmon remained sheltered safely in that position until all the shrapnel and debris from the exploding craft had settled and the flames had died down.

Partially buried in rocks, dirt and fragments of the wreckage, Ahrmon finally emerged from his sanctuary, shaking off the debris. Turning around, the picture before him was devastating. The Class Ten Destroyer had been reduced to nothing more than a burnt-out hull. It was hardly recognisable. Inside the shell, Ahrmon could just make out the smoking charred remains of his attacker and a scorched sleeve of his own spare robe with the remaining ancient gold insignias still partly visible. Not only had he missed the opportunity to question his attacker about where he was from and the whereabouts of his Blader leader, but also he was now without an escape craft.

Ahrmon suddenly realised that the explosion would have activated the Destroyer's tracking device, alerting the Communications Control Centre of the exact location of the incident. The Federation would soon come looking for their craft, accompanied by the Security Forces, perhaps led by Chief Zarkwin. A Federation patrol already cruising in this sector could quickly be diverted to Nebularis.

Anxious at first, Ahrmon then began to wonder whether this could provide an opportunity for him. *Might a Federation search party that discovered the wreckage falsely conclude that the cremated remains in the craft were his? After all, the remnants of his Sentinel regimental robe were right near the body and the intensity of the magma blast would have eliminated any DNA evidence. If the Federation accepted that the blast that destroyed the spacecraft had also killed their fugitive, this disaster might fool them into ceasing their efforts to hunt him down.*

Ahrmon removed the medallion from his neck, took one final close look at his parents' images, and then tossed the medallion near the sleeve remnant in the burnt-out hull. *The metallic insignias in the robe together with the medallion might convince the Federation of his death.*

Ahrmon had planned to take refuge on Nebularis. But now he needed to flee to a new haven, and very soon, just in case the Federation patrol began scanning the planet for life forms. However, until he could find a craft in which to escape he would need a secure hiding place, perhaps in a cave where the rock formation would shield his body heat signature.

The atmosphere was saturated in grey smoke partially blotting out the afternoon sun. In a few hours it would be dark and Ahrmon needed somewhere to set up a temporary camp and find some food. He decided to investigate the crash site of the Bladers' ship to see if there were any more survivors and to assess the condition of their craft. *Perhaps there might be food supplies and other salvageable items if the ship was still intact?*

The last reading Ahrmon had taken indicated that the wreck was due north from the spot where his own craft had landed. On his remote control device there was a guidance locater which he used to take his bearings.

After trekking for a short time through the mountainous terrain covered with lush vegetation of tall trees and thick underbrush, Ahrmon reached the Bladers' crash site. The thick scrub had cushioned the impact, leaving the ship intact but badly battered. The power thrusters were burnt out from the lasers fired from Ahrmon's craft. There was no sign of movement on board the wreckage, but Ahrmon was not convinced that his attacker was the only survivor.

Ahrmon decided to risk a closer inspection and cautiously approached the craft with all his senses heightened, anticipating the unexpected. The vessel was on its side and on the underside a hatch was open. He peered inside the hatch, half expecting a similar attack like the one he had just encountered. There was none. And inside he could see five bodies in twisted positions all dressed in the vivid, recognisable colours of Blader attire.

Ahrmon entered the vessel and carefully examined the bodies for any signs of life. They were all dead from the impact of the crash. So, Ahrmon looked around for any navigational aids that might give him a clue about where they had travelled from, where they were headed and why they were hovering around this planet.

Scattered around the flight console were several opaque memory rods which Ahrmon thought might give him the answers. The ship's communications system appeared to still be functioning so Ahrmon inserted one of the rods into the console. The large screen on the console came to life but the image flickered rapidly, showing the face of a Treldarian communicating in a broken transmission. It was unintelligible.

Assuming that the rod had been damaged from the crash, Ahrmon removed it and inserted another. Luckily this recording was not corrupted. It displayed the inventory manifest from the Federation cargo transporter, Kargnaus 23, on the date that the transporter, under Ahrmon's command, had been attacked by Bladers. The manifest recorded the quantity of the stolen Xytrinium. Other Federation inventories from past raids were also listed, giving the names of the targeted transporters and their manifests. Some of these vessels had never been found and Ahrmon suspected that this could well be the planet where the stolen ships with their consignments were stored prior to the sale of the cargo. This would explain why the planet was so zealously guarded by the Bladers who attacked any foreign ships that strayed into their territory.

Ahrmon couldn't contact the Security Forces to alert them of his find without jeopardising his own freedom. So he collected all the memory rods and searched for any food stowed on board. At the back of the vessel where the galley was located, he found all the provisions he needed. It was not the type of food that Tzuracians would normally eat, but it would be sufficient to sustain his needs for several days. He bundled the supplies into a carry bag along with a small emergency medi-kit which he found in the galley and then gathered several navigation holo-discs pertaining to the Sideros-Hudor system in the Western Quadrant. Finally, before leaving the vessel, he strapped one of the Blader's laser pistols to his belt.

Ahrmon considered it was not a good idea to linger near the scene. If this was one of their known rendezvous points, there may be other Bladers heading this way. The sun was setting and the light was fading fast. Before it became too dark Ahrmon decided to backtrack to find a cave he had passed earlier. The cave was situated several hundred feet up the side of the mountain range and would provide a strategic and secure position to view the surrounding landscape for any unusual activity. It was protected from behind by a very steep rugged mountain-side and was not easily accessible to anything approaching from below. The hard rock formation would also provide an anti-heat detection shield.

Night had fallen by the time Ahrmon climbed to the entrance. He illuminated the cave by shining the tip of his staff into the opening. Without warning, something large and black about the size of an eagle rushed towards the light, rapidly flapping its wings while screeching in a high pitched squeal and clasping Ahrmon's wrist with a large powerful claw.

It shocked the life out of Ahrmon, knocking the staff from his right hand and throwing him to the ground. Using his full strength, Ahrmon managed to pull his left arm free from its grip and the creature, still frantically flapping its wings, flew off screeching into the dark void. Ahrmon swung around and managed to grab hold of a jutting rock with the other hand, stopping himself from rolling down the steep incline. Still stunned from the encounter, he lay there for several minutes to take in what had just happened.

Eventually Ahrmon hauled himself back to the entrance of the cave. Retrieving his staff, he carefully ventured inside. There was sufficient blue light from the staff to provide some illumination, and it was clear that the cave was quite large inside and deserted of any other life forms. Ahrmon noticed another smaller opening the size of a porthole at the right side of the cavern. This would offer an escape route if anything was to attack the front entrance. Ahrmon felt that this would be an adequate haven for the night. But before he settled in, he barricaded the main entrance with a small dead bush. He didn't want another unexpected close encounter with the flying creature.

He was tired, cold and hungry and suffering mild pain from the wound inflicted by the creature. He searched his carry bag and pulled out one of the Blader's metal food capsules and a metal scoop with which to eat the meal. He placed the capsule on the ground, withdrew the laser pistol from his holster and fired a quick blast. The lid sprung open revealing a steaming, compacted, light-orange cake mixture. He scraped a small amount with the scoop from the metal capsule and hesitantly tasted the mixture. Surprisingly, it was quite palatable and he hurriedly consumed the contents.

Now satisfied with something warm in his stomach, Ahrmon was ready to get a solid night's rest, planning to rise early and start a systematic search for any spacecraft that may be docked on the planet. The last thing he needed was to attract any unwanted guests to the light in his cave, so Ahrmon reasoned that an early night was a good idea.

Before settling down for the night, Ahrmon examined the wound to his arm. The sleeve of his jacket had been partially ripped but the cut to his arm was only superficial. In the medical kit he found an antibiotic laser sealer which he administered as a precautionary measure against any unknown diseases the winged creature may have been carrying.

Making a pillow from the carry bag, Ahrmon threw his robe over himself like a blanket, placed his compact staff in his right hand and clicked off the glowing blue light. The cave offered safety and warmth and before long Ahrmon was asleep. Sentinels are trained to keep an ear open for any unfamiliar sounds and their highly acute hearing allows them to always be on guard, even when sleeping. But in spite of strange noises during the night from creatures that inhabited this planet, Ahrmon slept well, without interruption. He had earned the rest.

He rose at sunrise, performed his ritual martial arts exercises, and ate a light meal. The portal at the side of the cave allowed sufficient sunlight to illuminate the cavern. While enjoying the nourishments from his cache, he examined some of the navigation holo-discs he had collected from the Bladers' ship. Amongst these was a charted map of Nebularis showing the contours of the landscape. Three circles were marked on the map within a five mile radius of the Bladers' crashed vessel. Ahrmon calculated that he could cover these within a day's travel there and back, returning to his temporary base in the cave before nightfall. He quickly finished his meal and readied for the excursion.

He packed the carry bag with his disc charts, shook out his robe and swung it over his shoulders, picked up the carry bag and climbed out the entrance. He camouflaged the entrance with a small fallen dead tree. Outside the high elevated cave entrance, he had an excellent 180-degree view of the landscape and could detect no unusual activity. He took his bearings for the first circled point on the navigational chart and headed off.

Trekking at a fast pace through the forest, Ahrmon compared the landscape to that of Tzurac. Nebularis was lush with a greater variety of birdlife. He was struck by the bright colours of the birds and their exquisite calls. Other strange forms of small wildlife appeared as fast as they disappeared and, every so often, he could hear distant echoes of what sounded like the roars of larger wild beasts. This made Ahrmon constantly vigilant of his surroundings.

The water supply was plentiful, with flowing creeks and lagoons from which Ahrmon replenished his water capsule. The temperature in the forest was warm, cooled by intermittent rainfall through the day. The canopies of the tall trees provided shade from the hot sun and reduced the humidity, allowing him to make good headway.

After two hours of walking, Ahrmon rested to check his bearings using a tall mountain peak in the distance as a landmark against the co-ordinates he had earlier input into the guidance locator. According to his calculations he should, by now, have reached the spot marked by one of the circles.

Spying a tall tree about thirty paces to his left he strode towards it and started climbing to get a better view. Nearing the top, Ahrmon stopped and sat astride a thick limb. Approximately a hundred yards to the west, he spied a huge clearing covered by camouflaged sail cloth, at the same height as his seated position, stretched between the trees. Aerial surveillance would be unable to detect this as the colourings blended perfectly with the surrounding vegetation.

What aroused Ahrmon's interest were the clearly recognisable objects housed under the canopy — two Federation cargo transporters. Ahrmon's keen eyesight honed in like a bird of prey on some activity around the hut near the transporters. Three Bladers were loading one of the transporters with containers. He could hear their muffled voices calling to one another. *Here was an opportunity not only to commandeer one of the transporters to escape the planet, but also to question the Bladers about their leader.*

Ahrmon scampered down the tree as fast as he could, leaping from branch to branch. On reaching the ground, he scooped up his chattels and ran swiftly towards the edge of the clearing. He was there in no time at all and could easily distinguish the faces of the marauders and clearly hear their coarse language. He remained hidden and focused on their conversation.

"Hurry up with those crates," yelled one of them in a husky voice. "You know we have to leave before dark!"

The other, standing near the open hatch, responded casually with a thick accent.

"Relax will you, we have plenty of time and these are the last of them."

The words 'leaving before dark' echoed in Ahrmon's mind. He knew that this would be his only opportunity to escape the planet, especially with the Security Forces hot on his trail. Ahrmon was quickly working out a plan of attack in his mind. *The ground around the hut made it difficult for a surprise attack. He could charge at the Bladers with his laser pistol blasting, but that would risk possible damage to the vessels, and him, if the Bladers returned fire.*

As Ahrmon was formulating his strategy, he heard the hatch door close on one of the transporters. One of the Bladers near the doorway of the hut yelled to the other two.

"You two take that one and I'll be right behind you, after I destroy this place and any traces that we were here."

"We'll meet you at the main base," replied one of the other Bladers.

With that, the power blasters started up, making a humming vibration. The transporter hovered about a foot from the ground, moving slowly out from under the sail cover. Within minutes, it sped off into space at high velocity.

Ahrmon watched the other Blader disappear into the hut. *Now was the only chance to make his move.* He activated his two-sided blade and ran as fast as he could towards the hut. Reaching the side of the hut, he threw his carry bag on the ground. Moving to the hut's entrance he could see the Blader about ten feet away, hastily placing a device onto a container marked with Treldarian symbols that Ahrmon translated as 'highly explosive'.

Then, sensing Ahrmon's presence, the Blader turned sharply and made an attempt to draw his laser pistol from the holster at his right side. But before he could, Ahrmon leaped the distance and with one clean slice of his blade, severed the Blader's right arm. The Blader reeled back, screaming in pain and clasping his bloodied shoulder with the other hand.

"Where's this other base? Where is it that you and your two friends are planning to meet?" shouted Ahrmon angrily, while pointing the end of his sword at the Blader's heart. "Is your leader there?"

"Go to hell you Federation swine!" the wounded Blader courageously spluttered, before collapsing unconscious in a heap on the floor. He was rapidly losing blood and would soon be dead.

Ahrmon wiped his blood-stained blade on the Blader's clothes, retracted it and holstered it back onto his belt. He quickly disconnected the device on the container to ensure that the place was not going to be destroyed, then went over to a metal crate tipped over on its side that was being used as a crude table.

On the crate top was a navigation holo-disc. Ahrmon activated the disc, which showed Treldarian symbols highlighting the quadrant where the planet Xannox was circled. The planet was surrounded by a dense asteroid belt, but the chart clearly marked out a safe passageway through the hazardous field. Ahrmon wondered whether he should take the transporter and follow after the Bladers in the hope of finding their arranged rendezvous and perhaps even catching their leader. But knowing that there would be a high risk of being caught or killed and that he would be outnumbered with limited fire power, Ahrmon decided he would take the transporter to find a safe haven, leaving the hunt for the Bladers to the Security Forces.

Ahrmon returned to where he had dropped his carry bag and took out the memory rods he had retrieved from the Bladers' crashed spacecraft, placing them on the crate top along with the holo-disc as a trail to Xannox for any pursuers. Then he strode to the transporter and climbed on board.

Sitting in the pilot's console, Ahrmon noticed some loose fibre optics dangling from underneath. The Bladers had found the tracking device and had somehow worked out how to permanently disconnect it, preventing the Federation from tracking them.

Ahrmon retrieved the navigation holo-disc from his carry bag and examined the Sideros-Hudor system, looking for another habitable planet. He compared these to the information stored in the computer of the transporter. On the charts he identified a small habitable planet within range of Nebularis, nestled in a solar system that contained thirteen other uninhabitable planets. The planet was called Terra Major. Ahrmon requested an update on this planet and the information flashed onto the green fluorescent screen.

» PLANET TERRA MAJOR (EARTH) CURRENT STATUS – SIMILAR
  ATMOSPHERE TO TZURAC
» GRAVITY 0.5 TIMES THAT OF TZURAC DUE TO SIDEROS (IRON)
  BASE ELEMENT STRUCTURE
» INHABITED BY ALIEN BI-PED LIFE FORMS, SIMILAR BIOLOGICAL
  AND PHYSIOLOGICAL STRUCTURE TO TZURACIANS
» LUSH VEGETATION, FRESH WATER, SUPPORTS MACRO SYSTEM
  OF CARBON PLANTS AND ANIMALS, MICRO SYSTEMS OF
  ORGANISMS
» DISTANCE 100 LIGHT YEARS FROM CURRENT POSITION
» EST. TIME TO REACH TARGET AT HYPER SPEED – 1 MONTH

Ahrmon went to the galley to assess the food provisions. There was more than enough for the long journey to this planet, Terra Major. He returned to the flight console, activated the power blasters and checked the energy gauges, which gave a reading of full capacity. Then, on manual, he guided the vessel clear of the sail covers, set the co-ordinates on the tracking monitor for planet Terra Major, switched the navigation panel to 'auto' and hit the thruster levers. The craft accelerated to hyper-speed and disappeared into space.

***

During the four-week voyage, Ahrmon researched the computer's memory to glean an insight into Terra Major's inhabitants and prepare for a new future, living amongst a primitive and alien life form. Selecting the relevant programs, he performed a mind transfer of their many languages. He also gathered information about the Terranian culture and customs to help him assimilate to this planet. The history of this planet showed that over the last two thousand years Terranian tribes had been in constant conflict.

Ahrmon reflected on what he was about to face. *Wars appeared to be a part of their barbaric culture, in a continuous struggle for greed and power. They seemed to have little regard for life, with their tribes involved in torture, enslavement and killing. Even now, wars were still raging, mainly in the northern hemisphere of the planet. He would need to prepare for the worst if he was to encounter these barbarians with their crude weapons. His survival would rest with his ability to adapt and blend in with the political climate of the day.*

He was now feeling somewhat isolated and alone being well out of his comfort zone and missing his old life with his fellow soldiers. *There was no one to share stories with about their military escapades, laugh at their weird humour and join in their silly pranks. No more indulging in a friendly drink on social occasions or toasting to their achievements. He must now focus on the present and never let his guard down. He reminded himself that the head must rule the heart when it comes to strategic decisions. His life depended on it. His freedom was not to be taken for granted.*

Suddenly the intercom announced Ahrmon's arrival in the orbiting range of Terra Major. Four weeks had passed quickly, but it had given him ample time to absorb the vital information necessary for his survival. To avoid detection on Earth, Ahrmon needed to land his craft in a place where it could not be found either by Terranians or by the Federation Security Forces. The ideal place he thought would be in one of the deepest cavities in one of the planet's oceans.

Ahrmon voiced a command to the computer for the Terra Major marine charts. He identified several deep sea channels around the planet and focussed on one near a place called the Azores Islands. Ahrmon input a trajectory course on the navigation screen and calculated a night time entry when there would be less chance of being seen. A message flashed on the screen:

» EST. TIME TO REACH TARGET – 4 HOURS
» TERRA MAJOR PERIOD MARCH 15 1785
» PRIMITIVE HOSTILE ENVIRONMENT – WARRING BETWEEN NATIONS

This gave Ahrmon enough time to prepare for the landing. He found a metal security case on board in which to place all his items and programmed the code to the case using his pledge ring. He placed his robe, staff, navigation charts and two days' rations of food provisions into the case and sealed it shut. He packed the metal case inside his waterproof carry bag. The craft started its descent in stealth mode.

While waiting for the impact, Ahrmon pondered in anticipation. *What was his life going be like living amongst hostile Terranians? Although he looked very similar to Earthlings, what would he need to do to blend into their world without being detected as an alien?*

EXPOSED

ONE week after Ahrmon departed Nebularis for Earth, the Tzuracian Security Forces, led by Chief Zarkwin, arrived at the burnt-out hull on Nebularis, having tracked the distress signal from Ahrmon's stolen Destroyer. Inside the wreck they saw the charred remains of what looked like the pilot, Captain Ahrmon Tyros, recognisable only by a portion of the sleeve of his Sentinel robe and a gold medallion containing the portraits of his parents. No other life force the size of a Tzuracian had been detected by the heat sensors of the Security Force computers, but the intense incineration from the super-magma fuel had destroyed any evidence that might determine conclusively that the victim was Ahrmon Tyros.

Zarkwin cursed inwardly. All that careful planning to fulfil his quest for revenge on the one who had humiliated him seemed to be wasted. He was infuriated and frustrated. He wanted desperately to believe that Ahrmon was dead and that the charred remains were his, but there was some doubt and he knew that the uncertainty would eat at his conscience and play on his mind. It would haunt him for the rest of his life.

"Search the area within a five-hundred yard radius for anything unusual," ordered Zarkwin, angrily, to his fifty security guards.

Within an hour of the Security Forces' craft arriving on Nebularis, a second Federation patrol craft received the automatic distress signal from the Class Ten Destroyer and answered the call. Stepping out of the craft, the leader, followed by his unit of twenty Federation soldiers, approached Zarkwin. Saluting to the higher rank, the leader introduced himself.

"Captain Aztark, FQT Division, at your service sir! We came as soon as we could to assist." Aztark lowered his arm and maintained a rigid stance at attention.

"Stand easy, Captain," said Zarkwin. "As you can see, those charred remnants over there are all that's left of the stolen Class Ten Destroyer and the vaporised pilot who we suspect was Ahrmon Tyros."

"Sir," said the Captain. "We have been on the lookout for Captain Tyros since we received notice of his escape. We have been charting the planets in the Western Quadrant where we believed he might seek refuge. This was the last planet we were planning to survey before returning to Tzurac for our rejuvenation and re-assignment."

Zarkwin was quick to respond to the information. He could see no reason to stay any longer than needed on Nebularis. Although he was still unsure that this was the end of Captain Ahrmon Tyros, he reasoned that the case would be considered closed when evidence of the crash was submitted to the Senate. The Senate would consider Tyros dead and feel satisfied that the death sentence had been imposed, indirectly. Deciding that his pursuit of Ahrmon was over, Zarkwin decided to return with Captain Aztark, report to the Senate on Captain Tyros's demise, and get on with his life with his recently betrothed.

"Captain Aztark, I'll return with you to Tzurac and leave my Security Forces here to complete the operation with a wider search of the area."

"Yes sir, honoured to have you aboard," replied the excited officer.

Zarkwin, in his raspy voice, called out to his First Lieutenant who was busily searching the open grassy area.

"Brantz, come over here!"

The Lieutenant instantly turned in his tracks, and approached Zarkwin with a dutiful salute.

"Yes sir, what is it?"

"Lieutenant, I'm placing you in charge. Sweep the area to confirm that we haven't overlooked anything of importance. I'm returning with Captain Aztark to Tzurac to submit my formal report to the Senate on what we have found. Keep me posted if you find anything relevant, and I'll see you soon, back at Khazor."

The Lieutenant snapped to attention and saluted Zarkwin.

"Yes sir!"

"Alright, Captain, let's go," ordered Zarkwin, turning about and strutting briskly towards the other craft. Captain Aztark followed immediately with his troops marching in set formation. In no time the craft was on its way, disappearing into space.

***

Lieutenant Brantz ordered his guards to widen the circle of their search without delay and, within minutes of the new order, one of the guards called out to him.

"Over here, sir, I think I've found something!"

Brantz was there in seconds, with the others following suit. The ground was severely scorched, but on close inspection, they had found shallow boot prints behind the outcrop of rocks where Ahrmon had taken shelter from the blast. The footprints headed off in a northerly direction and faded out after about twenty paces.

Brantz rallied his guards and called out his orders.

"Sergeant Orkund, I want you to select five of your guards and take the Mag-hawks for an aerial reconnaissance within a ten-mile radius in the northern area, ahead of these footprints. The rest of you, follow me and spread out."

Soon after the command was given, six Mag-hawks took to the air, flying in a stretched-out line formation in a northern direction. On the ground, Brantz and his fifteen guards also spread out and slowly advanced through the dense vegetation on foot, leaving behind them the open grassy area.

Suddenly, Brantz's communicator activated with the sound of Orkund's voice.

"Lieutenant, we've sighted what appears to be a wreckage of an unknown craft, a thousand yards ahead of you, approximately 30 degrees in a north-westerly direction. We'll continue the sector search and keep you posted. Out."

Brantz gave another command, raising his arm to indicate the direction of the sighted wreckage.

"Change course!"

Within ten minutes of searching the area, one of the guards sighted the alien craft. He signalled to the others through his communicator so as not to alert any inhabitants who may have survived the crash.

Cautiously the others approached with lasers primed. They were all familiar with the craft's origin. This was not the first time they had encountered a Blader's craft. The heat sensors from the Tzuracian craft had been calibrated to detect heat above 20 degrees centigrade and, being a cold-blooded race that relied on food for fuel and solar energy to self regulate their internal heat, the Bladers had not registered.

Brantz signalled for two of his guards to check the open hatch, while the others surrounded the craft. The two guards entered apprehensively. The smell of rotting flesh was disgusting. After quickly examining the corpses, one of the guards leaned out of the hatch and signalled the 'all clear' to Brantz, who passed the signal on his communicator to the rest of his unit.

"Stand easy troops, but be on the alert as there may be Bladers around," ordered Brantz as he climbed through the hatch.

Brantz was also affected by the stench, but he wanted to search the wreckage for any evidence that might shed some light on the Bladers' activities or base hideouts. After a quick and unsuccessful exercise, Brantz ordered the guards out of the craft, following close behind them.

Brantz was in two minds whether to march on further north or retreat back to his Federation ship, when his communicator activated with another message from Sergeant Orkund.

"Lieutenant, we've spotted a small building about one-and-a-half miles due north from the wreckage we first sighted. Do you want us to investigate?"

"Yes, Sergeant, but be careful. We have found some dead Bladers in the wrecked craft and there may be live ones in that building. We will meet you there."

"Yes sir! Out."

Brantz raised his hand and indicated to his troops to press on in a northerly direction in spread-out formation.

Around ninety minutes later the Lieutenant and his unit rendezvoused at the building. Sergeant Orkund came rushing out of the small hut holding a holo-disc and greeted Brantz with a formal salute. The excited expression on his face showed that he could not wait to report what he had found.

"Sir," he blurted out. "We've had a breakthrough. We know where the Bladers may be hiding."

The Sergeant now had Brantz's full attention.

"Okay Sergeant, what have you discovered?"

"Sir, we've found another dead Blader in the hut. His arm has been severed and he appears to have been dead for over a week."

Orkund offered Brantz the holo-disc he had in his hand.

"These Treldarian navigation charts show a safe course plotted to Planet Xannox as well as the coordinates of a base camp on the contour map of that planet. There are also manifests of Xytrinium cargos from our transporters on some of the memory rods."

"Good work, Sergeant," said Brantz. "They must have been in a hurry if they left these behind or they weren't expecting us to be here and may be returning. It's a bit of good luck in either case. I think we need to pursue these renegades, and fast, while the trail's still hot. I won't report this to the Chief until I'm sure we have something more to show. Prepare to return to our craft with the Mag-hawks and I'll meet you back there in one hour with the rest of the troops."

"Yes sir!"

Orkund saluted and immediately called to his guards to prepare to leave while Lieutenant Brantz gave the order for his ground unit to ready themselves for a fast retreat to the Federation craft.

In less than an hour they had returned to their craft and, using an encrypted security code, undecipherable to any Bladers who might be tuning into transmissions, notified the Communications Centre at Khazor of their intention to fly to Xannox. Brantz gave the orders to set the course to Xannox, following the path plotted on the Treldarian chart. Using hyper-drive they would be there within a day, hopefully avoiding any collisions with the orbiting asteroids.

***

Most of Xannox's surface was similar to the Blader's home planet, Treldar. It was a dry, barren, sandy wasteland with the exception of a small mountain range surrounded by swamp vegetation. The planet had not been colonised as the sand contained toxins that destroyed crops and the strange creatures that inhabited the swamps and the mountains were extremely dangerous. It was an ideal sanctuary for cut-throat rogue smugglers. No-one else would even consider trying to navigate through the hazardous asteroid belt to land on an uninviting dead planet.

The Federation craft, using stealth and camouflage modes, landed at the base of one of the smaller mountains about half a mile from the Blader's campsite. According to the map, the Bladers had established their hideaway in a valley over the other side of the mountain. The Security Forces donned their battle outfits in readiness, attaching emergency breathing apparatus to their belts. They did not know the size of the enemy that they would encounter or the fire power they possessed. The surprise attack which Brantz had planned would avoid the use of unnecessary brute force and casualties. Brantz briefed his troops to use hand signals only and to set their pistols on stun. The plan was to encircle the campsite and converge on it, taking the Bladers alive.

Once outside the craft, Lieutenant Brantz and Sergeant Orkund re-examined the chart to confirm their bearings and signalled the unit to commence the trek up the mountain. Halfway up, the unit encountered dank heavy smog, permeated with the odour of rotting vegetation and decaying animal carcasses, making it difficult for the troops to breathe. The atmosphere was eerie, filled with strange unfamiliar noises that sounded like a thousand varieties of insects, intermittently interrupted by the faint wailings of the carnivorous creatures that stalked the marshes. Brantz gave the order to use their breathing apparatus and keep an eye out for anything that moved.

By the time they had reached the top of the mountain some twenty minutes later, they needed their night visors for clearer vision. With the aid of these visors they could now distinguish the Bladers' campsite in the valley below. The only activity at the campsite seemed to be in a central hut. A light shining inside projected shadows of figures on the windows and there were sounds of talking, laughing and strange music. There was a Federation transporter sitting idle nearby, but there appeared to be no sentries on guard.

Waving his arm high in a circular motion, Brantz gave a signal to surround the campsite. The unit of twenty guards silently manoeuvred themselves into position in a forty-yard circle, completely surrounding the hut. Their pistols set on pulse stun were now unholstered and raised in the direction of the target. They waited silently in anticipation for the Lieutenant's signal.

Suddenly there was a crashing sound in the undergrowth behind them and one of the guards swung around to see what it was. A huge fur-covered, yellow-eyed creature was screaming towards him on its hind legs, clawing madly and salivating from its open jaws filled with large jagged teeth.

The guard's reflexes were fast. He drew his dagger from his boot in an instant, but it was too late. The creature was faster, and with one powerful swipe of its long claws it tore the guard's throat open, leaving blood spurting from the deep gashes. Death was instant. The huge creature disappeared as fast as it had appeared, dragging its victim into the black void.

The guards nearby were horrified. *Could more of these vicious creatures strike without warning?*

Brantz waited a few moments to give his troops a chance to regain their composure and to see whether the noise from the animal attack had alerted the Bladers. Fortunately, the noise coming from the hut had drowned out the sound outside.

Without further delay, Brantz gave the signal to advance and in no time they reached their target, crashing through the doors and windows, and taking the seven Bladers by surprise.

"None of you move!" shouted Brantz, pointing his weapon in the direction of one of the Bladers.

Two of the Bladers dived for their weapons, but before they could reach them, they were blasted by Brantz's soldiers and stunned unconscious, falling to the floor. Realising that they were out-numbered, the other Bladers raised their arms above their heads in surrender.

"Sergeant!" ordered Brantz. "Bind their wrists." The guards reacted instantly.

Brantz, who spoke the Treldarian language fluently, started interrogating them.

"Who's the leader of this rogue outfit?"

There was no response from the captives.

"How many more of you are here on Xannox?"

Again there was no reply.

Then, with an air of contempt, one of the meaner looking Bladers spat on Brantz's boots and eyed him vengefully.

"Okay, if that's your attitude, we'll get the answers from you back at our craft. Sergeant, we'll use the stolen transporter to return to our craft. Take your troops and escort the prisoners on board. Lance Corporal Norak, seeing that you have your flight stripes, I want you to pilot it. I'll be with your shortly."

"Yes sir," responded Norak with a formal salute as they departed the makeshift hut.

Brantz cast his eyes around the interior of the hut looking for any clues that might tell him more about the intentions of these Bladers and the whereabouts of any other splinter groups. His attention was drawn to a dark-brown leather folder tucked into the loose covers of a chair in the corner of the room. He strode over to the chair and picked up the folder for a closer inspection.

As he thumbed through the documents contained inside, he could not believe what he saw — Tzuracian text with the name of 'Zarkwin' heading the page! The imprint was dated the week before the attack on the Xytrinium transporter craft that Captain Tyros had been escorting. There were schematics of flight co-ordinates and planet configurations in the sector where the craft was flying.

The Lieutenant was shocked, realising immediately that his Senior Officer had been involved in the plot to steal a payload of Xytrinium from the Federation. *Could it be that Ahrmon Tyros was innocent and that Zarkwin had deceived everyone?* Brantz quickly closed the folder, tucked it into his belt and hurriedly left the hut to catch up with his unit.

Safely on board their own craft, Lieutenant Brantz assembled his troops to address and debrief them.

"Let me commend you on your good work today and the success of the mission in spite of the loss of one of our colleagues. Private Bhardox was a brave and loyal soldier who died in the line of duty. He could have used his laser pistol to save himself, but thinking that it might have alerted the Bladers to our presence, he went for his dagger instead. He did not die in vain and he will be given a full military funeral service when we arrive back at Tzurac.

"Sergeant Orkund, I want you to commence interrogating the captives to extract information about their activities, the locations of the stolen Xytrinium, and details of the recipients of the stolen goods. Record the interrogations and make copies to a disc."

Brantz was anxious to find out the truth behind the attack on Captain Tyros and his company of Sentinels.

It didn't take long. Within an hour, Orkund reported back, warning Brantz that he would be surprised and appalled by the truth. But Orkund's report only confirmed Brantz's suspicions. The Blader's leader, Captain Cronaz, who was amongst the seven captives, had admitted that Khane Zarkwin was responsible for planning the attack on Kargnaus 23, providing all names, locations and schedules. Zarkwin had wanted no financial payment, only revenge against Tyros, and had promised the Bladers the spoils with no interference from the Federation. Lieutenant Dakhar had been killed in a struggle with Captain Cronaz and Ahrmon Tyros had not been involved.

"I suspected as much, Orkund," said Brantz in a disgusted voice. "It seems that our 'honourable' leader has deceived everyone. It makes me sick to my stomach that such a high ranking officer has used his trusted position to deceive the Senate, the Sentinels and the citizens of Tzurac and all this to gain personal revenge on an innocent, honourable soldier. He framed Captain Tyros, knowing that it would lead to his execution."

Both Brantz and Orkund realised the gravity of the situation. *How could they expose Zarkwin without endangering their own lives?* Brantz swore Orkund to secrecy.

"We must be careful. No-one must know about what we've just learnt until I can report in person to the Senate, back on Tzurac. If Zarkwin suspects that we know about his conspiracy, he won't hesitate to destroy the evidence, and us."

ZARKWIN'S LEGACY

FOUR days later Brantz and his unit, accompanied by Lance Corporal Norak in the retrieved transporter, arrived back at Khazor. It was nightfall and the rebel prisoners were escorted secretly to holding cells just outside the city; Brantz was trying to avoid making their presence known to the traitor, Zarkwin. Brantz immediately headed to the temple where the Senate resided to report his discovery to the highest ranking elder, Senator Sulkhram, and present him with the evidence.

As Brantz approached the temple, he was surprised to see Zarkwin coming down the stairs towards him. Trying to avoid any delay, the Lieutenant gave his Chief a respectful, if nervous, passing salute. But Zarkwin deliberately blocked Brantz's pathway and, returning his salute, began to question him sternly.

"Lieutenant Brantz, I haven't heard from you for the last four days. Is there a reason for your non-communication?"

"Well sir," responded Brantz timidly, "I didn't want to bother you as I had nothing to report."

For a moment Zarkwin stared intently at the Lieutenant, raising a questioning eyebrow.

"But you *do* have something to report, Lieutenant, don't you?" he teased, provocatively.

Brantz felt the tension increase in the back of his neck. *Was it possible Zarkwin had somehow found out he had uncovered the conspiracy?*

"What do you mean, sir?" replied Brantz, trying to look and sound innocent.

"Well, Lieutenant, when I saw on the Comm-nav screen that your Federation craft was landing back on Tzurac this evening, I contacted your pilot to ask him where you were."

Brantz was feeling increasingly uncomfortable. All sorts of excuses were racing through his head. *He needed to stall Chief Zarkwin until he could present his evidence to the Senate.*

"And you know what he told me Lieutenant?" Zarkwin continued.

"No sir, I don't."

"He said you were on your way to the Senate with some very important information and he would let you know I was trying to contact you. What is *so* important that you want to report it to the Senate before reporting it to me?"

Brantz tried to hide his nervousness.

"I'd rather not say, sir, until I have consulted with the Senate," he said as calmly and firmly as he could.

"Well, Lieutenant," said Zarkwin raising his voice menacingly, "as your Commanding Officer, I order you to hand over whatever you have that is so important and I will judge whether or not it is worthy of passing on to the Senate."

The Lieutenant stood his ground.

"With respect, Chief, I can't give you what I have," he said defiantly.

They glared intently at each other, trying to anticipate the other's next move. Then suddenly, without warning, Zarkwin pulled his laser pistol from his holster and pointed it directly at Brantz's head.

"Don't make me have to use this, Lieutenant!" said Zarkwin in a threatening tone. "Just hand over what you have!"

Without flinching, and still staring into Zarkwin's cold fixed eyes, Brantz reached into his pocket and slowly took out the disc containing the Bladers' confessions. He watched as Zarkwin's eyes momentarily shifted to focus on the disc. In that split second, the young Lieutenant made his move. Reaching across with his other hand, he tried to wrestle the weapon from Zarkwin's grip. But given his Sentinel bloodline, Zarkwin was far too powerful. In the struggle, the pistol discharged and Brantz winced with agony from the sudden pain he felt in his upper chest. He slumped to the ground.

Thinking that no-one could survive a direct charge to the heart at close range, Zarkwin believed he had killed one of his own guards. Instinctively, he checked up and down the dimly-lit street to ensure that there were no witnesses. There were none in sight. He quickly rolled Brantz over with his foot, bent down, and snatched the disc from the Lieutenant's clenched palm. Surveying the street once more, he quickly dragged Brantz's body out of sight off the main thoroughfare and fled the scene.

He headed for his nearby quarters to read the information on the disc. His suspicions were confirmed. On hearing the Bladers' confessions, Zarkwin knew he was doomed. Once Brantz's body was discovered and the authorities accessed the interrogation log on board the returned craft, he would be a hunted fugitive. Time was crucial. He needed to make an immediate escape from Tzurac.

The unscrupulous Zarkwin was now experiencing what it was like to be on the other side of the law. The symptoms of panic were starting to take effect. Adrenalin was racing through his body. He was in a cold sweat and his heart was pounding at twice the normal rate. Outnumbered, and with no contingency plan, he had to rely on his wits and animal cunning. He knew he couldn't hide for long and needed to get off the planet if he had any chance of avoiding capture. So he headed straight for the spacecraft hangars before the guards had a chance to mobilise.

But Zarkwin had misjudged the extent of Brantz's injuries. Shortly after Zarkwin disappeared from the scene, the Lieutenant regained consciousness, groaning with excruciating pain from the wound in his lower left shoulder, just beneath his collar bone. Fortunately, the laser blast had penetrated his torso at an acute angle, missing his heart and sealing the wound, leaving injury only to his chest muscles.

Using all his strength, Brantz slowly dragged himself to his feet and staggered painfully up the temple stairs. He collapsed as he opened the door to Senator Sulkhram's quarters. Recognising Brantz not only as a security officer but also as the son of a fellow elder, Senator Sulkhram rushed to assist him.

"Don't try to move. I'll get some help."

In a strained voice, Brantz tried to explain.

"Wait, there's something I must tell you first, before it's too late."

Despite his pain, Brantz quickly confided details of the conspiracy and the attack upon him by Zarkwin. Sulkhram was amazed by the revelations but he knew Brantz personally and trusted what Brantz said. It was now clear to Sulkhram that he had condemned an innocent man. Picturing the trial again, he could see the innocence on Ahrmon Tyros's face and the gloating on Khane Zarkwin's.

Sulkhram wasted no time in sounding the alarm. All attention was now focused on capturing the real traitor.

***

The hangars were a large underground multi-layered complex that housed various types of craft on dedicated levels. Transporters were housed on the lower levels for easier loading from the underground transport system. Fighter craft were kept closer to the surface for easier and quicker access to combat any possible alien invasion. The complex was guarded at the main entrance and had electronic surveillance throughout.

As Chief Security Officer, Zarkwin had full access to all facilities and knew the access codes to all the exits and entrances. But he realised it was only a matter of time before Security revoked his access. All he had to do was disarm the guards on the main entrance, get inside the complex and knock out the Communications Control Centre. This would deactivate the complex's surveillance, giving him easy access to the fighters on the second level.

Darting back and forth in the shadows of the dark laneways around the citadel and avoiding contact with the occasional citizen, Zarkwin was making good time. The colours of his black-and-red uniform camouflaged him well in the night shades. Through his communicator he was monitoring conversations transmitted between the Security Forces and the Sentinels, allowing him to follow their progress in trying to track him down. He heard the order being given to the hangar guards to be on the alert in case he attempted to hijack one of the craft.

Fifty yards diagonally across from the main entrance, Zarkwin hid behind one of the walls of a building in a laneway. He could clearly see the two guards in the flood lights but they couldn't see him in the shadows. Quietly sliding the laser pistol from his holster, he set the power on stun pulse and fired two blasts at the guards. Zarkwin charged towards them pointing his pistol in their direction as they fell to the ground. They were both unconscious by the time he reached them.

Re-holstering his weapon and removing his leather glove he waved his left hand at the code recognition access on the reinforced metal door. Zarkwin was rather surprised when the door slid sideways. *Good, Security has not yet shut down my access to the complex.*

He redrew his pistol and crouched down in anticipation of a welcoming party. There was no movement of any kind in the silent, brightly lit main hall.

Zarkwin holstered his pistol and ran towards the Communications Control Centre. Then, as he reached the access door, twenty Security Force guards appeared from nowhere, surrounding him with their weapons all pointing in his direction.

"Hello Chief, what took you so long?"

Zarkwin turned in the direction of the familiar voice. It was Sergeant Orkund from the recently arrived transporter.

"What the …?"

Before Zarkwin could finish his words, Orkund cut in with orders to his guards.

"Take his weapon and put him in hand restraints!" He turned to Zarkwin.

"You played into our trap, Zarkwin, you scum. We knew you could listen into Central transmissions to Security on your communicator but you couldn't monitor communications from Central to our transporter where we were still disembarking. Central suspected you would try to reach the hangars and alerted us. All we had to do was wait for your arrival."

The Sergeant tapped his communicator.

"Sergeant Orkund here, we have Zarkwin in custody. Out"

***

On the second day in custody while awaiting his trial, Syrina Penzark, Zarkwin's betrothed, came to visit him. She was desperately seeking answers to many questions arising from his capture. A Sentinel herself, Syrina had heard rumours within the ranks about Zarkwin's involvement with the Bladers. She found it hard to accept these accusations and needed to hear the truth from the man she loved.

When Syrina was escorted into Zarkwin's cell, she immediately threw her arms around him, holding him tightly for some time before speaking.

"Khane, tell me it's not true. They're just lies aren't they? Someone's trying to discredit you and your position. You'll be released as soon as they find the real traitor."

Zarkwin did not respond straight away, but stared into Syrina's eyes as if looking through her. He was searching for the right words. In that moment he realised that he had never looked for the beauty in his life, and Syrina was beautiful. He had been so filled with vengeance and hate that he'd never fully appreciated her and what she had to give. Now he saw her soft textured skin on her small round face, curly ringlets of golden hair that covered her ears and draped around the nape of her slender neck, rosebud lips, and bright sparkling round blue eyes.

After a long pause, he spoke to her, quietly and ashamed.

"Syrina, I can't lie to you. It is true what they are saying. I am that traitor."

Syrina pulled away, bewildered, and stood speechless in disbelief. She tilted her head slightly to one side, confused by the words she had just heard. Then, tears started to trickle down her now-distorted face. After several moments, she spoke.

"Why would you do this? What would possibly drive you to commit such horrible things? How could the person I trusted, that everyone trusted as a high ranking security officer, do such a thing?"

Again, after another long pause, Zarkwin began to explain, trying to restrain his pent-up anger.

"I did it out of revenge. I've never told you exactly how I lost my hand, only that it was severed in a fencing match. It was Cadet Ahrmon Tyros who, with a sword, ruined my career as a Sentinel and he did this in the presence of a roomful of cadets. I was the only Sentinel cadet in over a hundred years to be so disgraced and humiliated. It brought shame on my family who turned their backs on me. The Elders offered me a position in the Security Forces, which I reluctantly accepted, but I vowed that I would climb the ranks and one day be in a powerful position where I could make Ahrmon Tyros pay for what he did to me. I would have succeeded if Tyros hadn't escaped and the Bladers had not been captured."

Syrina paused for a moment, pondering the anger that Zarkwin had obviously felt for Captain Tyros all this time.

"Oh Khane, I understand how humiliated you must have felt, but you should've known that revenge leads to self destruction. No-one really wins. We would have had a wonderful life together, you, me and the baby, but you've ruined that dream."

Zarkwin was caught off guard by Syrina's words.

"What are you saying, Syrina?"

Trying to hold back the tears, Syrina looked deeply into Zarkwin's eyes.

"Yes Khane, I am bearing your child. I am five weeks pregnant and, until today, I had been looking forward to telling you."

Zarkwin shook his head in disbelief, then leant forward and embraced Syrina. He knelt down beside her, placing his left hand on her stomach and his head on her waist. His face was contorted with emotion from the realisation that he had lost more than he had gained. He held that embrace for some time and then stood slowly and spoke in a sorrowful voice.

"Syrina, I'm so sorry for what I've done and I'm overwhelmed to learn that we will have a child of our own. You've made me very happy."

Zarkwin was remorseful and overcome with emotion, faced with the realisation that he had created a life while trying to destroy another. All too late, something inside him had suddenly changed and his only desire was to protect Syrina and their unborn child.

"You're right, Syrina, I have wronged us all. I am not fit to be a father to our child and, as much as it pains me, I advise you to forget about me as my life is at an end. You should find another to take my place as your husband and provide a father figure for our child to look up to. But don't tell anyone that you are bearing my child. It would only bring shame on both of you. Perhaps you should leave Tzurac to make a new life. I'll always love you Syrina and I hope that you'll forgive me in time."

Syrina stood in silence for some time struggling with her feelings.

Emotionally she was torn between her love and loyalty for the person who had won her heart and the anger and disappointment she felt towards Zarkwin for what he had done. Deep down inside she knew that Zarkwin was right. She and her child could never live amongst the Tzuracian citizens with this shame.

Finally, she whispered in Zarkwin's ear, softly stroking his hair one last time.

"I will never really understand what you have done or forgive you for ruining our lives. But you are right my love, I must leave Tzurac. I will resign my commission as a Sentinel and go immediately to Urgellan. No-one there will know of our troubles and no-one will know the child is yours. I will name her Khaneera, and when she is old enough I will tell her that her father was once a noble figure, the Chief of Security, who protected the citizens of Tzurac."

Syrina kissed Zarkwin briefly on the lips, turned, and departed in silence, with tears streaming down her face.

Zarkwin watched his betrothed as she disappeared out of sight down the passageway, then he slumped onto the cold white marble bench seat alone once more. He placed his heavy head into his cupped hands to cover his face, still reflecting on what Syrina had told him and feeling his heart being torn apart. If he was not executed for his foolish crimes, he would live in torment, imprisoned and in solitude, for the rest of his remaining years.

PART 2

EARTH 2055

KYRON awoke with a start, disturbed by an ear-piercing high-pitched sound. It threw him out of bed and onto the floor, forcing him to block his ears with both hands — he'd had ultra-sensitive hearing since birth. The noise stopped after thirty seconds, but Kyron's ear drums continued to ache and ring and, for a time, he could not comprehend where he was or what he was doing in these strange surroundings. As the effects of the ear blast started to subside, he heard a soft, well-spoken female voice coming from somewhere in the room.

"Good morning Kyron, the time is zero-six-hundred hours, Day 10, Monday 2055."

Kyron looked around to see who was there in his sleeping quarters. He couldn't see anyone or any movement, but then he realised that a holographic screen had activated itself on the wall in front of him. An image of a young woman's perfectly symmetrical face, with deep-red straight hair and striking green eyes, was staring at him.

"I hope you slept well and that your accommodation is to your liking," came the voice again. "I can change the colour scheme to suit your mood at your request."

"Who are you?" snapped Kyron angrily, still only half conscious after being woken from a much needed sleep. "Why are you invading my privacy?"

The voice responded very apologetically, "Sorry Kyron, I did not mean to alarm you. I thought that you had already been briefed on the protocol of living as a tenant in the Company's apartments."

Kyron had arrived at the Central Reception Control Quadrant for the Company's high-rise apartments late the night before. He vaguely remembered some instructions that his assigned host had hastily given him.

"Yes, I was briefed, but I was taken a little by surprise, especially when I heard a feminine voice and then saw the image of you," responded Kyron, rubbing his eyes to help him focus on the image and become more accustomed to the over bright lighting.

"What do they call you?" he asked in a more pleasant manner.

"VALERI," she responded.

"That's a nice name," he replied.

"Oh that is not my name. It is an acronym for my technical classification — Voice Activated Laser Enhanced Response Interchanger, VALERI."

"Mmm, I still think it sounds nice. It adds that human touch," replied Kyron, thinking about what the world had come to with all its impersonal electronic devices. "Do you mind if I close you down for a short time while I get myself prepared for my first day on the job?"

"Kyron, you do not have to ask my permission to suspend communication as I am void of emotion and sensitivity. Just give the order 'VALERI close' or 'VALERI open' and I will respond accordingly.

"However, before you suspend communication, I am to remind you that you have an appointment at zero-eight-thirty hours with Mr Samuel Jensen at the MERIC Building. A transporter will take you directly there. On your way, you should familiarise yourself with the information on the transcorder that you received from your host last night. Access to the building will require your holographic identity card which was processed prior to your arrival. It is in the security folder along with the transcorder. Your thumb and retinal code print will also be required for access. When you get through security, the Information Services Directory in the foyer will indicate the correct floor and suite for your meeting."

"Thank you VALERI for the 'Intel'. Would you mind opening a panel on the wall for a window? I assume they have windows in these apartments?"

On the wall opposite the bed, a floor to ceiling panel about four feet wide slid sideways and disappeared into a slot encased in the wall, revealing a large window.

"Affirmative Kyron, your breakfast is already prepared in the servery and dinner will be in the servery on your return tonight. Your Company uniforms are hanging in the dressing compartment."

"Thank you, VALERI. Close!"

Now that he was alone and adjusted to his environment, Kyron could perform his daily workout. He had practised the regime every morning, just before sun-up, in the store-house back on the family farm. He and his father, Rhamon, had practised martial arts together ever since Kyron was old enough. Kyron's father had trained him in advanced martial arts including the use of the staff as well as the blade, and other types of weaponry. Rhamon had told Kyron that these vital skills would protect him and his mother when needed throughout his life. The physical training had also been combined with mind control through meditation. Rhamon continuously reinforced his teachings to Kyron as they practised together, sometimes in synchronisation and sometimes individually or when sparring. On many occasions they practised blind-folded to heighten awareness of their other senses.

"You must practise every day with focus and deep concentration, Kyron. Block out all other thoughts, but always be aware of your surroundings and never let your guard down. Trust only in your instincts and your keen senses. Mind over matter is the way of the warrior."

These words, spoken by his father, always echoed in Kyron's mind. Rhamon explained that most humans do not fully utilise the power of their minds and remain unaware of hidden abilities that exist in those who practise the art. His father told him that these powers, if developed, have superior healing abilities. They enhance the senses of hearing, sight and mind-vision and increase the speed of reflexes. They also allow thought reading or telepathy and the accurate sensing of others' moods.

Kyron's mind was brought back to the present by the sound of meditative music being piped through the room. He rose from his bed and tidied the blankets in a rough fashion before leaning over to what appeared to be a control panel at the side of the bed-head. He assessed the half-dozen sensor buttons, pressed the button marked 'retract', then took a step well back in anticipation. The bed silently withdrew into a cavity in the wall and a sliding mirrored panel covered the space into which the bed had disappeared.

Kyron strolled over to the double-glazed window on the other side of the room. The view was familiar to the climate he had just left behind in the country. A hazy sun was filtering through grey overcast skies. Pollution from industry world-wide was encasing the Earth and the planet was choking on its own debris, slowly suffocating itself into extinction. Kyron's location gave him an excellent view of the drab, carbon-coated, lifeless buildings, and the streets below where shuttle transporters busily collected and delivered the daily commuters.

New York was one of the many satellite-cities that had become the principal places to find work and accommodation. Food supplies were now being manufactured through advanced automation and the farms from the outlying countryside were rapidly being phased out. Those with limited education had a choice either of labouring in the mines or processing in the factories. Only a handful of primary producers remained to grow fresh fruit and vegetables that were cultivated under giant glass-houses and supplied to the privileged.

Kyron's father, Rhamon Shield, had been one of those few isolated farmers whose livelihood was supported by an underground natural spring and limited solar power with a back-up generator fuelled by methane gas. Kyron stood pondering why he was here in the city and not back in the open spaces on the family farm.

But Rhamon had planned a different life for his son, sending Kyron to an engineering college to acquire the education and skills that would secure his future. Rhamon and his wife, Zelda, had arranged for the planting and harvesting seasons to coincide with Kyron's college breaks, allowing Kyron to study full-time, while spending some time with them on the farm when he was most needed.

As soon as Kyron graduated from college, Rhamon had encouraged him to leave the farm and find a position with a reputable enterprising company based in the city. Kyron had just procured a position with a company known as MERIC when his father passed away.

It seemed that Rhamon had known, almost instinctively, that his life was coming to an end and realised that Kyron and his mother would be unable to manage and protect the farm without him. So he pre-arranged to sell the farm and for Kyron's mother to return to her own family. Kyron found it hard coming to terms with what appeared to be a cold decision to sell the family farm, but he appreciated that his father had done what he considered was best for the family. He missed his father so much.

Kyron sighed deeply and turned away from the window, walking across to his luggage in the corner of the room. He bent down to one of the smaller cases and, with his right hand, took out a small, thick wooden stick about one-and-a-half inches in diameter and two feet in length.

He stood up, slowly turned around and, with a quick flick of his right wrist, the stick suddenly expanded into a staff approximately five feet in length. Clutching the middle of the staff with both hands and holding it parallel to the floor, outstretched at arms' length level with his shoulders, he stood motionless like a marble statue with his eyes closed. He breathed deeply and slowly and remained unwavering in this position, as if frozen in time.

Then his eyes snapped open and, with incredible speed, his lithe gymnastic body started to lunge and twist while spinning the staff in rapid motion first to one side, then the other, wrapping it around his body. He made rapid jabbing and retracting movements and swung the staff in all directions with powerful controlled accuracy. Like a professional dancer he was performing the patterns and forms his father had practised with him year after year. The choreographed movements became more complex and intricate as he practised ways of fending off and attacking invisible foes. Then, all of a sudden, Kyron's frenzied activity stopped as abruptly as it had started and was replaced by stillness and quiet.

Kyron always completed his ritual training with fifteen minutes of meditation to calm the mind, relax the body and provide clear thoughts and an open mind with which to start the day. In the past, when practising in unison with his father, Kyron would 'mind link' to communicate at high speed, without uttering a sound. And, in these moments, Rhamon had passed his knowledge and wisdom to Kyron at three to five times the speed of the spoken word.

Coming out of this morning's ritual, Kyron thought that perhaps this was the reason why he had excelled in his studies and in his application of new knowledge. In some way, this meditative mind-link had expanded his mind's capacity so that he was able to absorb and process volumes of information, increase his reasoning ability, and enhance his senses. Kyron decided that he would continue to practise his martial art routines of staff and short-stick followed by meditation in the mornings, and his blade techniques and gym workouts in the afternoons, after work.

Just as he was slowly opening his eyes from his meditation, Kyron caught sight of the digital read-out pulsating in luminous red across the screen on the wall.

...0700 hrs...0700 hrs ...0700 hrs ...

This prompted him to spring into action in time for a quick breakfast.

Kyron was amazed at the variety of food choices offered in his servery. He was used to eating simple home-grown farm produce, and he felt guilty with the abundance of food, especially knowing that others were scraping a life together from meagre earnings. His father's words of wisdom returned to him.

"Remember Kyron, we all have our roles to fulfil in life. Some have more and some have less, but we do what we can to help our brethren, giving to others what we can afford to give of ourselves and our possessions." Kyron was determined to maintain the generosity and love that his father had instilled in him, and to have a clear conscience with a true heart.

After breakfast Kyron found the steam-cleansing suite, another retractable booth that slid out of the mirrored wall. After a brief time in the suite, Kyron donned the bathrobe and activated the dressing compartment.

Examining the contents of the compartment, Kyron could see several different coloured outfits made up of different coloured jacket-shirts with black trousers and black boots. The long sleeved jacket-shirts with round mandarin collars had two bands of gold braiding on the epaulets and matching braiding on the cuffs of the sleeves. *What a smart looking outfit for a company uniform.*

On the inside panel of the compartment was a sign that read.

"Dress Code: *WHITE – Formal Dress: BLUE - Day Shift: RED – After Hours"*. Kyron quickly dressed in the azure-blue jacket-shirt, black trousers and boots, finding them to be a surprisingly perfect fit. With his outfit complete, he retracted the closet into the wall and the panel slid back into position.

Kyron grabbed the security folder and headed for the front exit. As he strode past the mirrored panels he caught a glimpse of his reflection. He stopped for an instant to take in his new look. There in the mirror he saw a tall, well-built man with wavy short-cropped fair hair, steel blue eyes and a smooth fair complexion, dressed in a perfectly tailored crisp, blue and black uniform.

"Quite spruce if I do say so myself," he said out loud, as he headed for the shuttle terminal at the Central Reception Control Quadrant.

The shuttles arrived and departed every fifteen minutes and, according to the information directory at the terminal, the MERIC Building was only five minutes away. The terminal was crowded with commuters of all shapes and sizes and their pale, unemotional, facial expressions said it all: another week of toil for little reward, and not much quality of life. The commuters were dressed in different coloured and styled uniforms representing their particular company and most of them carried slim metallic briefcases. They darted about in all directions, making a beeline for their regular platforms.

Large illuminated signs dominated the complex with timetables and platform numbers displayed in flashing lights on billboards suspended in the air. Monotone, digitised voices blurted out simultaneously from hidden speakers, announcing arrival and departure times, as well as alerts and warnings. The whole scene appeared like a circus carnival.

The noise and the lights did not seem to bother the commuters but it took Kyron's total concentration to tone down the overbearing effects and sensations inflicted on his sensitive vision and hearing. Despite the grey overcast skies, his eyes were irritated by the glare. Kyron realised that he would also need to control his ultra-sensitive hearing in order to adjust to the unfamiliar, increased volume of his new surroundings. He decided that if he was to encounter this every morning he would need to acquire dark eye shades as well as ear plugs, similar to the other commuters.

On board the shuttle Kyron observed that those carrying small metallic cases had now opened them and were resting them on their laps. They also had receptors in their ears. The woman sitting beside him, who was occupied with her silver case, was focused on a hologram screen. There was a man's face on the screen and the text streaming across the top of the screen indicated he was reading the news. In the background flashed images of cities, maps and footage of other countries' populations.

Kyron thought that this was a good opportunity to inspect the contents of his security folder. First he pulled out his hologram ID card. His photo appeared three dimensional and very life-like. Positioned diagonally across the top right hand corner, in bold capital letters, was the Company name *MERIC* and impregnated into the base of the card was a raised multicoloured bar code containing seven digits. Embedded into the card beside his photo was printed his Name, Title and Rank — *KYRON SHIELD, ENGINEER, LEVEL 2, INTERPLANETARY SPACE DIVISION (ISD)*.

Kyron had recently graduated from the same Royal College of Engineers attended by the MERIC Company Director, Samuel Jensen, the man he was about to meet. His references from the College were as impressive as those of Samuel Jensen and, unknown to him, this was one of the reasons Samuel Jensen had selected him for the position in charge of the ISD unit. This unit was responsible for the design, implementation and maintenance of all the engineering machinery and equipment used in the Company's mining operations for newly discovered planets.

Peering into the folder again, Kyron spied the miniature transcorder which he switched on, and began reading the text on the small screen. It told him everything he needed to know about his security card, the organisational structure of the Company, and the senior personnel. The briefing also provided him with some basic information about his specific role within the Company, but not about the current project on which he would be working. Given security restrictions, advice about the project would be provided when he met his Divisional team.

Kyron started to reflect on the fact that he was now employed with the largest and most successful mining company on Earth.

MERIC (Mining and Engineering Resource Industrial Company) had originated from a small enterprise early in the twenty-first century and was solely owned by Samuel Jensen, an engineer by profession, having gained his qualifications on a scholarship to the Royal College of Engineers. Jensen had been a very astute student and highly advanced in his thinking, developing futuristic ideas and applications. Some of the engineering prototype models that he had developed in his spare time as a student had been patented and sold to industrial companies. And by the time he had graduated, Jensen had accumulated enough money to purchase the machinery and equipment to start his own mining company. In twenty-five years, MERIC had grown into the most productive mining enterprise in the world. The Board of Company Directors now comprised influential senior members from government as well as private enterprise.

Although he was in the mining business, Samuel Jensen was an advocate for conservation of the planet and Jensen only mined in those areas that were considered uninhabitable or unsuitable for establishing productive crops. He had developed methods of capturing, containing and neutralising the exhaust fumes from his mining machinery, preventing harmful chemicals from being released into the atmosphere. This made his Company a major contributor to carbon emission control.

While studying at the Royal College of Engineers, Kyron had read much about Samuel Jensen's innovative mechanical designs that could extract raw mineral resources whilst preserving the environment. Striving to maintain a balance between nature and man's needs for survival was something that resonated with Kyron's philosophy and that of his father. Samuel Jensen's papers had given Kyron great respect for the man and his company.

Kyron's thoughts were immediately interrupted by a shuttle broadcast.

"MERIC Building, next platform," blurted an electronic voice over the intercom.

Kyron hurriedly placed the transcorder back into the security folder and clipped his ID card onto his jacket pocket. He was ready to commence his new job.

THE COMPANY

THE shuttle slowed to a gentle stop in a terminal directly in front of the foyer of the MERIC Building and most of the commuters, including Kyron, hurriedly disembarked, pushed along by the impatient crowd. At first sight, Kyron thought the MERIC Building was daunting, a sort of modern day fortress. The foyer was cordoned off with thick glass panels from ceiling to floor and, to enter the foyer, commuters had to pass through a sophisticated security booth monitored by a number of multi-directional detector cameras.

There was a choice of three security booths at which to queue. Each was guarded by a security officer, dressed in black, with knee-high leather boots. The security officers were well armed with laser pistols and retractable black metal truncheons strapped to their waist. Kyron waited his turn in one of the queues.

Security was tight and three forms of ID were required of all those who wished to enter. He watched the commuters as they filed through the entry, sliding their identification cards across an illuminated plate on the counter, then stepping one pace forward and looking straight ahead at a camera lens on the wall panel for retinal scanning, while pressing their thumbs for fingerprinting on a small illuminated plate just beneath the camera lens. When the light turned green, a section of the thick glass panel slid open to allow the person to enter, and then quickly closed behind them.

Beside the entry booth was an exit space with another glass panel. Those leaving the building needed only to swipe their access card to allow an easy exit. It was intimidating and, as a newcomer to the building, Kyron was relieved that no alarms were activated when he passed through the security checks for the first time.

He found himself in the centre of a vast white marble floor. Three of the surrounding walls were also covered in matching white marble, and the fourth housed two internal transporters with plate-glass sliding doors. There was a miniature obelisk of black onyx several paces in front of him which listed the building directory. All the fifty or so departments' names and suites were illuminated on the obelisk in alphabetical order. There were thirty floors and Samuel Jensen's name appeared in gold lettering at the top of the Directory:

SAMUEL JENSEN, EXECUTIVE BOARD DIRECTOR PENTHOUSE SUITE, LEVEL 30

Underneath the directory list was a square gold coloured plaque engraved with the words:

MERIC

ESTABLISHED 2030

BUILT ON TRUST, LOYALTY AND DEDICATION

Kyron walked briskly through the crowd in the foyer towards one of the empty internal transporters. A digital read-out above it flashed the time:

...0800 hrs...0800 hrs...0800 hrs...

Stepping inside, he pressed the sensor pad numbered '30' on the illuminated strip beside the door and the doors began to close slowly.

"You are not authorised to access this level sir!" came a stern synthesized feminine voice over the intercom. "You have pressed the sensor pad in error. Please try again."

Kyron noticed a small red sensor light flashing on the security monitor in one of the corners of the transporter. He looked directly at the lens and spoke slowly, but decisively.

"No, unless your directory is incorrect, I did not make an error. I have an appointment with Mr Samuel Jensen at 08.30 hours in his Penthouse suite."

There was a long pause before the same voice responded.

"Please place your ID access card in the open tray to your left."

Kyron hadn't noticed the small tray that had silently slid out beside him while he was waiting for a response. As he placed his ID access card in the tray as instructed, a thin green beam of light automatically scanned it and the voice activated again.

"Verified, you may pick up the card, sir. Sorry for the inconvenience."

Kyron quickly retrieved his card and clipped it back onto his pocket. He was not familiar with such strict security.

The transporter began to speed towards Level 30, sensor pads lighting up in turn as each floor was passed. Then the transporter slowly came to rest at the top floor and the doors parted. The time readout above the door was 08.25 hrs.

In front of Kyron was a wide dark-red carpeted passageway lined with subdued wall lighting. On both pastel grey walls, between rows of fashionable light shades, were gold-framed portraits of past members of the Board of Directors. Soft, tranquil music emanated from an undetectable source as Kyron paced quickly down the thoroughfare. As he neared the end and looked to turn left or right, a friendly, mellow voice, which contrasted to the voice in the internal transporter, came from the passageway to his right.

"Kyron, my boy, you managed to find us and right on time too. Glad to see you."

Kyron turned his head to see a distinguished, silver-haired gentleman approaching him, his right arm outstretched to welcome him with a warm handshake. His host sported a well-groomed, steel-grey moustache and beard and wore a smart, dark-grey tailored suit, fashioned into a type of uniform with silver buttons on the blazer and a handkerchief pocket monogrammed with the initials 'S.J.' in silver thread. The black mandarin-collared shirt beneath the blazer gave his host a refined appearance. He was clearly a man of good taste.

"Samuel Jensen's the name, but you can call me sir or Mr Jensen".

Kyron felt Jensen's firm but warm hand grip and noticed that he wore a silver and onyx ring encrusted with a tiny diamond in the centre. He sensed from this contact that Samuel Jensen was a genuine person with a good heart, a man who could be trusted.

"Hello, Mr Jensen," responded Kyron in a respectful tone. "Nice to finally meet you."

"We are one big happy family here, Kyron," said Jensen, "and I want you to feel that you are a part of this family. I have an open door policy and if you have any problems or concerns, I want you to come and see me to talk about them. Alright, Kyron?"

"Yes sir, thank you, I will." Kyron was very relaxed in Samuel Jensen's presence and felt instantly at home.

"Excellent, now come along and I will introduce you to the family. The Board of Directors is assembled today for our scheduled monthly meeting, so you will have the opportunity to be introduced to them all."

Jensen led Kyron briskly through a maze of passageways past polished wooden doors with gold nameplates displaying the names and titles of each occupant.

Inside the diffusely lit Board Room were ten figures talking amongst themselves around a large, oval table made from the same polished black onyx as the miniature Directory obelisk in the foyer on the ground floor.

"Ladies and gentlemen, may I have your undivided attention," commanded Jensen. The group suddenly quietened and their faces immediately focussed on Jensen and Kyron.

"I would like you all to meet our new Level 2 Engineer, Kyron Shield, and welcome him to our family. Starting on my right, I would like to introduce you to the Board members one by one. Mr John Sykes from the Department of Mineral Resources; Mr Evan Montcliffe from the Environment and Natural Resources Commission; Miss Mandy Harrison, Health and Welfare Commission; Mr Randolph Jacobs from the Lands Department; Mrs Susan Langley, Industry and Manufacturing Board; Mr James Harcourt, the Energy Commission; Mr Alfred Piper, Society of Royal Engineers; Miss Korie Davis from Aero Space Program for Exploration, Colonisation and Transportation or ASPECT; and, last but not least, my son, Jackson, newly appointed head of the Commercial Administration Department."

As each member was introduced in turn Kyron nodded politely, sensing their warmth and sincerity. However, as he was introduced to Samuel Jensen's son, Jackson, Kyron immediately felt uneasy. Jackson was cold and aloof and Kyron sensed negative undertones.

Samuel Jensen's only son, Jackson Bartholomew (JB) Jensen, was of similar physical appearance to his father. He was tall and wiry with an olive complexion, but his thick, black, gelled hair and dark brown eyes were distinctive. Like his father, Jackson was gifted in commercial and financial matters, and before joining his father's Company he had graduated from university with a double major in business and financial administration. On graduation, Samuel Jensen had insisted that Jackson join his company, MERIC, and use his expertise to help control and maintain the company's finances. Samuel Jensen hoped to groom his son to take over the reins of the company one day.

However, the similarities between father and son ended there with Jackson having a more shrewd and competitive nature. Although Jackson had been an excellent student at university, receiving top marks in his subjects, he had not been well liked by his peers because of his 'winner-take-all' approach. Those who did associate with him followed Jackson largely out of fear. Jackson was extremely manipulative, finding unsportsmanlike ways to eliminate his competition, particularly in his chosen sports of boxing and fencing, sports he had captained for three years.

"Well Kyron, now that you have formally met all our members, you need to see the manager in Personnel to arrange your orientation. Miss Blake, my Personal Assistant, will escort you. Glad to have you on board, Kyron."

"Thank you Mr Jensen, I look forward to working with all of you," replied Kyron, as he turned towards Miss Blake.

Miss Blake was about thirty-five years of age, of slender build and pleasant appearance with dark, short hair and she was wearing a dark-grey corporate trouser suit. They exchanged friendly smiles as Kyron left with her to continue the next stage of his orientation.

Using the Speed Memory Transfer (SMT) method, Kyron's orientation lasted four hours. A specially-designed helmet allowed visual and audio information to be transmitted at ultra-high speed and Kyron was soon familiar with the Company's structure and its achievements to date, those responsible, access limitations, reporting processes, and the credit and debit point program that had replaced the previous monetary system.

On completion of his orientation, Kyron was escorted by a MERIC security officer to the Interplanetary Space Division, located on the 15th floor. And, en route, Kyron couldn't help but notice the security surveillance cameras in all the passageways and internal transporters.

Soon Kyron arrived at his new workplace, which was a very large room with walls of thick tinted glass. Kyron swiped his ID badge and, on entering, noticed more security surveillance cameras, strategically placed around the room. He reflected on his new environment: *Why so much tight security?*

Without hesitation, Kyron introduced himself warmly to the three occupants who were dressed in white laboratory coats and located at various workstations around the room.

"Good afternoon, everyone. I'm Kyron Shield, the new Level 2 Engineer."

"Welcome Kyron, I'm Brenton White the hardware engineer, but everyone calls me Whitey," said a young man in a southern drawl who was the first to approach, holding out his right hand to Kyron, while clasping a small sonic calibrator in his left.

Whitey was about twenty years of age, relatively thin and short of stature, with long dark hair swept into a ponytail. His smile was partially hidden by a neatly trimmed beard and moustache and he wore round, gold wire-framed prescription shades with lightly tinted blue lenses.

"We've been waiting to show you our progress on a new sonic amplified frequency excavator or SAFE, as we call it. The team's been working on it for the last eighteen months," he said excitedly.

"Thank you Brenton, I'm looking forward to working on this project with all of you."

By now the others had wandered over to greet the new recruit and introduce themselves.

"Hello Kyron, my name is Torri Madison and I'm the computer

systems engineer for MERIC," said the only female amongst them, speaking eloquently in a soft, British accent. But Kyron wasn't listening. He was preoccupied with her very recognisable face.

"You're the same as …"

Before he could finish his sentence, Torri cut in sharply.

"Same face as VALERI?"

"Yes," replied Kyron, "an incredible likeness."

"The Company used my face to generate a computer enhanced image," Torri explained. "They thought it projected a warm, friendly and welcoming impression."

Kyron instantly felt a strong rapport with Torri and sensed that she had a pure heart. She was a beautiful woman, about the same age as him, with a slim petite body. Her soft red hair was longer than that of the hologram image, now down to her shoulders, and her eyes were deep green with a healthy sparkle. Her complexion was very clear with a hint of rose colour in her cheeks. She had pale pink lips and, when she smiled, small dimples showed on her cheeks. And her teeth were so white and perfect. There was a glow to her aura and her hand felt very soft yet energising when Kyron shook it.

Kyron was immediately unsettled by some unusual sensations; his heart raced and his face flushed, his hand trembling slightly in Torri's.

"I wholeheartedly agree with the Company's choice and I will enjoy working with you, Torri," stammered Kyron, gathering himself to greet the last member of the team.

Finally Kyron was approached by the third room member, an older gentleman with greying hair, taller and more heavily built than Brenton White.

"Good afternoon, Kyron," the man said in an articulate baritone voice as he extended his hand in a welcoming gesture. "I'm Guy, Guy Simmons, the energy resources scientist, also involved in this major project. Welcome aboard the team."

"Thank you," replied Kyron gratefully before turning to address the group.

"I would just like to explain my role to all of you so that you know where I fit into the team. I have been appointed as the Level 2 Engineer in my specialisation, application design and mechanical engineering. I am charged with responsibility for the administration of this Division, and for overseeing the mining equipment on the planets Terra Iota and Terra Upsilon.

"But my main role is to work with the team as a team member, to help complete the project on schedule. I am to submit monthly progress reports to the Board of Directors and authorise the acquisition of resources necessary to complete this project within six months. So please, treat me as an equal member of the team and I will lend my assistance and knowledge as the need requires. I am also keen to learn from *your* knowledge and experience. Be patient with me while I get up to speed."

Kyron was surprised to receive a spontaneous round of applause from his new team. They obviously appreciated his arrival and his impromptu speech and he felt immediately comfortable with his new co-workers.

The rest of the day Kyron spent listening to each member of the team and learning what they had achieved to date in their specialised field. Whitey had joined MERIC as a graduate cadet two years ago. He had been interested in computerised mechanics since he was six years old, helping his dad build anti-gravity hovercrafts and experimenting with different powerpacs. He had the philosophy that there was always a way to improve on what already existed.

Guy, on the other hand, had been head-hunted from the military branch of scientific research after he had revolutionised the method of nuclear fusion, producing channelled energy that could be stored and released as required.

Torri had formerly been employed by a London technology firm supplying hi-tech equipment to one of the British space program companies stationed in the USA. She had originally intended to transfer back to the UK when her tenure expired but, when the time came, two years ago, Torri had wanted to stay in the States. So she had landed a position with MERIC and gained American citizenship.

At the end of the day, when the team had left and all was quiet, Kyron sat in his new office observing his surroundings and absorbing all that had taken place in the ten hours since his arrival at MERIC. He reflected on the members of his team: Whitey, the enthusiastic techno and ex-university radical, keen to see the newly developed machine operational; Guy, in his fifties, reserved and methodical;

and Torri, confident and logical with leadership qualities and a face like VALERI's. He liked the team members, especially Torri, as well as the project he had been assigned and the Company, MERIC. His thoughts were suddenly interrupted by someone calling.

"Kyron, my boy, you're still here?" It was Samuel Jensen who had surprised him, having access to the office after hours. "Just wanted to see how your first day went with the Company and the team."

"Oh, Mr Jensen, you startled me. Thank you for asking, I was just collecting my thoughts. I'm very happy with the Company and the team. They seem to be very skilled in their professions and work well as a team with a friendly attitude."

"Glad to hear," cut in Jensen. "They were all hand picked by me to ensure compatibility, competence and commitment. I'm confident that you will all work well together."

Then, Jensen added a more personal note.

"Kyron, you may think I'm a little premature in my judgement seeing as this is your first day on the job, but I've been monitoring your progress since you were a student at the Royal College. Some of your mentors brought you to my attention because they thought you reminded them of me when I was a student."

Kyron was a little taken aback by the thought that his progress had been monitored but he was reassured when Jensen continued.

"I selected you for the job because you remind me of myself when I was younger, studying the same subjects at College. And I know that you have the same passion about nature and the protection of life and want to see things through to the benefit of all. I have faith in your ability and honesty to be a strong leader and maintain the code of this company. After all, my boy, there aren't many honest people left in this world that can be trusted. Well, better be off now, it's getting late. Are you joining me, Kyron? It's been a long day for you."

"Yes, thank you sir. I'll try to meet your expectations," said Kyron, packing some documents into his new briefcase.

"I'm sure you'll do well, my boy. I haven't been wrong yet about my employees. Now come on, it's time to go home."

As they left the building, Kyron had a good feeling about his future with MERIC.

UNEXPECTED
CHANGES

FOR the next six months, Kyron enjoyed working with his team at MERIC. They were all enthusiastic about the SAFE project and its innovative approach to diminishing air and noise pollution. Their aim was to develop superior equipment for mining in the field using sonic amplified frequencies and an alternative power source and Kyron quickly adapted to his lead role in coordinating the project.

The new SAFE technology used vibrating sound waves to fracture densely compacted, geo-rock formations similar to the way a high-pitched voice-frequency shatters glass. The fragmented rubble required no further crushing as the fragments were already reduced to the required size and were easily captured in a trough directly in front of the machine. The rubble was then conveyed in sealed capsules to a processing unit. The SAFE machine could be modified to mine all types of minerals and metals and, having no mechanical drilling components, required no ongoing replacement of parts. Other benefits of the silent sonic frequency were that it had no adverse affects on the auditory senses and caused no interference with neurological activity.

Whitey was mainly responsible for the design and implementation of the high frequency technology, while Torri was working on incorporating a remote control program, allowing the apparatus to be operated by miners stationed well away from the excavation site, thereby minimising danger.

The SAFE prototype was also designed to work on nuclear fusion energy. Current excavators used rechargeable solar energy packs and, while large solar panels on Terra Iota and Terra Upsilon ensured the effectiveness of this traditional energy source for above-ground operations, solar energy was not effective for sub-surface excavation over long periods. Guy Simmons, with Whitey's assistance, was experimenting to perfect the new power source.

Over time, working alongside one another, Kyron and Torri became more than fond of each other and, every opportunity they had outside work they would be together sharing a meal and each other's company. They talked at length about the project, sharing ideas and theories that could be pursued or experimented on within the development of the prototype. They also discovered and talked endlessly about each other's likes and dislikes, their past, their family and their future aspirations. They found they had similar interests and felt the same way about protecting the environment and conserving natural resources. There was natural electricity between them.

Being nature lovers they would often take weekend treks together to the mountains or to the coast, escaping the pollution of the city and the more settled areas. They enjoyed rock climbing, abseiling, kayaking, fishing and camping. It was not unusual for them to pitch a tent by one of the mountain streams, catch a fish for dinner, throw it on a campfire and sleep under the stars. They enjoyed cuddling up together in their sleeping bags and making love next to a warm fire without any inhibitions. Kyron loved the feel of Torri's muscle-toned athletic body, nicely sculpted in all the right places, yet sensual to the touch. Her soft skin had a sweet smell and her lips were moist and inviting. He wanted to be with her forever and wished that weekends never ended.

It came as no surprise to Whitey and Guy when Kyron eventually announced that he and Torri were engaged and would be married in six months' time. They had watched Kyron and Torri's romance blossom. Samuel Jensen was also delighted with the couple because he liked them both and recognised them as good people dedicated to each other and to the Company.

The only person who was not happy with news of the engagement was Jackson Jensen. Jackson had wanted Torri from the first time he met her but, on several occasions, Torri had rejected his advances. He was not attractive to her in any way: She didn't like Jackson's overbearing egotistical attitude and the disrespect he showed to others. Jackson was offended by her response and he resented the fact that Torri had become more interested in Kyron. In the past, Jackson had never lost out to another man and he was loath to accept defeat.

***

One morning, while preparing to leave for work, an unexpected incoming call signalled on Kyron's transceiver.

"Hello, Kyron speaking." There was a pause, and then a familiar voice responded.

"Hello son, how are you this morning?" There was a slight quiver in his mother's voice and Kyron knew instinctively that something was wrong.

"I'm alright, mum, what's wrong, you sound a little upset?"

"Oh, Kyron," she paused, and he could hear her taking a deep breath. "I called to tell you that the farm is being sold to a mining company that specialises in artesian well drilling. The good news is that the credits they are offering will support me comfortably for the future. I know how much the farm means to you, Kyron, but it only makes me sad when I'm there, because it reminds me of those wonderful times we all once shared."

Kyron could sense the tears that his mother was shedding while telling him the unwelcome news. He wished he could be there to comfort her now that she was growing old and frail. He had kept in touch with his mother regularly, telling her about the project he was involved in, the team, the Company and, of course, Torri. But Kyron missed seeing his mother, as they had always been very close.

"I need you to come home Kyron for a short stay at the farm to help me sort through our belongings and to collect some of your father's things that he wanted you to have. Can you let me know when you are able to come? I'm very much looking forward to seeing you, Kyron. You could bring Torri with you. It would be nice to meet the girl who has made my son so happy."

Despite the sadness, her voice still had a warm tone to it.

Kyron was disappointed that the farm was being sold. It was a major part of him and the happy life he shared with his parents, a life he had once hoped would never change. But he remembered the words of his father:

"Nothing stays the same forever and we continue to evolve and change. We need to adapt if we are to grow and expand our spirit and our minds. If we accept this, then life is full of endless possibilities and can be an enriching experience. If we reject change and struggle to maintain the status quo, we will surely stagnate. Ride the tide and stay alive."

Kyron missed the sound of his father's tranquil voice and words of wisdom, but he knew that they would remain in his head and heart for the rest of his life.

"Alright, mum, I'm sure that Mr Jensen will let me have the time off under the circumstances. I'll let you know by tomorrow. Will you be okay until I get there?"

"Yes Kyron, thank you for asking. I'll wait for your call. Bye for now, love you son."

"Same to you, mum. Bye."

The transceiver went silent.

"VALERI open!" commanded Kyron.

"Good morning Kyron, what would you like?" came the instant response as the hologram screen on the wall illuminated.

"I need an appointment with Samuel Jensen first thing this morning."

Within seconds, VALERI responded, "He is available for an hour at 09.00."

"Thank you VALERI, confirm that. And I won't be home for dinner tonight. VALERI close."

Kyron hastily finished his breakfast, packed his compact staff and training outfit into his metal briefcase and rushed off to catch the shuttle. He was planning his moves in his mind as he went. He would ask Torri to have dinner with him tonight to let her know that he would be taking leave in two days time to visit his mother at the farm. *Perhaps she would like to accompany him?*

Soon after arriving at the Division, Kyron went to see Samuel Jensen for his appointment.

"Come in my boy, take a seat and tell me what's on your mind that you so urgently wanted to see me about. Miss Blake! Could you please bring us some refreshments while Kyron and I have a chat?"

"Yes, Mr Jensen," she replied, warmly.

Samuel Jensen made Kyron feel at home on every occasion. In fact Samuel Jensen had become almost like a second father to Kyron and Kyron would ask his advice from time to time, not only on business but also on personal matters.

"Well sir, I've just received word that my mother is selling the farm and would like me to be there to sort things out. I would like to take some time off, if that's possible, to assist her. The SAFE project is on schedule, the prototype's ready to be tested and, by the time I return, it should be in operation for the field."

"Oh, I see, Kyron," responded Jensen. "Well I want you to know that I have been very pleased with the results of the SAFE project, and I'm looking forward to the demonstration of the prototype in the next few weeks."

"Excuse me Mr Jensen."

They were momentarily interrupted by Miss Blake bringing in some iced green tea served in crystal glasses. Samuel Jensen was a keen advocate of natural health and did all he could to keep his body and mind healthy.

"Is there anything else you need, sir?" she enquired.

"No thank you, Miss Blake."

She departed, quietly closing the door behind her and leaving a faint essence of fragrant perfume permeating the air.

"I'm also proud of how you have become one of the family and, from what others have told me, they like working with you," Jensen continued. "You know Kyron, although you have not been here long and we only see each other every so often, I consider you as my second son."

Kyron was surprised but thrilled to hear those words from his employer.

"Thank you sir, I am honoured and I would like to say that you have been like a father to me."

Jensen had more to say.

"You have a positive attitude and refreshing honesty Kyron, which

I have not encountered with many others." He paused briefly before adding, "Including my own son."

There was an awkward moment and Jensen took a long sip of tea before continuing the conversation.

"I consider you as a valuable employee with whom I would trust my own life. I also believe in rewarding hard work and I think you deserve some leave for your efforts. Will four weeks be enough time to resolve things?"

"Yes, thank you sir, that should be plenty of time," replied Kyron, still thinking about the remark Jensen had just made about his own son. "It will be good to see my mother again. The team are very competent to handle the demonstration exercise, and I'm confident that it will be a success."

"But I want you to take the Company's transceiver with you just in case I need to contact you should there be any hiccups with the prototype and the demonstration," said Jensen. "So Kyron, when will you be leaving for the trip to the farm?"

"The day after tomorrow would be best, sir," Kyron replied. "This will give me a chance to brief the team and double-check the equipment as well as the control modules."

"Very good, Kyron. On your way back to ISD, just inform Personnel of your leave of absence, and I will see you on your return."

Jensen rose and shook Kyron's hand firmly for some time, emphasising the gesture of goodwill using both hands.

"You take good care of yourself and your mother," he said, sincerely.

"Thank you, sir, I will. See you soon."

As Kyron left Jensen's office, Jackson mysteriously appeared at the door as if he had been eaves-dropping, and he stared coldly at Kyron as he passed by. Kyron sensed jealousy and anger radiating from Jackson but, saying nothing, Kyron simply nodded an acknowledgement of Jackson's presence and continued on his way.

Arriving back at the Division, Kyron called the team together.

"Listen everyone; I need to inform you of some changes that have been made due to unforeseen circumstances."

The team looked a little alarmed until Kyron continued.

"No need to worry, but this morning I received word from home that I need to return to sort out some personal matters. I've been granted four weeks' leave by Mr Jensen and I've explained to him that I'm confident in the team being able to present the demonstration of the prototype in my absence.

"While I'm away, and if you all agree, I would like Guy to be in charge, that's if Guy accepts my proposal. I know this is very sudden and, I really wanted to be there for the unveiling of our project, to share in the success of SAFE. But you are the ones who really deserve all the credit. You have been involved in this project from the beginning, and for a lot longer than I have. I'll be leaving the day after tomorrow, so that gives me enough time for a final inspection just to ensure we have everything working perfectly. So, are you all okay with this?"

There were mixed feelings amongst the group. They all wanted Kyron to be there at the launch, but well understood his need to return home. Guy and Whitey approached Kyron separately to indicate their agreement with the arrangements. Then Kyron took Torri aside.

"I'm sorry for not preparing you for this sooner Torri, but it all happened so fast. I want you to come with me to the farm. Will you think about it? And can we have dinner tonight to talk about the situation?"

"Alright Kyron and thanks for the invitation to your farm; I'll think about it and let you know at dinner," Torri responded in an understanding voice. She knew Kyron would have informed her earlier if he'd had the opportunity.

"Shall we meet at 'The Zenith' at say, 19.00 hrs after I finish my training?"

"Yes, alright, I'll see you there."

The day passed without event although the atmosphere was somewhat more sombre than usual following Kyron's announcement of his impending absence.

After work, Kyron headed for the gym for his routine blade practice. The Company encouraged health and fitness for its employees and had installed a very large gymnasium, furnished with the most modern equipment. It was open twenty-four hours, seven days a week, to cater for staff members who were rostered on different shifts. This suited Kyron's commitment to his training, allowing him to practise even when he worked late or had early morning starts to keep the project on schedule.

As Kyron was coming out of the gym change-room that afternoon he sighted Jackson on the far side of the training hall, duelling with an opponent using a thin-bladed sword with the point of the blade protected to prevent a fatal blow. He had seen this style of fencing before but he watched intently the way Jackson had mastered the technique. Jackson seemed to be toying with his opponent like a cat playing with a captured mouse.

Jackson's sparring partner was also very well versed in the art, but Jackson was more agile, with very quick reflexes. He was easily blocking every strike and thrust, returning a counter-attack and marking his opponent with every blow. In the short time that he watched, Kyron saw Jackson become more and more aggressive in his attacks, working to defeat his opponent. *He's some swordsman.*

Kyron completed his training deliberately out of sight from Jackson and then prepared to meet Torri for dinner. When he arrived at 'The Zenith', Torri was already waiting and had seated herself at one of the more private booths, where the lighting was subdued.

"Hello sweetheart, have you been waiting long?"

"Hello, Kyron," she responded. "No not really, about five minutes."

"Sorry about today and the sudden notice without warning."

"That's alright, Kyron. I know you would've told me sooner if you'd had the chance. Are you okay? Is everything alright at home? I'm worried about you."

Over dinner, Kyron explained to Torri why he had to take leave urgently to return home and how he wanted to see his mother in person instead of talking to a hologram image of her, which he had done for the last six months. It was clear to Torri how sad it was going to be for Kyron parting with the farm where he had grown up under the watchful eye of his loving mother and father.

"You know how much I love you. I really want you to come with me to meet my mother. She's looking forward very much to seeing her son's fiancée," Kyron said.

"I feel the same way Kyron and I'd really love to meet your mother," Torri replied, "but this time, I feel that it would be better for you and your mother to be by yourselves, without anyone else intruding on your memories. Sorting through your family's belongings will most likely be very difficult for you and your mother. I feel I'd be in the way. I definitely want to meet her sometime soon, but it would be better to meet her under different circumstances, when she has settled into her new surroundings. I'll miss you very much, Kyron, and I'll be here for you when you return."

Kyron knew that Torri was right in her thoughts about the situation. It would be better if he went by himself this time.

"Thank you Torri, for being so understanding," Kyron said with a tear of affection in his eye. "I'll call you every day, without fail."

They finished their meal deep in thought.

***

Kyron spent the next day overseeing final preparations for the demonstration of the prototype. This involved diagnostic analysis and retesting the new equipment, ensuring that the mechanics and the electronics were failsafe.

By the end of the day everything was set to go and Kyron issued last-minute instructions to the team. They were all feeling very confident that the trials would be a success. By the time Kyron returned from his leave, the new machine should be ready for the production line.

Kyron and Torri were the last of the team to leave for the day and decided to have a quiet romantic dinner at one of the more up-market restaurants. Over the meal they talked about their future with the company, their ideas and plans for a family and children and their thoughts about when Kyron could meet Torri's family back in the United Kingdom.

They were so engrossed in their conversation they didn't realise how late it was getting. All the patrons, save for the romantic couple, had left some time ago. The head waiter, still looking amazingly sharp in his crisp, black-and-white uniform was anxious to retire for the night and approached their table to give them a subtle hint.

"Excuse me monsieur, 'ere iz your account," he said in a polite French accent.

It was then that Kyron, for the first time all evening, looked at the timepiece on his wrist.

"My God, is that the time? Sorry for keeping you so late," he exclaimed, thinking to himself how time was lost when he was with Torri.

"That iz alright, monsieur," replied the waiter with a smile. "I could see that you enjoyed the meal with the lovely mademoiselle and I did not want to change the mood."

Torri acknowledged the compliment.

"Thank you for being so considerate and patient."

"Yes," Kyron interrupted, handing the waiter the account, "here is my card and please add five credit points for your tip."

"Merci monsieur, you are most kind and if you don't mind me saying so, that iz an exquisite ring the lovely lady iz wearing."

"Yes," responded Kyron, "only the finest for the finest. This is Torri, my fiancée."

"Ah! Congratulations to you both," exclaimed the waiter, now grinning from ear to ear. "You are a very lucky man. You need to look after thiz delicate flower."

"I know I am sir and yes, I will guard her with my life."

After settling the account, they returned to Torri's apartment where they spent the rest of the night together, making the most of each other's company. This trip would part them for the first time since they had met.

DISCOVERY

KYRON arrived at the farm the following day to find his mother busily packing all sorts of items that had accumulated over a lifetime. His mind momentarily wandered back to the times when he and his parents would sit down to a meal together after a day's work on the farm, discussing the day that had just gone and planning the next year in an atmosphere of love and humour. But all had changed when old age finally caught up with his father.

According to Kyron's mother, his father had been seventy-five years of age when he died and although his mind had still been active, it was his physical body that had worn out. Rhamon's funeral service had been held on the farm and his ashes given to Kyron's mother in a sealed container.

It had taken some time for Kyron to overcome his grief and he channelled his emotions into his study and martial arts. Eventually he was able to accept the experience and move on with his life. However, returning to the farm brought back the trauma and emotion of an event which had deeply affected both Kyron and his mother.

Together they agreed that most of the furniture and his parents' personal items could be transported to the place where his mother now lived, close to her family. However, among his father's possessions were some items that had been bequeathed to Kyron and Kyron's mother spoke softly and sincerely as she handed him a gold signet ring and a shiny, metallic briefcase.

"Kyron, my son, your father wanted you to have these gifts and asked you to guard them with your life. I didn't know about these things until your father showed them to me just before he passed away. I have no idea what's in the case. Your father instructed me not to show them to anyone but you. He said to give them to you only when he was gone as this would be the right time to enlighten you. Your father didn't explain what he meant, so I hope you will be able work it out."

"Thank you mum, I'll look after them and honour my father's wishes," Kyron replied. He was curious to inspect the gifts and puzzled as to how they could enlighten him. After all, his father had taught him everything he needed to know.

As soon as Kyron had the opportunity to be by himself in his room, he started to examine the items. The first was an intricately designed gold ring. On the face of the ring, which resembled an ancient coin, was a circle with six equally-divided segments, each inscribed with a different symbol, and all unrecognisable to Kyron. On each side of the ring and set into the band were four small gemstones, deep blue in colour. Inscribed inside the band were more symbols which looked like a form of ancient language.

Kyron tried the ring on the middle finger of his right hand. It was a perfect fit. As he sat admiring the ring he felt an unusual faint tingling sensation pass through his hand and slowly work itself through the length of his arm, to the other arm, to his chest, down to his waist and finally through both his legs. The feeling was not unpleasant; quite the opposite. Within seconds the tingling ceased, leaving a warm inner glow through his entire body. Kyron enjoyed the sensation. Although unlike anything he had ever felt before, it felt completely natural.

Next, Kyron examined the silver case. It was unlike other metal cases he had encountered. The lid was locked tight with no locking device on the surface area. In place of where a slide-card would normally be located, there was a small triangular panel. He pressed the panel with his thumb and it illuminated with a blue fluorescence. Using all his strength, Kyron tried to open the container. It refused to budge. He pressed the triangular panel again and the illumination faded.

Having no success opening the case, Kyron decided to inspect the ring more closely. *What did the symbols in the segments mean?* He pressed the symbols randomly, triggering a very soft, high-pitched, harmonious sound, like a complex chord played on an electronic synthesizer. Suddenly, to Kyron's surprise, the catches on each side of the case flicked open and the triangle illuminated once more. Kyron pressed the triangle again and the case sprung apart.

Hesitantly, Kyron peered into the case. There were three items inside. One was a small silver box of similar size and shape to the obsolete transcorders that had been used two decades ago. Next to this was a tightly folded dark-blue cloth of an unusual material. And the third item was a length of rounded wood that appeared to be petrified wood. It was of a similar size and diameter to Kyron's expandable staff.

With great care Kyron lifted the silver transcorder out of the case and, on close examination, found the colour-coded sensor buttons. Peering over his shoulder, he quickly surveyed the room to ensure that he was alone and the door was closed. He then pressed the green sensor on the machine to listen to the recording. His father's voice was instantly recognisable although it sounded a little more apprehensive than usual.

"Kyron, by the time you hear this message, I will no longer be alive, and I hope that you, my son, will be safely listening to what I have to say. There is much to tell and I hope that you will forgive me for not telling you sooner, but it was necessary to withhold this vital information until I felt that the time was right not only for the protection of my family, especially you, Kyron, but also for the preservation of my race. I know this may come as a shock to you, my son, but I will explain the circumstances. So please listen carefully."

Kyron paused the recording and sat motionless for a moment while his mind raced with a myriad of questions. *What were these items in the case? Why had his father kept them secret for so long? What was his father hiding? What was this 'race' he mentioned? And why would Kyron and his mother need protecting?*

Kyron was struggling to understand the mysterious scenario and was eager to learn more about his father to resolve these questions. He checked over his shoulder again before restarting the transcorder.

"I am not from this planet, Kyron. I originate from a planet named Tzurac which is located three hundred light years away in a star system yet to be discovered by Terranians. I arrived here two-hundred-and-seventy years ago in the Earth year of 1785, around the time of the Napoleonic wars. Tzuracians are very similar to humans in their physiological and biological structure so I was able to blend easily into this society. And, by moving from country to country over a long period of time, I was able to maintain my secret.

"You're probably wondering how it is that I have lived for so long. A Tzuracian's life span is similar to Earthlings, approximately eighty years. However, I am a soldier or 'Sentinel' as they are known on Tzurac and, like all Sentinels, my DNA had been specially treated in such a way as to increase my lifespan to four hundred years by slowing down the ageing process. I was one-hundred-and-thirty years old when I arrived on Earth.

"I would've been quite content to live out my life on Tzurac if I hadn't been framed for the murder of my best friend and sentenced to death. With the aid of my loyal soldiers, who knew that I had been falsely accused, I was able to escape from Tzurac and its Security Forces, eventually navigating my craft to Terra Major. I remained anonymous for fear of exposure by humans and of discovery by the Tzuracian search party they would have sent to hunt me down.

"I met and married your wonderful mother forty years ago. She was unaware of my origin and still is to this day. I did all this for the family's protection and trained you in martial combat techniques to help you and your mother survive any unwanted encounters. It appears that my DNA has been passed on to you Kyron, which explains why you have enhanced sensitivity and unique physical attributes. I want you, Kyron, to hide these special qualities from others as they will not understand or accept the powers you have and will only try to destroy you.

"Keep these objects hidden and take good care of your mother. Remember, I will always be with you in spirit and, in time of need, you will sense my presence. Follow your teachings, use your heart as your guide and always have a clear mind. Do not let the hatred of others lead you astray. Do all these things and you will lead a good and healthy long life."

Kyron's pulse was racing, his body was flushed by a rush of adrenalin, and small beads of perspiration dampened his forehead. He let the recording run until it stopped automatically within seconds of those last words. He was finding all this very hard to believe.

He had known his father so well and his father had appeared to be a normal human being, living a normal life. Yet his father had also seemed to possess a deeper knowledge of life than most and, when he and Kyron meditated together, Kyron had sensed an area in his father's mind that would not reveal itself in mind-linking. Perhaps this was where his father had kept his secret tightly locked, to protect Kyron and Kyron's mother from sceptics and from those who would ridicule and destroy what they couldn't understand out of fear or jealously.

Kyron replaced the transcorder carefully in the metal case and picked up the dark-blue cloth. He unravelled the strange material. It had an unusual feel to it, like liquid metal or mercury only coarser, but not heavy. The cloth was fashioned in the shape of a robe or cape with wide flared sleeves and an ample hood. Embossed on the sides of each sleeve were gold symbols similar to the six symbols that appeared on the face of his signet ring.

After carefully refolding the robe and placing it back in the case, Kyron reached for the short petrified wooden rod. He found it much lighter than expected and as soon as he touched it, he experienced the same tingling sensation taking over his entire body as he had experienced with the ring. As Kyron returned the wooden rod to the case, the tingling sensation slowly dissipated.

At that moment Kyron's mother called out to him from outside his room. Kyron was momentarily caught by surprise. He quickly closed the lid of the case and placed it out of sight under the desk where he was sitting. There was a gentle knock and the door slowly opened.

"Hello Kyron, sorry to disturb you, but your transceiver screen is flashing. Are you alright? You seem a little on edge."

Kyron did his best to look like nothing out of the ordinary had happened.

"Yes thanks mum, I'm okay," said Kyron as his mother handed him the device. She turned and left the room, closing the door quietly behind her.

Kyron was surprised to see that the cryptic message on the screen was from Samuel Jensen. Samuel Jensen rarely communicated by transceiver and this was out of character for him. The message read:

"Sorry to interrupt your leave, Kyron, but I must instruct you to return to headquarters immediately. There has been an incident in the last twenty-four hours that only you can attend to and time is of the essence. I cannot tell you any more due to security protocol. Please come immediately and please apologise to your mother for me, as I know how much she was looking forward to spending some time with you."

Kyron was immediately anxious. *What a curious message? Perhaps something had gone wrong with the demonstration of the SAFE prototype? But why would Samuel Jensen make personal contact when there were other engineers he could have approached?* Kyron had no option; the only thing to do was to return immediately as ordered.

"It's probably not that serious, mum," said Kyron, trying to reassure his mother about why he would need to return immediately to MERIC. "I'll probably return very soon to continue helping you with all the sorting and packing."

Kyron was tempted to tell his mother about the items in his father's metal case and the history of his father's life. But Rhamon had suggested that this might endanger her. And now Kyron didn't have time to think it through. Kyron's mother interrupted his thoughts with a simple and direct question.

"May I ask what your father left you, Kyron?"

Kyron could not tell a lie — he was too honest, even for his own good. Besides, even when he was trying to hide something from his mother, she always knew.

"Well, I haven't had much time to study the things in detail inside the metal case but I can tell you that he left me a staff and a robe. They may have more of a story to them when I get the chance to re-examine them but, at this stage, I really don't know or understand where they came from. The gold ring is intriguing and I'm fascinated by the strange symbols marked on it."

Kyron held his right hand out to his mother to give her a closer look at the intricacies of the ring.

"Yes, they *are* strange symbols, Kyron. I too would like to know what they mean." She paused for some time while examining the ring. Then she enquired sincerely, "Do you intend to wear the ring from now on, Kyron?"

"Yes, of course," said Kyron. "I'll always wear it. It belonged to my dad and I'll feel very proud to wear his ring as a symbol of my love and respect for him. I think he would appreciate that, don't you mum?

I'll take the case with me back to the city and look at those things more closely when I find some spare time."

Kyron's mother pondered for a moment, reflecting on her beloved late husband.

"How interesting. You know your father never did explain exactly where he was raised and what he did before he met me. He seemed to have a troubled past and I often wondered if there was something serious that he wasn't telling me. He would sometimes wake up in the middle of the night in a cold sweat, calling out a name like 'Dagger'. When I asked him if he was having a bad dream, he would say it was just the past catching up and that it best be forgotten. I wonder if these things that he left for you were trappings of his past? Oh well, I suppose you will uncover more when you have time to inspect them."

"Yes, I suppose so," said Kyron kindly. "It's all rather mysterious. Well, I must get a move on and catch the next transport shuttle so I'm back before morning. I'm sorry my stay was cut short. Will you be able to manage without my help for a while, mum?"

"It saddens me that you have to leave so soon Kyron, but I'm sure we'll catch up again in the very near future. Your Uncle Trent is coming over in a couple of days and he will be able to help out. Please keep in touch and let me know how everything is when you get back there."

On that note, Kyron leant over to kiss his mother on the cheek and give her a warm hug.

"I love you mum," he whispered affectionately in her ear.

She returned a quick peck on his cheek and a warm embrace.

"It was good to see you again Kyron. Take care of yourself and stay in touch. Give my regards to Torri, and tell her I look forward to meeting my son's future wife."

"I will," said Kyron, as he slipped away and headed for his room to collect his father's metal case.

***

Kyron was soon on the night shuttle express heading to the city, his mind fully preoccupied not only with his father's mysterious past, but also with the mysterious incident that had occurred back at MERIC.

Travelling at ultra-high speed, it took little time to arrive at the Central Reception Control Quadrant which was busy as usual, crowded with shift workers. And, Kyron was back in his apartment by midnight.

He was too tired to examine the contents of the metal case and needed to conceal the case where it would not be found easily. He had always suspected the security in his apartment and felt as if he was being spied upon. So, while the apartment was still in darkness, he hung a large towel across the hologram screen and then placed the case in the hollow compartment in the wall cavity just behind his bed. He wondered momentarily whether he should remove his father's ring, but decided to leave it on as it felt very comfortable and gave him that 'good-feeling' glow that he had experienced when he first slid it onto his finger. Kyron removed the towel from the hologram screen, ordered VALERI to turn the lights on dimmer mode and prepared himself for bed.

CONSPIRACY

KYRON was startled from his slumber next morning by the sound of VALERI.

"Good morning Kyron, did you sleep well? And did you have a good trip?"

"Thank you VALERI, yes I did, to both your questions."

Kyron swung his legs over the side of the bed and sat on the edge thinking about the dream still vivid in his head. Although he had slept deeply, he'd had an unusual dream he hadn't experienced before that felt very real to him. He couldn't recall a complete story, only coloured flashes of images and places. There were soldiers wearing dark-blue robes similar to the robe he found in his father's case and the soldiers were brandishing swords as if in battle. Voices were yelling and horses were being ridden hard, sweat pouring down their drenched manes onto their necks.

The scene suddenly switched and he was standing in a large cobble-stoned courtyard with huge towering white mosques surrounded by high, white stone walls. On the terraces were people, some very old, and all were dressed in pastel-coloured tunics. And on the grounds within the courtyard, more of the robed soldiers were marching in regimented formation, the sound of their leather, knee-high boots thudding on the hard cobblestones and echoing loudly within the walls.

Kyron shook his head trying to clear the images, but they still lingered in his memory. The time flashing on the hologram screen showed -**...06.30 hrs...**- and he needed to make haste.

After performing his martial art exercises, Kyron had a quick breakfast, steam bathed and dressed for work. Arriving at work at 08.00 hours he went straight to Samuel Jensen's office. Samuel Jensen, who always arrived earlier than anyone else in the Company, was already at his desk.

"Come in my boy," said Jensen. "I'm glad you've returned promptly as the matter is quite serious." Jensen appeared worried.

"Did something go wrong with the SAFE prototype demonstration, sir?" enquired Kyron in a concerned voice.

"No, no Kyron," replied Jensen in a more business-like tone. "The demonstration was a great success and I'm very pleased with you and your team. The sonic excavator is working perfectly and it will be replacing most of the equipment in the field almost immediately. That's not the issue, my boy."

Now Kyron was even more concerned. Samuel Jensen had his complete attention.

Before he spoke, Jensen rose from his chair and walked over to the doorway. He quickly checked the outside passageway and closed the door, before returning to his seat.

"What I'm about to tell you Kyron is in the strictest confidence and you are not to repeat anything I say on this matter to anyone."

Kyron nodded in agreement and Jensen continued.

"I have only recently been informed by transmissions from Terra Iota that there was an explosion in the main open mine two weeks ago which killed several of the miners and injured two of the engineers. I'm not sure why I wasn't informed sooner. It's most unusual and I wonder whether there's more to it than meets the eye. The explosion appears to have been caused by some sort of unusual crystallized blue rock which the geologists stationed there cannot identify. It is a substance unknown to us. I want you to accompany an investigation team that I'm sending to Terra Iota to follow up. The team comprises geophysicists, science officers and senior engineers from MERIC as well as some astrophysicists from ASPECT. I've already contacted ASPECT and they are arranging for a space transporter to leave the day after tomorrow."

Kyron's memory quickly flashed back to his research days when he had first encountered ASPECT and their involvement with the mining industry. Fifteen years ago, a contract had been signed between ASPECT and MERIC giving MERIC sole mining rights to those planets discovered by ASPECT in exchange for a percentage of the profits from the sale of the mined minerals to fund ASPECT's space programs. Given Earth's limited future to sustain life, ASPECT was searching desperately to find new solar systems to colonise. They had found two other habitable planets, Terra Iota and Terra Upsilon, within the same solar system as Earth. These planets could sustain local flora and fauna not unlike Earth's, and had a similar climate to that enjoyed on Earth a century earlier. Mining had since commenced on Terra Iota.

"They will send you travel arrangements and briefing schedules and other information to help you prepare for your trip," Jensen continued. "You can inform your project team that you are undertaking an investigation of an explosion in one of the machines on Terra Iota, but say nothing about what might have caused the incident. The round trip should take approximately three months."

Jensen leaned closer to Kyron and continued in hushed tones.

"The reason I'm keeping this information highly confidential is that there have been some unusual events happening within the Company. I have nothing tangible as yet to confirm my suspicions, but I feel that there is some sort of conspiracy afoot and you, Kyron, are one of the few people I can trust. I want you to be my eyes and ears while on Terra Iota, to be my 'confidante' so to speak. I would like you not only to examine the machinery and the probable cause of the explosion, but also to observe those around you and their behaviour. I know you well Kyron, and I believe you have a special gift for perceiving the real character of those with whom you come into contact."

Jensen lowered his head, and the disappointment in his voice was clear.

"I'm also having some doubts about my own son, Jackson, and I'm reluctant to place complete trust in him."

Raising his head again and, looking Kyron in the eye, Jensen implored:

"I want you to be extremely careful and to watch your back, Kyron. Keep me posted. I'll look forward to your reports and to your return."

"Thank you Mr Jensen, I won't let you down," said Kyron as they shook hands.

Kyron strode to the door and out of Jensen's office.

***

On the way back to the project team, Kyron's mind was preoccupied with what Samuel Jensen had just told him. Kyron had been suspicious of Jackson since their first encounter at the Board meeting on Kyron's first day with MERIC. He had also sensed a change in the environment in the MERIC Building this morning when he had entered. At first he had attributed it to the fact that he had been away on the farm and was over-sensitive to a change in surroundings, but now he began to think differently.

Kyron was quite concerned and alarmed about a suspected conspiracy and he was glad that Samuel Jensen had trusted him enough to confide in him. His mind turned to thinking how much he wanted to be with Torri tonight. Although he had only been away for a short time, he had missed her warmth and affection and this three-month journey to Terra Iota would certainly test their emotional commitment to each other. Before he left again, Kyron also wanted to share with Torri what he had learnt about his father.

As he entered the internal transporter on the 30th floor, Kyron encountered Jackson, who was also catching the transporter.

"Hello Kyron," said Jackson. "I see you have returned early from your leave. Any particular reason?"

Jackson's face was cold and expressionless and he spoke in a manner that made Kyron feel as if he was being interrogated. He was glaring at Kyron waiting for him to respond.

"Good day, Jackson," Kyron replied, "Yes, your father requested that I return from my leave to discuss a specific issue. It's a nice feeling to be needed. Oh! This is my floor. Have a nice day Jackson, won't you. Bye."

Kyron felt as if he'd had the upper hand. He had avoided giving any information to Jackson about the conversation with his father, keeping Samuel Jensen's wish of confidentiality.

Arriving at his Division, Kyron was greeted warmly by the team.

"Kyron, good to see you back," exclaimed Whitey. "But why so early?"

The others were also keen to hear his response, especially Torri.

"Yes Kyron, what's wrong?"

"There's nothing wrong," said Kyron. "Mr Jensen asked me to return early because I was the only engineer available to undertake an investigation of an explosion in one of the machines on Terra Iota. The machine might need replacing and I have to leave the day after tomorrow. I was only notified last night."

The team seemed to accept what Kyron had told them, although the expression on Torri's face told Kyron that she was not completely convinced. Kyron quickly changed the subject.

"On a brighter note, I was informed by Mr Jensen that the demonstration was a success, and he asked me to tell you that he is very proud of all of you, as am I. He'd like to start line production operations of the sonic excavator immediately for use in the field."

Kyron's words were rewarding to the team and Whitey and Guy happily returned to their work stations to continue with what they had been doing before the surprise interruption. But Torri approached Kyron for a more private conversation.

"How is your mother managing, Kyron? She must have been upset that you had to cut short your leave."

"Thanks for asking, Torri. I'm sorry I didn't have time to contact you, but I wanted to explain to you in person. Can we have dinner tonight?"

"That would be great, Kyron. My place?"

"Perfect."

Kyron gently held Torri's arm as a gesture of his affection for her and pulled her slightly closer to him while he spoke quietly. Even in her white lab coat she still looked fabulous and the scent of her jasmine perfume made her even more enticing. Kyron knew that it was going to be difficult being away from her for three months and that he would have to focus all his energy on the task at hand.

"Sorry I can't talk right now Torri but I have so much to do and so little time to do it before I report to ASPECT. I need to collect all the specs and reports on the Terra Iota machine and contact the relevant personnel. We'll talk more in depth after work. I need to tell you about some very interesting things I came across while I was away. I missed you so much Torri. It's good to be back, even for just a little while."

Torri didn't need to say anything. Her eyes and her smile expressed the same thoughts.

The rest of the day Kyron was kept busy extracting as much information as he could about Terra Iota's equipment. This included hologram images of the mine and the machinery before and after the incident, the mining crew, the ore being transported and the communications received and transmitted over the last month.

In the afternoon Kyron went to see the Communications Officer to obtain a transcript on disc of the Terra Iota transmissions. But, when he requested the disc, the young officer on duty appeared to be quite hesitant about releasing this information to him.

"Sorry, sir," the newly recruited officer said in a slightly nervous, high-pitched voice and then with a smug smile on his face, "but the rules are that I need authorisation from your senior manager before releasing this confidential information."

Kyron knew that this would probably take another week of paperwork and bureaucratic red tape and he didn't have time for the delay.

"Okay, if that's what you need," responded Kyron, frustrated. He reached for the transceiver on his belt with his left hand, thumb-pressed the direct line button to Samuel Jensen and placed the transceiver to his ear. There was a few seconds delay. Then Kyron spoke into the transceiver.

"Mr Jensen, Kyron here. I am having some difficulty in acquiring the information I need regarding transcripts of the transmissions over the last month between Terra Iota and the Communications Centre. I was wondering if you could authorise this if I hand the transceiver over to the Communications Officer."

There was a slight pause and then Kyron placed the transceiver to the ear of the Communication Officer, who was taken aback by Kyron's direct line to Samuel Jensen.

"Hello, CO Martin here, sir."

Kyron watched the young officer's facial expression change as he listened to Samuel Jensen, the blood draining from his face.

"Yes, sir. Sorry sir, I... ah, yes, alright, thank you sir. I am doing it now. Okay sir."

The officer pushed the transceiver away from his ear and began frantically manipulating the computer controls.

Kyron placed the transceiver to his ear again.

"Thank you, sir." There was a brief pause while Kyron listened to Samuel Jensen. Then Kyron spoke once more. "Yes, he's retrieving it now. Thank you, sir. Over and out."

While the information was being collated, Kyron noticed from the output on the screen that there had been a surprisingly large number of transmissions. He made a mental note to investigate these more closely. Within minutes Kyron had the information on disc and left the young officer still dumbfounded by his brush with Samuel Jensen.

By the end of the day, Kyron had collated all the necessary information onto another disc. Placing both discs in a sealed folder, he packed the 'Confidential' folder into his brief case. It was his intention to make the most of his remaining time with Torri, leaving examination of the material until the space flight.

There were so many issues on his mind that he needed to share with Torri. He wanted to tell her about the items in his father's case, although he was fearful of breaching his father's confidentiality. He also wanted to tell her the real reason for his excursion to Terra Iota and about the probable conspiracy within the Company. He knew that this would breach the trust that Samuel Jensen had placed in him but he remembered the words of his father echoing in his memory: "Have clear thought and an honest heart." Kyron knew he could trust Torri implicitly with this confidential information. Besides, he wanted her to be as safe as possible and to be prepared and aware of anything that might affect her safety. Kyron mulled this over in his mind for some time. Satisfied with his decision, Kyron left work and headed for the gym. He would do his daily blade practice before continuing on to Torri's place.

***

Kyron was overwhelmed by the passionate greeting he received from Torri before a word was exchanged. When they finally broke from their embrace, Kyron spoke quietly to her.

"We don't have much time tonight, Torri, so I'll talk quickly to tell you all the things that have been happening over the last few days."

Kyron raised his right hand to his face and placed a finger to his lips, gesturing silence. He rose slowly from his seat and went over to the music system, turning the volume up to muffle any of his words. Torri looked at Kyron with a puzzled expression, but before she could utter a sound, Kyron began.

"For some time now I've suspected that the security systems within these apartments have been monitoring everyone's behaviour with audio and visuals. Increasing the volume on the music will muffle our conversation. The visual monitoring may still be operating on the hologram screen so I suggest we move to another area of the apartment if we don't want to be detected. Sorry to alarm you Torri, but after the discussion I had this afternoon with Mr Jensen, I am even more suspicious of the Company's activities. I trust you Torri with my life and I need to confide in you for both our safety. This is just between you and me, so please don't say anything to anyone about the things that I'm about to tell you. I don't want to lose Samuel Jensen's trust in me."

Looking somewhat perplexed, Torri nodded her head in assurance.

"Yes, of course Kyron, you have my word and my heart. But, why all the 'cloak and dagger'? What's going on?"

Over dinner Kyron described to Torri the items bequeathed to him by his father and the story left on the transcorder about his father's origin. Torri listened with keen interest to what seemed like an incredible tale out of a fantasy novel. She admired the ring on Kyron's finger and probed him for more detail about the blue robe with the unique texture and the short stick that resembled petrified wood. Kyron also explained the real reason for his trip to Terra Iota, the discovery of the blue crystal rock, and Mr Jensen's suspicions of a conspiracy. He cautioned Torri to be on the alert while he was away and observe any 'out of the ordinary' behaviour, but to act innocent about everything. Torri was intrigued and a little alarmed by what Kyron told her and she looked to Kyron for reassurance that everything would be alright.

"Don't look so worried my darling," said Kyron, comforting her. "I'm sure all will be revealed in time with no harm coming to anyone. I won't let anything happen to you, Torri. I'll always be there for you."

Torri raised a smile knowing that she was safe with Kyron. She hugged him tightly and they embraced with a long, lingering kiss so passionate that it promised to stay with him through the three months ahead.

Kyron stayed with Torri that night, but before retiring, they placed a cover over the hologram screen on the wall and left the meditative music playing to dampen their conversation and their close and sensuous encounter.

THE JOURNEY

KYRON stirred early the following morning and sat for a moment on the side of the bed, basking in the filtered morning sunlight that shone through the small strip of tinted windows on the eastern wall of the bedroom. The wall screen had not yet activated, giving him time to ponder in solitude without disruption. He had been awakened by the same recurring vivid dream that he'd had the night before. This time Kyron clearly remembered the faces of the characters and some of the foreign words that were spoken. *But what was the significance of these repeated dreams? Who were these military characters? And where were these strange places that appeared each night in his slumber?* They felt strangely familiar to Kyron, giving him a sense of déjà-vu. Kyron realised that the dreams had commenced soon after he had started wearing his father's ring and he hoped that he would eventually uncover the answers.

Kyron looked across at Torri who was still sound asleep. She looked so beautiful lying beside him with her long, dark red hair partially covering her angelic face. Her complexion was so soft and smooth. It felt nice just being there with her. Travelling on this mission to Terra Iota and being away from her for so many weeks was not really what he wanted in his life right now.

Leaving Torri sleeping, Kyron dressed and slipped silently out of her apartment, arriving back at his own place in time to prepare for his voyage. There, he packed all the essentials, leaving his short-staff until last in order to complete his routine exercises before breakfast.

After breakfast he took his usual steam bath, dressed and finished packing the rest of his travel gear. Kyron left his father's case where he had stashed it for safe keeping and notified the Central Reception Control Quadrant that he would be away for approximately three months, asking them to keep his apartment secure until his return. Picking up his travel pack and his work case containing all the information he had collected, Kyron left for the MERIC Building.

Arriving at his office before the rest of the team, Kyron had time to check the messages on his computer. Amongst them was a confidential message from ASPECT which read:

KYRON SHIELD YOU HAVE BEEN GIVEN CLEARANCE TO ACCOMPANY A SCIENTIFIC PARTY TRAVELLING TO TERRA IOTA DEPARTING TODAY 5 JUNE 2055 AT 20:00 HOURS. A SECURITY OFFICER WILL MEET YOU AT 16:00 HOURS AT YOUR OFFICE TO ESCORT YOU TO THE ASPECT SPACE ADMINISTRATION BUREAU FOR BRIEFING AND PREPARATION. PLEASE NOTIFY YOUR SUPERIORS OF YOUR DEPARTURE.
CHIEF CONTROLLER..........GENERAL M. A. BLAKE.

"Interesting coincidence," Kyron said aloud, as he continued to sort through his messages. "The General has the same name as Samuel Jensen's Personal Assistant."

While Kyron was busy making an appointment to see Samuel Jensen and say his farewells, the rest of the team started to appear: First came Whitey, who greeted him with a 'thumb's up' and a wide grin, then Guy who nodded discreetly, followed soon after by Torri, who smiled sweetly as she brushed past him, trailing a faint fragrance of jasmine. For a moment Kyron was mesmerised, but a cold harsh voice behind him instantly brought him back to reality. It was Jackson.

"So Kyron, you're going to Terra Iota? Any particular reason for the trip?"

Kyron tried to be diplomatic and find a polite way of telling Jackson to mind his own business.

"Hello, Jackson. What brings you to our humble quarters? Say hello everyone."

The team reluctantly, but coldly, responded to Kyron's request. They all disliked Jackson's condescending attitude.

Impatient with Kyron's overwhelming niceness, Jackson ended the conversation abruptly.

"Well, try not to lose yourself out there and while you're away," he paused momentarily and turned his head in Torri's direction, "I'll keep an eye on Torri for you. After all, we wouldn't want any harm coming to your fiancée, would we?"

With those words, Jackson stormed off.

Kyron turned to the team, smiled and said tongue-in-cheek, "Thank you for your keen hospitality." They all laughed at having had the upper hand. But Kyron addressed them with a word of caution.

"Team, just between us, I believe that in the near future our mutual friend may cause some trouble and I want you all to be extra careful with what you say and do in order to avoid any possible conflict with him or his close associates. I can't explain to you in what way this trouble may arise, but I have grown to appreciate your friendship and respect, and would not like to see any of you harmed or lose your positions in the Company. I'll be back in about three months' time, so take care of yourselves and watch out for each other."

During the day, Whitey, Guy and Torri each thanked Kyron in their own way, letting him know just how much they enjoyed working with him as a colleague and a friend and wishing him a safe return. Torri told Kyron that she would keep in constant contact with him and reassured him not to worry about Jackson and his threatening comments.

When it was time for his appointment with Samuel Jensen, Kyron made his way to the penthouse office. Over a cup of herbal tea he exchanged information about the data he had collected on the equipment and voiced his concern about the large number of transmissions that had been sent from Terra Iota over the last month.

"That's odd," said Jensen, "I've only received about half a dozen transmissions from there lately to inform me about the damage to the machine, the related deaths and injuries of the miners and engineers, and a very brief note about this strange blue crystal rock. Have you read any of these transmissions, Kyron?"

"No, sir, I haven't as yet," said Kyron, "but I intend reviewing them on the trip. There are around fifty or more of these you know."

"About *fifty* you say!" exclaimed Jensen, looking both surprised and angry. "Please try and look into this as soon as you can, Kyron. I'll be *extremely* interested in knowing the content of those transmissions and the parties involved. Keep me informed of developments on a regular basis during your absence."

Jensen reached into the top drawer of his desk and retrieved a small metallic disc and, as he handed it to Kyron, he spoke in a whisper.

"This memory disc contains the dedicated frequency of my transceiver as well as restricted information about the Company and my future plans. Guard it with your life Kyron and communicate to me only on this frequency."

As Kyron reached out for the disc, Jensen noticed the signet ring on his finger.

"That's a uniquely designed piece of jewellery you're wearing, Kyron. I hadn't noticed it before."

"It belonged to my father, sir. He bequeathed it to me when he died and my mother passed it on to me when I was home on leave. I wear it with pride to keep the memory of my father alive."

"That's very decent of you, Kyron," said Samuel Jensen. "I'm sure your father was very proud to have a son like you and I'm also proud to have you here in the Company. So watch your back and take good care of yourself."

Jensen rose from his seat and shook hands with Kyron.

"Good luck my boy and come back safely."

"Thank you Mr Jensen, I will."

As Kyron was leaving Jensen's office he paused to have a word with Miss Blake who was sitting at her desk in the adjoining office.

"Hello and goodbye Miss Blake. I'll see you when I return from my trip in three months' time. By the way, I received a message today from a General Blake of ASPECT. Is he any relation of yours, or is his name just a coincidence?"

"Oh, hello Kyron. No, it's not a coincidence. General Blake is my father. Mr Jensen and my father have known each other since the Company was formed. When this position became available, I applied for it because I wanted to be in close contact with my father. It has worked out really well as I can also pass on messages informally between Mr Jensen and my father."

"How convenient," responded Kyron, thinking to himself about the possible conflict of interest. Kyron was starting to become more suspicious of staff in the Company since hearing of a possible conspiracy.

"Well, I best be on my way. Bye for now."

As he headed for his office, Kyron's thoughts were still on Miss Blake and her informal communications. *But Samuel Jensen was usually a good judge of people and he would certainly trust the daughter of a long term associate.* So, after some reflection, Kyron dismissed his suspicion as ill-founded and concentrated his efforts on preparing for the long trip ahead.

On his return to the office Kyron saw Torri engrossed in her programming. The time on the panel display read 13.00 hours.

"Hi Torri, are you too busy to stop for some lunch now?"

"Kyron, I'm never too busy to enjoy your company. You left this morning without a word. Is everything alright?"

"Sorry for not saying anything when I left, but it was very early and you looked so peaceful in your deep sleep that I didn't want to disturb you. I was in a hurry to get back to my place to pack my gear for the trip and get to work to check all the messages that had piled up since being on leave."

They left the office together and headed for the staff cafeteria where they talked non-stop over lunch. Kyron told Torri about the conversation he'd just had with Samuel Jensen, every now and then casting an observant eye around the room to ensure that they weren't being monitored. Again, Kyron cautioned Torri to be extra careful while he was away, trusting no-one just in case they were involved in the suspected conspiracy. He assured Torri that he would keep her informed while he was on Terra Iota but, to guard against possible interception, he would use a special transmission code they had devised when he and Torri were first courting.

No sooner had Kyron and Torri arrived back at the office than Whitey, carrying his compu-logbook, approached Kyron.

"Have you got a spare moment to discuss something in private, Kyron?" asked Whitey in a hurried, yet nervous tone.

"Yes, what is it Whitey?" said Kyron, ushering Whitey into his office and closing the door.

"Well, I didn't want to say anything in front of the others. But, while you were away on leave last week Jackson came down with some engineering schematics of our sonar excavator. It had some major draft modifications to our blueprint. Here, take a look at this."

Whitey activated the compu-logbook and placed it on the desk. Kyron could see that the frequency modulator and the trough compartment had been modified to equip the excavator for diamond mining rather than metal ore drilling. The modified blueprint resembled sketches that Kyron's team had been working on before the priority had changed to metal ore drilling. Jackson had made these modifications without following proper protocol and Kyron was very curious to know what Jackson was planning.

"What did Jackson say to you when he gave you these schematics?" Kyron asked.

Whitey looked cautiously over his shoulder before replying.

"Jackson said he'd been instructed by his father to see me about these changes because you were on leave. He said there was some urgency to have the modifications in place before commencing production of the sonar excavator. Jackson said not to bother his father with any problems, and just report them to him. He insisted I didn't talk to anyone else about the matter either. I knew that we needed sign-off approval from Samuel Jensen counter-signed by you, Kyron, before any changes could be made to blueprints, so I didn't proceed with his request immediately. But I'm sure he'll soon be following up to see what I've done."

"You did the right thing, Whitey," said Kyron, nodding knowingly as though all his suspicions had been confirmed. "Jackson wasn't expecting me to return early. No wonder he was a little surprised to see me in the lift today. I guess that's why he was here in our section this morning to see if I had found out what he'd asked you to do. Most likely he is still under the impression that I know nothing and thinks I will soon be departing the scene without finding out. But I am very curious to know why he wants these modifications done without my knowledge. Who was the engineer that drafted them?"

Whitey and Kyron examined the blueprints more closely. The senior engineer's name that appeared as the Authorising Officer on the modified blueprint was Peter Brennan from the Production plant.

"Thanks Whitey for bringing this to my notice. It's good to know that I have trusted and loyal staff on my team. I want you to pretend for the time being that this meeting didn't take place and see if you can somehow delay constructing this equipment. I'll discreetly inform Samuel Jensen about his son's actions and let him handle this. Is that alright with you, Whitey?"

"Yeh, I can do that Kyron," Whitey replied, relieved to know that he was not being left to deal with this on his own. "Thanks for your help."

"I'll be in contact with Torri while I'm travelling, so if I need to let you know of anything, or you need to contact me, Torri will keep us both posted. Okay?"

"Yeh, okay Kyron. Catch you later and have a safe trip," said Whitey, leaving Kyron's office with the compu-logbook under his arm and returning to his workstation.

Before the security officer from ASPECT arrived, Kyron contacted Samuel Jensen via the transcorder using the dedicated code on the disc Jensen had given him.

"Sorry, sir. There has been a breach of protocol. It seems that Jackson has requested my staff to modify the SAFE's blueprints for diamond mining. Without my knowledge or authorisation the modifications were approved last week by the Senior Production Engineer, Peter Brennan. Your son also instructed my staff not to let anyone know about this request."

Samuel Jensen was obviously alarmed.

"Are you sure about this, Kyron? Have you any evidence?"

"Yes Mr Jensen, I sighted Brennan's name and signature on the blueprints. I would trust my staff member with my life and his honesty is beyond reproach."

Samuel Jensen did not want to believe what he was hearing. With disappointment in his voice he reiterated that his suspicions of a conspiracy were being confirmed.

"Thanks for the information, Kyron. I'll get to the bottom of this while you're away. Just focus on what's happening on Terra Iota, while I look after these matters here in the Company."

No sooner had Kyron finished the conversation than the security officer from ASPECT arrived to escort Kyron to the briefing. The officer was a tall, rugged, solidly-built man; unshaved with short, black, grease-slicked hair, combed straight back in a severe style. The standard black uniform was well-tailored to his sculpted physique. Like the security officers at MERIC, he was armed with a laser pistol and a short black metal truncheon, anchored to his wide black-leather belt.

"Good afternoon, sir," the officer said in a confident, low accented voice while saluting. "I am officer Drammon and I am here to accompany you to ASPECT Administration for your briefing."

"Hello, Officer Drammon. I've been expecting you. I'll just let my team know that I'm leaving." Kyron picked up his travel bag and his metal briefcase and approached his colleagues.

In turn, each wished him a safe return trip and urged him to take care. Torri, who was the last to farewell Kyron, could not help giving him a long lingering kiss and a hug while shedding a brief tear.

"Be careful Kyron and bring yourself back to me in one piece. Remember, you have a wedding to attend!"

"I promise I will sweetheart. Look after yourself," Kyron said, adding in a whisper, "And watch your back."

Torri smiled and nodded as Kyron turned away and left with his escort.

***

It was only a ten-minute journey by fleet shuttle to ASPECT Headquarters. This was Kyron's first visit to the huge complex and he was overwhelmed by what he encountered. The outside of the entire building was formed of dark reflective windows making it impossible to see inside. The main entrance led into the reception area and could not be passed without a security check. There Kyron was issued a security pass, complete with his hologram portrait and a tracking bracelet.

Kyron was processed through a stringent security check before being greeted by General Blake. Kyron observed the close family resemblance, his daughter, Miss Blake, having the same dark eyes and bone structure. The General was smartly clothed in a modern navy-blue blazer covered with strategically-placed shiny brass buttons and matching navy trousers. A brass chain looped through an epaulet on his right shoulder, wrapping around and under the shoulder sleeve.

On the cuff of his sleeves were matching wide bands of shiny gold material identifying his rank. He was carrying a matching cap laced with brass-coloured braiding on the peak.

On one of the walls in the reception area there was a hologram floor plan showing the layout of the building. A tower in the centre of the structure housed the internal transporters and communications. It was surrounded by four colour-coded domes: orange for maintenance and workshops, blue for engineering and design, green for aeronautics and red for administration and security.

The main reception area of administration and security where Kyron was being 'processed' was a very busy thoroughfare. People dressed in their designated coloured uniforms were eagerly strutting across the wide expanse of highly polished white marble floors carrying items, talking to each other, or carting boxes and equipment, interrupted by intermittent broadcasting over the public address system. There was a large number of surveillance cameras placed around the ceiling.

Without warning, a high-pitched alarm suddenly activated. The sound, amplified threefold, caused Kyron to immediately clasp his hands over his sensitive ears. Four security officers appeared from nowhere, laser pistols drawn. In an instant they bundled up someone at the door of one of the internal transporters, which was flashing a bright red light.

Within seconds the scuffle was over, the sound was silenced and the flashing light ceased.

"Are you alright, Kyron?" enquired the General with a concerned expression on his weathered face.

"Yes, sir, not used to the noise. It caught me by surprise," responded Kyron, his ears still ringing.

The General reassured him.

"I don't think it's anything to worry about. An alarm is often activated when someone tries to carry something into the transporters without it being properly demagnetised and it triggers the sensors. The expensive equipment in this facility is extremely sensitive to electromagnetism so we must have tight security. Objects coming into this facility have the potential to severely disrupt and possibly damage the equipment. Well, shall we continue to the briefing room?"

In the briefing room of the administration dome, Kyron met the other travellers who were being entertained with light refreshments while waiting for everyone to arrive. The travellers were specialists from a wide range of disciplines and among them was the engineer from the MERIC production plant, Peter Brennan.

Kyron was surprised to see Brennan, but when they were introduced, Brennan didn't seem to flinch at all. It was only when Kyron introduced himself and stated that he worked for MERIC as an engineer that Brennan became unsettled, fidgeting nervously with his ear. Kyron decided to wait until the voyage was underway before having an in-depth conversation with Brennan about the modifications he had authorised to the SAFE blueprints.

The General welcomed everyone and gave a brief talk on space travel before handing the group over to the Psych Officer and the Medical Officer. The majority of the group, including Kyron, had not undertaken space travel before and listened for two hours to the information presented, taking notes and asking questions. Then the captain of the craft arrived to inform the group about their self-contained living quarters, the dining schedules and general house-keeping rules.

The briefing finished, leaving time for the passengers and crew to have dinner and a steam bath and then change into their special charcoal-coloured anti-static jumpsuits.

At 20.00 hours, they boarded the craft and strapped themselves into their allotted seats. The craft was powered by anti-matter delivered through particle accelerators, technology that had been introduced at the end of the last decade. This technology had revolutionised interplanetary travel, significantly reducing the time taken to leave and return to Earth at hyper-speed.

The craft departed Earth with no technical problems, just as it had done so many times before, and then it was set on autopilot, on course for Terra Iota.

UNRAVELLING
THE PLOT

ADJUSTING to space time travel where there was no day or night was a strange phenomenon. Weightlessness was a thing of the past as the gravitational problem had been mastered some ten years earlier, but there were still side-effects. These were similar to the jetlag that had once plagued international flights, however in outer space the effects were exaggerated threefold. Within two days, most of the passengers, including Kyron, had adjusted and settled into their respective routines. But some still had anxieties about space travel and were struggling with the side-effects.

Kyron considered that the ship's quarters were well appointed with all the modern conveniences. There was room in the cabin for dining 'in house' at a small meal servery, a bunk bed with temperature control and mood lighting, steam bath with laser fixtures for lighting, heating and drying, and an audio-visual system to select music and broadcasts as an alternative to the music piped through the craft's public address system. Kyron was also pleased to have a gymnasium onboard the ship. This not only allowed him somewhere to continue his martial art routines and keep his skills sharp, but also the exercise helped him to overcome the side-effects of space travel.

Group discussions had been scheduled during the flight for those members who wanted to attend. The discussions allowed the passengers to present their professional views on the newly-discovered planets. Kyron attended the lectures relating to Terra Iota's geological composition but found that none of the speakers, or any of the other members of the group, had been told about the blue crystallized rock. They were aware only that some equipment had exploded at the open-cut mine, exposing deep subterranean fossils of plants and animals.

Kyron socialised with the others on board while trying to piece together like a jigsaw snippets of information that would help him reconstruct the incident on Terra Iota. At every opportunity, he also spent time reading, in chronological order, the copies of the transmissions to and from Terra Iota. It was most revealing.

First, he downloaded the data onto his compu-logbook and stowed the device in a safe place in his cabin. Then, using the in-house computer in his cabin, he inserted one of the discs and began his examination.

DATE: 16 MAY
TO: SAMUEL JENSEN
FROM: SENIOR ENGINEER GRANT THOMPSON –
TERRA IOTA
TEXT: HUGE EXPLOSION OPEN CUT MINE. 5
MINERS KILLED. 2 ENGINEERS BADLY INJURED.
MAY BE DUE TO FAULTY MACHINERY OR
GAS IGNITION FROM PRESSURE. FURTHER
INVESTIGATION WARRANTED. WILL KEEP YOU
POSTED.- END

DATE: 17 MAY
TO: SENIOR ENGINEER GRANT THOMPSON-
TERRA IOTA
FROM: SAMUEL JENSEN
TEXT: ARRANGING WITH ASPECT TO SEND SPACE
SHUTTLE WITH MEDICAL TEAM AND SCIENCE
FIELD SPECIALISTS AS SOON AS POSSIBLE.
ANYTHING ELSE NEEDED? –END

DATE: 18 MAY
TO: SAMUEL JENSEN
FROM: SENIOR ENGINEER GRANT THOMPSON
-TERRA IOTA
TEXT: MAINTENANCE CHECKED. MACHINERY
DOES NOT APPEAR TO BE FAULTY. NO GAS
DETECTION IDENTIFIED IN MINE. MINUTE
PARTICLES OF BLUE CRYSTAL SIMILAR SIZE
AND SHAPE TO TABLE SALT CRYSTALS FOUND
ON EXCAVATION BLADES AND IN RUBBLE
OF MINE OPENING. SENT TO FIELD LAB FOR
EXAMINATION - END

DATE: 20 MAY
TO: SAMUEL JENSEN
FROM: SENIOR ENGINEER GRANT THOMPSON
TEXT: LAB TESTS SHOW BLUE CRYSTAL
UNKNOWN CHEMICAL COMPOUND. HIGH
EXPLOSIVE POTENTIAL EQUAL TO 10 TIMES
URANIUM STRENGTH, NO RADIATION EFFECTS.
- END

DATE: 21 MAY
TO: SENIOR ENGINEER GRANT THOMPSON
FROM: SAMUEL JENSEN
TEXT: CEASE MINING OPERATIONS UNTIL
FURTHER NOTICE–END

DATE: 21 MAY
TO: JACKSON JENSEN
FROM: ENGINEER DON CARSON – TERRA IOTA
TEXT: LAB TESTS SHOW BLUE CRYSTAL
UNKNOWN CHEMICAL COMPOUND. HIGH
EXPLOSIVE TENDENCY EQUAL TO 10 TIMES

URANIUM STRENGTH, NO RADIATION EFFECTS.
DIRECTIONS RECEIVED TO CEASE MINING.
AWAITING FURTHER INSTRUCTIONS - END

Kyron paused momentarily. He wondered why another engineer in the same mining outfit would transmit the same message to Jackson Jensen, unless Jackson was secretly keeping something from his father. He read on.

DATE: 22 MAY
TO: ENGINEER DON CARSON – TERRA IOTA
FROM: JACKSON JENSEN
TEXT: WHAT IS THE MASS QUANTITY VEIN OF
BLUE CRYSTAL ROCK IN MINE AND AT WHAT
DEPTH? - END

DATE: 22 MAY
TO: JACKSON JENSEN
FROM: ENGINEER DON CARSON – TERRA IOTA
TEXT: APPEARS TO BE IN EXCESS OF 500,000 TONS
APPROX. 2,000 FEET BELOW SURFACE LEVEL –
END

DATE: 23 MAY
TO: ENGINEER DON CARSON – TERRA IOTA
FROM: JACKSON JENSEN
TEXT: AM WORKING ON REDESIGN OF NEW
SONIC EXCAVATOR TO SAFELY EXTRACT BLUE
CRYSTAL ROCK AND TRANSPORT TO EARTH.
WILL BE SENDING 50 SECURITY OFFICERS IN
DUE COURSE TO ENSURE SAFEGUARDING
OF MINE AND SECURE PASSAGE FOR THE
TRANSPORTATION OF BLUE CRYSTAL ROCK BACK
TO EARTH – END

The transmissions between Jackson and Don Carson continued, requesting information about time schedules, loading capacity, hauling delays, labour resources and other costings. There were no further transmissions from Senior Engineer Grant Thompson or Samuel Jensen other than notification of the space shuttle transporter departure and the passengers on board.

Kyron decided it was time to have a talk with engineer, Peter Brennan, to find out what his involvement was in all of this and discover what Jackson had told him. The evidence was pointing to what appeared to be a conspiracy, but Kyron was not going to make any presumptions or accusations until he had the facts. He packed the discs away in his briefcase and turned in for the night.

After a restless sleep, Kyron rose early and, before breakfast, went to the gymnasium for his daily workout, taking with him his short-staff. After performing his martial arts routine, he returned to his quarters to complete his meditation ritual.

On his return, Kyron noticed that the sliding hatch door to his quarters was partially open. His pulse quickened slightly as he cautiously entered. No-one was inside, but his briefcase had been jemmied open and the discs were gone!

It was now obvious to Kyron that he was being watched and his movements were being closely monitored. *But by whom? And for how long?* His suspicions pointed to Peter Brennan. His psychological readings of the other passengers had not raised any concerns, but Brennan had appeared nervous after they had been introduced. He had kept looking over his shoulder, checking the time on his watch and frowning while rubbing his ear in an agitated manner with his thumb and forefinger.

Kyron decided not to report the incident. There was no need to frighten the other members of the group or create paranoia for the rest of the trip. However, he determined to be more on his guard. He would talk to Peter Brennan in private.

After steam bathing and dressing, Kyron went to the main dining room for breakfast, hoping to catch up with Brennan. He spied Brennan, eating alone and totally engrossed in reading some papers. Kyron collected his breakfast at the servery and sat down at Brennan's table, facing him.

"Hello again, Peter. Mind if I join you?"

Brennan's face suddenly gorged with blood and perspiration started to show on his forehead. He appeared very nervous as he replied.

"Hello Kyron, yes that's ...ah... alright. Have the table, I was just about to leave anyway," said Brennan as he hastily folded up the documents he had been reading.

"Please don't leave on my account; I need to discuss something with you."

Kyron stared at Brennan with steel piercing eyes and leant over towards him, placing a hand on his shoulder with deliberate downward pressure to prevent Brennan from trying to stand.

"I'm not sure if you are completely aware of my role at MERIC, Peter, so I will enlighten you. I am the Level 2 Engineer in the SAFE Project Team that developed the sonic excavator. I'm the only officer, apart from Samuel Jensen, who can authorise modifications or amendments to the SAFE blueprints."

Brennan's face turned from red to pale white.

"So, tell me Peter, who gave you the authority to change the SAFE blueprints without my consent?"

Brennan was hesitant to answer and responded in a higher pitched, nervous voice.

"It was J...Jackson who said I had the authority, because you were on l...leave and I was the s..s...senior engineer. Him being the boss's son and all, I felt it was inappropriate to question his word. He also said that he had already s..spoken with his father and it was all okay. So I made the modifications to his s..specifications. He asked me how soon I could start production on the machines once Brenton White produced the prototype."

"Is that right, Peter? Well, as far as you are concerned, this conversation never took place. Say nothing about it to Jackson Jensen when you are next talking to him, alright? That's if you still value your career with the Company...."

Brennan nodded his head vigorously in agreement.

"Oh, and by the way, you didn't happen to visit my quarters this morning, did you?"

"No," Brennan responded more confidently. "I've been here since six this morning reading my presentation papers. There were others here that can vouch for that."

"Alright Peter. Thank you for our little talk."

Brennan quickly gathered up his papers and left, obviously shaken by the encounter.

Convinced that Brennan was telling the truth, Kyron was even more curious to identify the intruder. *Perhaps someone else on the craft was working for Jackson?*

A picture was starting to take shape in Kyron's mind. He suspected that the Communications Officer had informed Jackson about his request for copies of the transmissions and that Jackson was trying to retrieve the disc before Kyron had a chance to read them. *Perhaps Jackson had attempted to access them at his place, the night before he left for the space excursion? But luckily he had spent the night at Torri's place with the discs in his briefcase.* Kyron realised that he had become a real threat to Jackson, especially if Jackson believed that Kyron had read the transmissions before they had been stolen.

Kyron now realised that his life was in danger and that he would need to be constantly vigilant throughout the journey. Through a process of elimination, Kyron deduced who the suspect might be. All the passengers had seemed harmless and Brennan had revealed all that he knew. That left the flight crew and the security officers. Kyron decided to meet them as soon as he could to assess their character. He was also determined to contact Samuel Jensen to let him know about the theft of the disc and warn him of the secret transmissions implicating his son, Jackson.

Kyron's transceiver was out of range so he was forced to make contact though the ship's datacom system. Arriving at the Data Communications room, Kyron was confronted by two security officers but, after submitting his ID, he was permitted entry. He seated himself in one of the individual booths and commenced his transmission using Jensen's security code.

DATE: 14 JUNE
TO: SAMUEL JENSEN
FROM: ENGINEER - KYRON SHIELD ONBOARD SHUTTLE
TEXT: HAVE READ SOME OF THE TRANSMISSIONS FROM TERRA IOTA CONCERNING EXPLOSION. EQUIPMENT NOT AT FAULT, EXPLOSION MAY

*BE DUE TO BLUE CRYSTAL ROCK. JACKSON
PLANNING TO MINE CRYSTAL WITH NEW
MODIFIED SONAR EXCAVATOR AND TRANSPORT
BLUE CRYSTAL ROCK TO EARTH. HE IS ALSO
SENDING 50 SECURITY OFFICERS TO TERRA IOTA
TO SECURE MINE. - END*

Realising that Torri might also be in danger, Kyron sent a coded transmission to her.

*DATE: 14 JUNE
TO: ENGINEER TORRI MADISON
FROM: ENGINEER KYRON SHIELD
TEXT: HI TORRI, MISS YOU ALREADY. WATCH
OUT FOR JACKSON. I HAVE EVIDENCE AGAINST
JACKSON AND HE MAY SUSPECT THAT YOU
KNOW ABOUT THIS. IF JACKSON APPROACHES
YOU, PLEAD IGNORANCE. YOU KNOW NOTHING
ABOUT ANY TRANSMISSIONS FROM TERRA IOTA.
BE ON GUARD AND ENSURE YOUR SECURITY
SYSTEMS ARE OPERATIONAL AT ALL TIMES –
LOVE KYRON -END*

***

While Kyron was preoccupied with his investigations on board the space shuttle, Jackson Bartholomew Jensen was following his own hidden agenda back at MERIC.

Soon after receiving the transmission from Kyron, Samuel Jensen called a meeting with his son, Jackson, to find out exactly what his son had in mind for the Company's future.

"Come in Jackson my boy, good to see you," said Samuel Jensen, welcoming his son warmly. He ushered Jackson into his office, his right hand outstretched for a handshake and a comforting left hand on his son's shoulder.

Jackson accepted the handshake.

"Good day dad, what did you want to see me about?"

Before he replied to Jackson, Samuel called out to his Personal Assistant.

"Miss Blake, would you be so kind as to bring us some tea?"

"I wouldn't mind a whiskey instead, if that's okay," blurted Jackson.

Samuel Jensen was taken aback.

"It's a bit early in the afternoon for that Jackson, and besides, you know the Company rules about alcohol on the premises."

"Company rules! It's about time we dispensed with some of these archaic rules," Jackson retorted in a resentful manner.

Samuel Jensen and his son had not always seen eye to eye, although Samuel had tolerated Jackson's rebellious nature, hoping that holding a responsible position in the Company would settle him down and improve his attitude. Samuel retaliated in a stern tone.

"This Company was built on the very foundations of moral and ethical standards, and the rules that evolved from these have made this Company what it is today, a modern enterprising and successful business that has kept pace with the growing technology and applications in a competitive market. I am excusing you for your attitude because of your youth and inexperience, but I will not have anyone, under any circumstances, insinuate that this Company is archaic. You should know of our financial successes."

Samuel Jensen was interrupted by Miss Blake with the refreshments.

"Thank you Miss Blake," said Samuel Jensen in a quieter tone. "That will be all for now."

"Very good, Mr Jensen," replied Miss Blake as she disappeared through the door, closing it behind her.

Jackson sat brooding, tapping his fingers impatiently on the arm of the leather chair. His father spoke again, noting his son's agitation.

"Now Jackson, what is this I hear about you making modifications to the SAFE blueprints and not informing me of these changes? What's this all about? You know that I have always had an open door policy, especially for my own family. Why didn't you come to me first to discuss this?"

Jackson tried to conceal his emotions, responding in a restrained, semi-whispered voice.

"Because you wouldn't have listened to my proposal and would have delayed it by processing it through the members of the Board, who most likely, would have rejected my idea for being too radical."

"And what is this idea that you have? I'm very interested to know," enquired Samuel Jensen, now sounding seriously concerned.

Jackson stood and spoke with some urgency in his voice, while pacing the floor.

"As you probably know by now, dad, the explosion on Terra Iota appears to have been caused by the open mine excavator coming into contact with a strange blue crystal rock. It's also been established from lab tests of a small particle that the substance has power ten times more potent than that of uranium, without the radiation effects. If this is the case, it will be the most sought-after material in the future as a potential power source. Now that I have modified the new sonar excavator to prevent further explosions, I think we should immediately start mining the stuff and transporting it back to Earth. I stress the urgency. We need to act before anyone else decides to do the same. MERIC will then have a total monopoly for production and marketing. What power! We'll be set for life!"

There was fire in Jackson's eyes as he spoke with passion at the thought of having total control of the valuable blue crystal.

Samuel Jensen was shocked at Jackson's obsession with power and tried to quell Jackson's excitement by directing him sternly to sit down and discuss this sensibly like mature adults. He spoke with authority.

"First of all, my son, there is no urgency as MERIC has the mining rights to prevent anyone else taking control. We need to undertake more lab tests to gain assurances about the stability of this substance and check for potential harmful effects before placing Earth at risk. We also need to have a comprehensive scientific report submitted to the Board for further discussion and MERIC is required by law to alert the World Assembly of this newly discovered substance as it is something that could dramatically affect the whole world and its future. All these things have to be done before we even think about stockpiling this substance."

With that response, Jackson slammed his clenched fist down on the table, and shouted.

"You don't understand you old fool! We don't have time for this bureaucratic red tape crap! We must act immediately!"

Jackson slammed the door open and stormed out of the office.

Samuel Jensen was furious and totally disappointed in his son's response. They'd had their differences in the past but now Samuel Jensen was questioning his son's true character. This confirmed that his son could no longer be trusted. He would be placing power in the wrong hands if he allowed Jackson to take over and run the Company.

He called Miss Blake to come into his office with her transcorder. Miss Blake entered the office slightly flustered from what she had overheard.

"Is he alright, Mr Jensen?" she asked timidly.

"We'll have to wait and see, Miss Blake. He seems to have his own agenda when it comes to company protocol. Now, let's get started as there is no time to waste."

Samuel Jensen began relaying directions with urgency in his voice.

"I want you to arrange an urgent meeting with the Board of Directors and inform them that I will discuss the agenda at the meeting. Oh, and I want you to leave Jackson off the attendance list. Instead, please contact your father and ask him if he could attend. This is top priority! Send the notice through the 'Personal-in-Confidence' system.

"I also want copies of all transmissions from Terra Iota that were sent over the last three weeks. See if there have been any reports released from the Terra Iota lab, and if there have been, I need them poste haste. Then arrange a meeting as soon as possible with our liaison officer in the World Assembly and reserve a flight on the transport shuttle to coincide with that meeting. Ah yes, and can you contact Kyron Shield and ask him to return on the next available space transporter from Terra Iota? Okay, Miss Blake, make haste and keep me posted as time is of the essence."

"Yes, Mr Jensen. So you want me to leave your son out of the loop for now?"

"Affirmative, Miss Blake."

THE AWAKENING

AFTER five days of thorough investigations, speaking to all the flight crew, Kyron narrowed the field of suspects to the security officers who were employed by Guardor. Guardor was an independent privately-owned international bureau that contracted out their security officers to commercial companies.

Distinguishable by their black uniforms and the weapons they brandished, Guardor security officers were essentially 'guns for hire' and a law unto their own, loyal to the bureau but obedient to the company to whom they were contracted. Some officers were (honourably or dishonourably) discharged veterans and deserters from pre-existing, old-world armies. Others were mercenaries, and a number were new recruits trained in the bureau's cadet training system. They were all a force to be reckoned with, trained in most forms of war tactics and martial fighting techniques.

Kyron was informed by the flight crew that there were six security officers on board; four from ASPECT and two from MERIC, alternating between shifts. Their security cards accessed all areas of the craft, including the passengers' living quarters. Kyron knew that as soon as he came into contact with these security officers, he would sense if they had intruded into his quarters.

Within two days he had spoken with all the ASPECT security officers, quickly establishing their innocence. He would find the last two security officers from MERIC, Krane and Largo, on the third late shift.

On the third night, Kyron found them in the dining room enjoying their meal before heading off to perform their nightly duties.

"Hello gentlemen, my name is…"

Kyron was cut off midstream by Largo, the larger of the two, who lowered the coffee mug from his mouth and blurted out in a deep threatening voice:

"We know who you are, and we heard you've been searching for us."

Kyron was taken by surprise. He thought he had been very discreet in his approach but his enquiries had become obvious and Kyron knew that he would have to take a direct approach with these two. A quick profile assessment suggested that they both had a deceptive nature.

"Yes, you are quite right," responded Kyron, unflinchingly, still maintaining eye contact, "I'd like to know if you two officers have, in the last few days, entered my quarters."

"Why ask us?" responded the other security officer defensively.

"Well, because the other morning when I returned from the gym I found the door to my cabin unlocked and partially open. I definitely locked my quarters that morning as I always do every time I leave. I've also been informed that all the security officers on board have total security clearance for access to all areas."

The larger officer grinned under his stubbled, unkempt face, and responded while giving a shifty sideways glance at his side-kick.

"We wouldn't do anything like that sir; it's not in our nature to do things behind people's backs. Besides, we're here to serve and protect."

There was a sarcastic tone in his voice and Kyron wondered who these officers really served and protected.

Using the better part of discretion, Kyron decided not to pursue his enquiry and rose from his seat.

"Well then, would you mind keeping an eye out for anyone trying to break into the passengers' quarters for the rest of the flight?"

"Oh, yes sir," was the abrupt response from the smaller one. "Thanks for telling us, we'll be real sure to let you know if we see anyone."

Kyron walked off, leaving both of them with smirks on their faces. He sensed that they were definitely lying and probably following orders from Jackson.

He returned to his quarters suffering mild indigestion from his hurried meal and anxiety from the encounter with the two security officers. The situation was dangerous and his life was clearly at risk.

There was no-one on this craft who could help him. Thousands of miles from anywhere, Kyron was feeling very alone and vulnerable. Even the ASPECT security officers would not believe what he sensed about Jackson's uniformed 'watchdogs'. They would probably think him paranoid. He would have to rely solely on his own inner strength and abilities.

The ship would be arriving at Terra Iota within the next twenty-four hours so Kyron decided that, with a clearer head in the morning, he would start planning his movements and finalising his investigations.

Back in his quarters and immersed in deep thought Kyron was startled when his cabin intercom suddenly came to life with its strange alert tone. He hit the digital response button and a voice came on the line.

"Mr Shield, are you there?"

"Yes, I'm here."

"You have a transmission from MERIC to collect at the Communications room."

"Thank you, I'll be there in five minutes."

The intercom went silent.

Kyron left his quarters, making sure the access was on lock, and headed for the Communications room. The Communications Officer handed him the printed transmission, explaining that one of the security officers had been present when it arrived. The security officer had read the message 'for security reasons.' Now Kyron was even more wary and apprehensive about Krane and Largo.

"Thanks, much appreciated," said Kyron.

While making his way back to his quarters, he began to read the message. It was brief.

DATE: 21 JUNE
TO: ENGINEER - KYRON SHIELD
FROM: MISS BLAKE
TEXT: MR SAMUEL JENSEN REQUESTS YOUR
URGENT RETURN ON THE NEXT AVAILABLE
TRANSPORTER. WILL EXPLAIN DETAILS ON YOUR
ARRIVAL AS THIS IS TOP SECURITY- END

Crap! What now? Kyron tried to imagine what had raised the alarm so suddenly.

Arriving back at his quarters, Kyron again found his hatch door unlocked. He cautiously slid back the hatch door. The automatic illumination for the room was not operating and it was pitch black inside. Kyron's enhanced nocturnal vision activated naturally and from the doorway he sighted a dark outline of a uniformed figure pressed against the wall to his right, arms raised with what looked like a club, clasped ready to strike. On the other wall to his left, pressed tightly against it, was a larger figure in the same pose. Kyron could feel the adrenalin rush. Although he had no weapons, his martial arts training in unarmed combat gave him the confidence to act.

With lightning speed, Kyron dived through the doorway, rolled into a tight ball onto the floor, sprung to his feet and simultaneously, with precise accuracy, struck the figure on the right with a knife-hand snap to the throat. Using a powerful side kick, Kyron struck the other assailant in the stomach. The figure on the right immediately collapsed, gasping for air. The other figure doubled over in pain, giving Kyron the opportunity to swivel around and deliver a forceful blow to the back of his neck with another knife-hand strike, leaving him sprawled, unconscious, face down on the floor.

Kyron turned the lights on, identifying the attackers as the two security officers from MERIC. Krane was kneeling and still gasping for air, so Kyron quickly retrieved the set of hand restraints from his security belt and strapped the officer's hands behind his back. He did the same to the unconscious Largo and then sounded the security alert.

While waiting for ASPECT Security to arrive, Kyron discreetly activated his transcorder and began to question Krane with the aid of the officer's own laser pistol which he had snapped from the officer's holster. Holding the pistol to Krane's head, Kyron, who was in no mood to have his patience tried, was determined to extract the truth.

"Who ordered you to do this?" he demanded. "Remember, I have the right to shoot an intruder in my quarters with no repercussions. Now, tell me, who was the one that gave you these orders?"

Krane knew that Kyron wasn't bluffing. If he confessed, he had a chance to live. His voice was trembling as he responded.

"It was Jackson Jensen who wanted you out of the way."

"Why would he want to do this?" threatened Kyron, tightening his hold on the officer.

"Because he said that you knew too much, and things would run more smoothly without your interference."

At that moment two of the ASPECT security officers arrived at the entrance to Kyron's quarters.

"What the hell's going on here? Why are these security officers handcuffed?" demanded one of them in an authoritative tone, his weapon drawn and pointed at Kyron.

Before answering, Kyron lowered his weapon and switched his transcorder on to replay.

"Before you jump to any wrong conclusions, officer, listen to this."

With the aid of the recording Kyron related exactly what had taken place.

By now Largo had gained consciousness and was trying to grapple free of his restraints.

"What the...?"

He was interrupted by the other ASPECT security officer, who had his laser pistol now trained on him.

"Don't move Largo!"

Then the other ASPECT security officer spoke.

"We'll place these two in the ship's brig until we arrive at our destination and immediately report the matter to our superiors. We've had concerns about these two ever since they joined up with us on this voyage." With that, the ASPECT security officers bundled the two prisoners together and escorted them out the door.

"Just a minute, Officer Tanner," said Kyron, who had sighted the officer's security ID badge. "Might I have a word in private?"

"Yes, Mr Shield. What is it?"

"Can I ask a favour of you? Could you delay reporting this? There may be accomplices on Terra Iota under the same orders and we don't want to alert them that Jackson Jensen's cronies have failed in their mission."

Tanner hesitated for a moment in his response while rubbing the furrows of his brow with his right hand.

"Yes sir, I well understand your situation but all matters of a security nature, particularly an assault on a passenger, are to be reported within twenty-four hours."

He paused again and then spoke.

"However, under the circumstances, I think this over-rides protocol."

"Thank you, Officer Tanner. Much appreciated."

"And may I say sir," responded Tanner, "I am most impressed with how you dealt with these two thugs. Let me know if you need anything else, Mr Shield. My men are at your disposal."

"Thank you Officer Tanner, that's good to know. But let's hope there are no other incidents."

Kyron closed the door behind them, giving him time to calm down and take in what had just happened. This was the first time that he had needed to put his skills to the test in a real life situation of a threat to his life. Kyron was quite relieved that he'd handled the attack so easily. He was feeling much more confident in the knowledge that his martial arts had worked so effectively.

He replayed the recording again, listening carefully to the words of the assailant and mulling over in his mind the consequences. *Jackson wanted him out of the way because he knew too much and Jackson believed things would run more smoothly without his interference. It was clear that there was a conspiracy and Jackson was behind it.*

Kyron needed to warn Samuel Jensen again about his son and alert him to the orders Jackson had given to murder anyone standing in his way. He also needed to warn Torri of the danger.

Kyron made his way back to the Communications room, contacting Torri about what had happened and assuring her that he was alright. Then he sent a transmission to Samuel Jensen via the security code, informing him of the attempt on his life ordered by Jackson.

At the flight control deck Kyron enquired when the next available transporter shuttle would be travelling to Earth. The Flight Officer, Lieutenant Cartwright, indicated that the next available passenger flight was due to leave Terra Iota in two weeks time.

Agitated by the news, Kyron emphasised the desperate need to return immediately.

"I'm afraid that's not soon enough. This is of great urgency. It's a matter of life and death! Are there any other transporters heading back to Earth sooner Lieutenant?"

Lieutenant Cartwright maintained his composure in spite of Kyron's desperate pleas.

"Would you be willing to hitch a ride in an ore transporter?" he said calmly. "It's a little cramped with only the bare necessities, but they travel faster and you could be back on Earth in less than two weeks."

"Yes, that's perfect, thank you," said Kyron, relieved and appreciative.

"It leaves in two day's time from Terra Iota," the Lieutenant continued, "and I could contact them now to let them know of your intentions if you wish?"

"Yes, that would be very helpful, but when do we land on Terra Iota?"

"In seven hour's time," came the response from Cartwright.

Kyron quickly calculated that he would still have a day and a half to inspect the mining site, assess the damage to the machinery and investigate the mystery of the blue crystal rock by talking to the laboratory scientists. He responded decisively.

"Yes, I will be ready to travel back with them, thank you."

The flight lieutenant communicated the confirmation to the ore transporter, which was in range, and received an instantaneous affirmation from the craft.

"It's done, sir, all confirmed."

Kyron couldn't thank him enough.

"That's very decent of you. You won't get into trouble will you?"

"No sir, but don't forget to cancel your other return trip, otherwise they will assume you have gone missing."

Kyron nodded in agreement and happily shook Cartwright's hand before departing for his quarters. To ensure the safety of the others back on Earth as well as himself he decided that it was better that no-one knew of his rescheduled plans.

When he finally bedded down for the night, Kyron found that he was still apprehensive about security officers having access to his quarters. Instead of totally switching off his mind, he went into a meditative state that kept him relaxed yet aware of his environment. He would be prepared if disturbed by uninvited guests.

But the night passed without further event and the next morning

Kyron rose early, packed his bag and ate breakfast in his quarters. He needed to organise a priority list of contacts to visit, arrange an inspection of the blast site at the mine and examine the damaged equipment. Kyron continued to finalise his list deciding that his first contact would be senior engineer Grant Thompson. While he was in the process of finalising this list, the intercom system activated with a broadcast.

"Attention, attention all personnel! This is the Captain speaking. The ship is preparing to land on Terra Iota. Please be seated and remain seated until you are advised that it is safe to disembark. Thank you for your assistance."

***

Within an hour the passengers started to leave the transporter, most encountering this new world for the first time. Terra Iota had an atmosphere very similar to Earth with rarefied air, the sky and vegetation much richer in colour. The moment Kyron stepped onto the surface he experienced the same familiar feeling that he had felt when first wearing his father's ring. His body had an inner glow and he could feel a strengthening in his muscles. His senses sharpened and there was a spring in his step. Strange!

When the entire group was assembled, they were escorted by one of the security officers to the main building complex, a huge dome with criss-crossed lattice work covering dark shaded windows that completely encircled the complex. After a head count they were shown to their assigned quarters.

Kyron was on a tight schedule, so after offloading his gear he went straight to the Engineering Department to find Grant Thompson. The staff informed him that Thompson was already at the mine and Kyron could catch a lift with a surveyor who was about to head out there. Before long, he was at the mine shed introducing himself to Grant Thompson.

Thompson was a well-built, tall character, with wild, unkempt, red hair and a rough stubble growth of red bristles on his chin. He had a leathery face with serious looking green eyes. His hands were rough from years of being in the field overseeing mining operations.

"Hello Mr Thompson, I'm Kyron Shield, Level 2 Engineer with MERIC."

Thompson responded in a strong lyrical Irish accent.

"Oh, hello there Kyron, Samuel Jensen told me you'd be comin'. Call me Grant, young fella. I assume you've read the report of the event. Come let me show you the damage."

They were about to step outside the shed when Kyron caught sight of something lying on one of the benches that stopped him dead in his tracks. It was a piece of blue material with faded gold-coloured circular symbols embossed on it. His face turned pale.

"Are ya' alright Kyron? You look like you've seen a ghost man," enquired Thompson.

Kyron pointed to the material on the bench.

"Where did this come from?"

Thompson was quick to respond, "Arrh, we found that amongst the debris from the explosion and we haven't yet had a chance to send it to the lab for further examination."

Kyron recognised the symbols on the material. They matched the symbols on his father's ring and those on his father's robe. A cold shiver ran through his body. He was now even more puzzled as to how this relic from the ancient past came to be here, buried over time, and now uncovered from the explosion.

His thoughts were suddenly interrupted by the sound of Thompson's voice close to his ear.

"Come on lad, I haven't got all day."

Kyron followed Thompson no more than about a hundred paces when they came to a huge crater, larger than three space transporters placed end to end, and so deep that it was hard to clearly see where it stopped.

"Amazing!" exclaimed Kyron, his eyes staring widely in disbelief.

"Kyron, ya see that excavator, or what's left of it, over the other side?" said Thompson. "Well that's where the open mine used to start. This large open area ya see here is what the explosion caused. We've located a main seam of the blue crystal rock another two thousand feet below the surface and from what we have assessed, this damage was caused by only a small piece about the size of a golf ball layin' close to the surface. We sent to the lab some of the mangled excavator blades that had speckled remnants of this blue stuff fused into them. We've ceased mining until further notice from Samuel Jensen. Manual clean-up operations will take some time to complete anyway. So Kyron, when do ya think we can have a replacement excavator that can mine this stuff?"

Kyron was still in awe of the devastation before him and did not respond immediately to the question raised by Thompson.

"I still can't get over the amount of damage, can you? This blue crystal is incredibly potent stuff. It would be extremely lethal in the hands of the wrong people."

"Arrh, you'd be right in sayin' that lad," said Thompson.

"Ah well, Grant, to answer your question about the replacement machinery, the Company is in the process of replacing these excavators with the new sonar excavators. They are super quiet, faster, environmentally-friendly and require very little maintenance. No crushing process is required and the machines are powered by nuclear fusion making them far more economical. Oh, and they can be operated by remote control from several hundred yards away. They should be here in about a month."

Thompson's eyes had opened wide. He was like a little boy anticipating a new toy for his birthday.

"However, Grant, I need to tell you something in the strictest confidence to fill you in on what has happened lately back at MERIC."

Kyron now spoke in a more serious hushed tone.

"You must not inform anyone else for your own safety, and I mean, no-one, no matter how much you think you can trust them. Do I have your word?"

"On me life sir, I swear on me mother's grave!" responded Thompson, curious to learn.

Kyron related to Thompson the events that had taken place during his voyage to Terra Iota and explained why he was here to investigate. He also informed Thompson about Don Carson's involvement with Jackson Jensen and the plan to send fifty of Jensen's MERIC security officers to take control of the mine. Kyron advised Thompson to be careful and keep a watchful eye on Carson.

Thompson was flabbergasted.

"Thanks Kyron for lettin' me know what's been happenin'. I had no idea about Carson and Jackson. After all these years of working with Carson ... I never!"

"Grant, I want to see the lab technicians before I leave on the next ore transporter. Things have taken an unexpected turn and I need to get back to Earth immediately. Don't tell anyone that I'm leaving as I want to keep my movements confidential and not alert anyone who may be conspiring with Jackson. My life's already been put in jeopardy once."

"I understand. You can trust me Kyron, and call on me if ya need anythin'."

"Thank you, Grant."

"I'll let ya know first thing, Kyron, when that ore transporter arrives. Now let's go see the lab techs."

The laboratory was located in the main dome and, within thirty minutes, Kyron was being introduced to the Senior Science Officer, Dr Robert Pearmont, who was leading the team on the examination of the blue crystal. Pearmont explained that the crystal was an unknown substance with a complex molecular structure with an atomic number higher than uranium and a weight heavier than gold. The lattice configuration of the molecular bonding also made it harder than diamond. He also informed Kyron that there could be many uses for this crystallised rock, and it would take several years to discover all its qualities other than its massive explosive properties.

While Pearmont was showing Kyron the embedded fragments of crystal in a piece of metal from the excavator, Kyron again experienced a pulsating glow and a mild tingling sensation in his hand. It emanated from the ring on his finger.

"Thank you Dr Pearmont, I would appreciate it if you could keep me informed of your progress."

As Kyron was finishing his conversation, a siren suddenly sounded over the public address system. It was followed by an urgent message.

"Attention all personnel, this is a red alert security warning! One of the MERIC security officers named Krane, who was under guard, has just escaped from custody. He is of medium build, has short cropped black hair, with a moustache. He is wearing a prison-orange uniform and is still handcuffed. Please remain inside while we attempt to apprehend the escapee. If you sight him do not approach, but immediately contact the Security Division. Thank you for your assistance in this matter."

"That's all I need to happen, a crazed assailant on the loose," said Kyron.

"Was that one of the assailants that made an attempt on ya' life, Kyron?" enquired Thompson.

"Yes, that was one of them," responded Kyron shaking his head in disgust. Not wanting to hang around while this escapee was on the loose, Kyron checked his timepiece. It was 13.00 hours.

"Has that ore transporter arrived yet, and what time does it depart?"

"I'll just check with the mine." Thompson retrieved his transceiver from his jacket pocket and activated it by flipping the lid. One of his crew answered instantly and Thompson reported back.

"Kyron, the transporter has just arrived and is departin' at 16.00 hours."

"Thank you, Grant. Well, I have all the information I need, but before I go, I'd like to see those engineers who were injured in the blast, just to see how they're recovering and if they need anything. Have you contacted the families of the miners who were killed in the blast and made arrangements to transport their bodies back to Earth? The Company will be paying for all expenses and compensation to their families."

"Yes Kyron, we've arranged all this, and have already been in contact with Samuel Jensen."

"Then I'd better see those engineers back at the base and then pick up my gear. Can you get me to the transporter from there Grant?"

"No problem, lad."

THE BATTLE BEGINS

THE ore transporter was very small in comparison to the passenger transporter. There were sleeping quarters for the two pilots, who alternated between shifts around the clock, and another two sleeping bays for any stray or surprise guests. Although the galley was small, it was well stocked with the essentials for long space flights; refrigerants, laser particle exciters and automated nutrient dispensers. The crew's dining and entertainment room outside the galley was just as cramped, but there was a hologram screen located on the wall which received continuous broadcasts of news bulletins. Kyron was quite comfortable with his sleeping bay and settled in quickly to the routine.

The first week was uneventful, although Kyron sensed some sort of negativity on the craft. He was unable to pinpoint what it was that made him feel slightly apprehensive. He passed his time by indulging in his ritual martial arts program in the empty storage hull, watching the news bulletins and having discussions with the pilots who had interesting stories to tell. He was content in the knowledge that he would soon be seeing Torri, even though he was unable to communicate with her for security reasons.

In the second week while taking refreshments in the dining room and watching the news bulletin, Kyron was utterly devastated by a news flash that came onto the screen. The distressed female newsreader announced:

"We have just received word that the Chief Executive Director and founder of the MERIC mining company, Mr Samuel Jensen, has been fatally injured. Details are not clear at present, but we understand that the accident occurred when Mr Jensen was travelling alone in one of the MERIC Building's internal transporters. The faulty transporter reportedly plunged from the penthouse suite on the 30th floor to the ground floor. Mr Jensen was pulled alive from the wreckage but he was pronounced dead on arrival at the hospital. Samuel Jensen's son, Jackson Jensen, is being interviewed by our on-the-scene reporter and we now switch to Jackson Jensen."

Kyron almost gagged.

The hologram showed Jackson being interviewed on the platform outside the MERIC Building where a noisy crowd of inquisitive onlookers had gathered. Amid a mob of journalists, and against a background of flashing lights and distant sirens, an earnest reporter forced a micro communicator towards Jackson's face.

"Can you tell us what happened, Mr Jensen?"

Jackson showed little emotion and spoke in a rehearsed or scripted manner. Those who didn't know him might have mistaken his demeanour as one of shock. But those who knew him thought otherwise.

"We're still investigating the incident which caused my father's death. Something has caused the internal transporter not to respond to the automatic braking mechanism and we're not sure whether it was a power failure or an equipment malfunction. We will inform the authorities when we know the reason. I have lost a great father and the world has lost a great man, but through his enterprising spirit and his vision of the future, MERIC will continue to carry on his legacy. Now if you will excuse me, I have work to do and serious matters to attend to."

Jackson turned abruptly away from the reporters, pushing them to one side as he strode off.

Kyron was stunned and could not believe what he had just heard. Samuel Jensen dead? *Was Jackson more ruthless than he had imagined? Had Jackson arranged for his father's death?* Kyron was now even more anxious to speed up his return to earth. He had to ensure that Torri as well as the other members of his team were alright.

Kyron jumped up from his chair and headed straight for the flight deck. When he arrived he found the senior flight officer at the controls.

"Captain Dawson, I have an extremely urgent matter to discuss with you."

"Please sit down, Mr Shield. What is so urgent?"

Captain Jake Dawson was a veteran pilot. He had flown fighter jets during the Gulf wars in his youth some forty five years ago, but now approaching retirement he was happy safely transporting ore.

Kyron began talking at twice his normal speed without stopping for breath.

"Well, according to the latest news bulletin on the screen, Samuel Jensen has been killed in an internal transporter malfunction in the MERIC Building. I need to get back to Earth as fast as I can. I was on a special mission on his orders and I suspect that this has something to do with his untimely death. I fear that he has been murdered and I am asking for your help Captain to arrive on Earth ahead of schedule."

The Captain pondered for a brief moment before replying.

"You say Jensen is dead? I'm sympathetic to your cause Kyron, as I knew Samuel Jensen personally when I first escorted him to the new mine on Terra Iota. He was keen to spend time with me at the flight controls and we became quite good friends during the space flight. He was a good man. This shouldn't happen to a person like him."

Captain Dawson paused a moment, trying to comprehend the news.

"The only way to increase speed in this craft would be to lighten the load, which would mean having to offload the ore capsule. Being an engineer, you'd know about speed being relative to increasing the mass weight. Exceeding the inertia in a vacuum would …"

Kyron cut him short of going through Einstein's relativity theory.

"Yes, I know all about that. So, when can we start?"

"Well first I'd need someone in authority to agree to your request," Captain Dawson replied.

"And who has that authority, Captain Dawson?" asked Kyron with urgency in his voice.

"General Blake is the only one with that power."

Kyron realised that he would have to breach the secrecy of his trip if he was to reach Earth sooner.

"Alright Captain, send a transmission to Miss Blake, his daughter, at MERIC. I'll give you the confidential security code which feeds directly into Samuel Jensen's transceiver without interception by the Communications Officer. I'm hoping that Miss Blake has his transceiver. This is the message I want you to send immediately."

Dawson reached for the control panel and switched on the transcorder, beckoning with his hand for Kyron to lean into the device and dictate his message.

"Miss Blake, I have just heard of Samuel Jensen's death and I am very sorry. I know how close you were to Mr Jensen and I have lost someone who was like a father to me. I'm on my way back to Earth as requested. You're the only one who knows, so don't tell anyone else of my travel arrangements. I need you to request your father's permission to offload the ore capsule in order to increase the speed of the ore transporter in which I am now travelling. I think you know the reason for the urgency and the secrecy. Please get back to me as soon as you can. I'm on stand by. Out."

Kyron gave the security code to the Captain who, without hesitation, inserted the code and started to transmit the message. Kyron waited anxiously for the reply from Earth, pacing backwards and forwards in the small confines of the flight deck and continuously checking his time piece.

"Would you like a coffee, sir?" suggested Dawson in an attempt to settle Kyron's nerves.

"No thanks, Captain. That would have no effect on the way I'm feeling at the moment."

Within the hour they received a reply directly from General Blake granting permission, with instructions for the flight officers to note the location where the load was to be jettisoned. Without the excess baggage, the estimated time of arrival at hyper-speed was in four days.

"I've been waiting years for the opportunity to officially crank this armoured tank to the max and see what she can do!" exclaimed Dawson, hardly containing his excitement. Kyron nodded in appreciation and headed back to his quarters.

Just as he was nearing the galley, Kyron heard the sounds of rummaging. As he turned the corner of the passageway Kyron was surprised to see a man with his back towards him, dressed in a prison-orange uniform and frantically pulling things out of the food storage cabinets. Sensing Kyron's presence, the intruder suddenly stopped what he was doing and swiftly swung around, gripping a large carving knife in his right hand.

Kyron was amazed to see Krane standing there with a half crazed look in his eyes and a nasty grin on his face. Krane spoke slowly with a harsh, vengeful voice.

"So glad to see you, Kyron. Now I can finish what I started and put you away for good before you reach Earth."

Kyron knew that he was confronting a hardened ex-mercenary, a killing machine who had no fear of injury or death, and a man who had nothing to lose. This gave strength to his enemy, but in Kyron's mind it was his weakness. Kyron's father had instilled in him that those who have no fear possess no caution, and those who care less are subjected to carelessness, which leads to errors of judgement. Free from the emotion of hate and destruction, Kyron was clear in his thinking and controlled in his actions.

Krane lunged at him with the knife, aiming for his stomach. Kyron, with lightning reflexes, stepped aside and tripped Krane with a side flick of his outstretched left leg. Krane fell face down, accidentally landing with his right shoulder on the knife edge. He winced in pain, but his anger forced him to roll over and quickly stand to his feet. His shoulder was bleeding badly and his nose was bloodied. His adrenalin, acting like a strong analgesic, over-rode the pain and he continued in his pursuit to destroy Kyron. He swapped the knife into his left hand and took a wild, back-handed swipe at Kyron's head.

Kyron ducked, sprang back up and, at the same time, gave an instant front snap kick to Krane's chest. This sent Krane reeling backwards, smashing him against the side metal panel of the craft. Partially dazed and winded, Krane charged like a madman at Kyron with his left arm raised in the air and the knife tightly clenched in his fist, ready to strike a downward blow.

Kyron was too fast and, leaning to one side, he produced a powerful roundhouse kick to Krane's stomach. Krane doubled up and again landed face down on the floor. Krane lay there, motionless.

Momentarily, Kyron stood his ground. Then he carefully approached Krane, his arms in a defensive position and his body ready to spring into action. Placing his right foot on Krane's left shoulder, Kyron gave a soft shove. There was no response. Slowly he bent over and tugged at Krane's right shoulder to roll him over. With Krane now on his back, Kyron could see why his attacker lay motionless. The knife was sticking out of his chest at an inclined angle near his heart. Krane's glazed eyes were frozen open. There was no apparent breathing and Kyron felt no pulse on Krane's neck. Krane was dead.

Kyron took a deep breath to compose himself. He was in partial shock. He had not intended killing the man and had wanted only to disarm him and place him back in custody. It was the first time he had been directly responsible for taking a life. In the silence, his adrenalin-pumped heart thumped loudly until his breathing started to deepen and the tension in his body began to subside. Kyron, in his mind, was trying to justify the death of this stranger. *Yes, it was self defence. Krane had initiated the attack with a weapon. I had to defend myself in a life and death confrontation.*

Now that he was reassured and in a more relaxed frame of mind, Kyron hurried back to Captain Dawson to report what had taken place.

"Captain, I have something I need to report to you. And perhaps you won't believe it…. On my way back to my quarters I was attacked by an escaped prisoner from Terra Iota who had obviously stowed away on board your ship. He was the MERIC security officer who had been placed in custody after attacking me on the flight from Earth. He came at me with a knife and I had no choice but to defend myself. Unfortunately, he is dead after accidentally falling on his knife in the scuffle."

Kyron was clearly unsettled.

"I'm aware that this needs to be reported to the Security Division back at Terra Iota straight away. But it's getting a little complicated. Would you mind asking security on Terra Iota to delay notifying MERIC security on Earth until after our arrival? I don't want to alert anyone else back home in case there's another attempt on my life when we dock."

The Captain was stunned by the news. Nothing like this had ever happened before on his ship. He spoke his thoughts aloud.

"Well, Kyron, in spite of the seriousness of the incident it certainly has disrupted the monotony of the long flight. Yes of course I'll transmit the message now. Are you alright?"

"Yes, thank you Captain, just a little shaken."

Kyron helped the Captain place Krane into a preservation capsule and secure the capsule in the storage bay.

"He's very heavy and quite large," panted the Captain after struggling with some difficulty. "I'm surprised you managed to fend him off, considering he's a trained mercenary."

Kyron, who was breathing easily, responded humbly.

"Just lucky I guess."

Kyron was now even more apprehensive of his surroundings. *Perhaps there were more of Jackson's stowaways lurking on board?* He returned to his quarters wondering how he would be able to get some sleep.

Lying there in the dark room with just the faint background noise of the pulsing thrusters, Kyron re-lived the events in his mind, questioning what had just taken place. *Could he have handled it better? Were there other moves he could have made to avoid Krane landing on the knife? Should he have tried to negotiate with Krane using words that could have diffused Krane's aggression?*

The more Kyron reflected, the more he was convinced there was nothing that could have stopped Krane's mission. On orders from Jackson, Krane was out to kill Kyron and it was Krane's own blatant carelessness that got him killed. Just before dozing off, Kyron heard the noises of the ore capsule being uncoupled and then the thrusters engage for full propulsion. They would soon be back on Earth.

Kyron was grateful that the next three days were uneventful, providing him the opportunity to plan a strategy for when he landed back on Earth. His first priority was to see Torri to assure himself that she was unharmed and that his team was safe. Next, he needed to see Miss Blake to find out what Samuel Jensen's plans were, and how far they had been carried out. He also wanted forensics to perform an autopsy on Samuel Jensen to determine if his death needed further investigation.

Kyron was feeling quite vulnerable. He was a threat to Jackson and his life was clearly in danger. He was very much alone and outnumbered, with Jackson in control of MERIC and the security officers. But Kyron felt that he had no choice but to expose the conspiracy and bring Jackson to justice. Jackson had gone too far.

At night, Kyron's strange dreams were becoming more vivid

and lifelike. He saw soldiers in blue velvet robes carrying swords as well as staffs, sometimes marching, sometimes in battle, in a strange countryside or in a courtyard within a citadel of domed buildings. He saw a younger version of his father, smiling and laughing with other soldiers. He heard the voice of his father talking to others in the dreams and heard the name 'Rhyk' mentioned often. It seemed very real and Kyron felt comfortable in this dream environment. Somehow, it was like being home.

THE PAST RETURNS

ON the third evening out from Earth, Kyron was preparing to retire for bed when he felt his father's gold ring start to vibrate more strongly than it had before. As he clasped his shaking right hand in the palm of his left to support it, an incandescent blue light suddenly shot out from the centre of the ring, filling the room and plunging it into an eerie silence.

A hazy holographic figure appeared within the blue light and slowly shaped itself into the outline of a person. As the haziness dissipated Kyron could see a uniformed figure cloaked in a similar blue robe as the one he had found in his father's case and carrying a familiar looking staff. The hologrammed figure spoke in a friendly, mellow voice which echoed through the cabin.

"Do not be afraid. You are not imagining this."

Kyron, although mesmerised by what was happening, felt at peace.

"I am Captain Ehrane Dakhar from the planet Tzurac, not within your solar system, and I have come in response to the activation of the ring that you are wearing. That pledge ring once belonged to a Sentinel by the name of Captain Ahrmon Tyros who we thought had died on the planet Nebularis some two hundred and seventy years ago. I would like to know who *you* are and how the ring came into *your* possession."

Kyron was temporarily stunned, but tried to hide his nervousness by feigning a superficial confidence in his voice.

"I am Kyron, son of the man who called himself Rhamon. He bequeathed this ring to me before he passed away last year. I have every intention of honouring my father and following his teachings."

"Ah," said Captain Dakhar, piecing the threads together. "The son of Rhamon…"

After a moment of reflection, he spoke again, in a more compassionate tone.

"Tell me about your father."

Kyron felt instinctively that he could trust Captain Dakhar and that no harm would come to him or his mother. So he explained the message left by his father on the transcorder.

"My father told me that he was falsely accused of murdering his friend and asked me to keep secret his identity and the story of where he came from for fear that the Tzuracians would come looking for him. He also left me his robe and staff."

"Ahh," said Dakhar, "Now all is clear. I believe that your father was Ahrmon, Ahrmon Tyros of Tzurac, and that he changed his name to Rhamon for protection when he started a new life on Terra Major.

"A long time ago your father was accused of murdering my father, Rhyk Dakhar, and sentenced to death, although he pleaded his innocence to the Senate, insisting that rogue Bladers had been responsible. Your father escaped from Tzurac in a stolen craft before the sentence was carried out. Soon after, a search party located the stolen craft through a tracking signal. The party, led by Chief Khane Zarkwin, traced the signal to the planet Nebularis, known by your Terranians as Terra Iota, where your father had crash landed. The craft had been burnt to a shell and, inside, was a body charred beyond recognition with only a sleeve of your father's robe identifiable by the gold symbols. They concluded that your father had been killed in the crash.

"While on this planet the Security Forces found charts that the marauders or Bladers, as they are known, had left behind and they were able to track down and capture them with their leader. The Bladers confessed that they had killed my father on direct orders from Khane Zarkwin, Chief of Security. Zarkwin was eventually captured. He admitted to the treason and was sentenced to life imprisonment. You have nothing to fear now from the Tzuracians, Kyron. You should be proud of your father and of your own name which is based on one of the planets in our star system, Kyronis."

The holographic figure spoke once more.

"I am pleased to know that your father survived his ordeal and lived a full life, raising a family. Being an offspring of a Tzuracian Sentinel you may have noticed that you have unusual qualities that are unique compared to other Terranians. You may also have experienced a strange vibration feeling whenever you are near the blue crystal rock."

"Yes," replied Kyron, excited by the information, "And things that my father did not explain clearly to me, like my keen eyesight, particularly at night, my increased strength and rapid healing, speed and agility – qualities that others do not possess. My father told me to conceal these unique qualities from others, fearing that those who didn't understand would attempt to destroy those who possessed these qualities out of fear or envy. There's more."

Kyron was stopped abruptly as the image raised his hand.

"Yes, I know and understand how you must have felt, but there will be time enough for you to tell me more when we meet again on Earth. I have very little time to prepare you for what is about to happen. But do not fear my brother. You are not alone and good will triumph over evil, trust me. I will see you in two days time, but do not disclose to anyone our encounter or the things of which we have spoken. I am happy to have found the son of my father's closest friend. I will let the other Sentinels know. If you need to contact me again before I see you, just press the first set of blue stones either side of the ring band simultaneously, and I will appear in holographic form within the hour."

The illumination of Captain Dakhar flickered and then vanished as suddenly as it had appeared.

Kyron sat motionless for almost ten minutes, trying to absorb what had taken place. His mind was racing with all sorts of questions that he wanted to ask this strange intruder from another world. The image, dressed in uniform with a robe and staff, was just like the soldiers he had seen in his dreams. *Perhaps they were not dreams, but remnant images of his father's past life triggered whenever he was wearing his father's ring?* Kyron was anxious to meet this strange figure again in person and felt more confident knowing that he was no longer alone in fighting the conspiracy at MERIC.

***

Two days later the ore transporter reached Earth and, having travelled incognito, there was no sign of any hostile security officers waiting to greet Kyron when he arrived.

After offloading his travel bag at his apartment and refreshing himself, Kyron went straight to the MERIC Building, where he managed to enter the building easily without raising any alarms. He was aware that he was in dangerous territory and realised that he could be captured at any time by the security officers if they were on full alert.

Surely the cameras and his access card would have been enough to give him away? But perhaps Jackson was unaware of his early return and had not issued a security alert? Or maybe Jackson had a plan? Perhaps he wanted to allow Kyron to walk into the MERIC Building without being stopped knowing that, once inside, he would be easy prey?

Kyron needed to see Miss Blake to find out what Jackson had been up to since he had taken control. But first he proceeded to his work unit.

As he entered the room, Torri let out a cry of excitement and surprise.

"Kyron! You're back!" She ran to him, smothered him with her arms and kissed him passionately.

The rest of the team soon gathered around them with wide grins on their faces and hands outstretched to welcome Kyron back. But before Kyron could utter a word, Torri began showering him with words of relief.

"We were worried about you, Kyron. We hadn't heard from you for over two weeks. All of us were concerned for your safety, particularly since the death of Samuel Jensen and since Jackson took total control. Why didn't you keep in touch?"

"I'm sorry for keeping you all in suspense, but it was for my safety as well as yours that I needed to stay under cover. I can't explain right now, but you'll all know more after I've spoken to Miss Blake."

"They're holding the funeral for Samuel Jensen tomorrow at the crematorium and we're all attending. Will you be there Kyron?" said Whitey.

"Yes, of course I will. Thank you Whitey for letting me know. Now, I must see Miss Blake urgently. It's great to see all of you again. If you see Jackson, try not to let him know that I'm back. Okay guys?"

They all nodded and returned to their workstations, Torri being the last one to leave his side. Kyron whispered in her ear.

"Can you come over tonight after work? God I missed you, Torri. I was so worried about your safety."

"I worried about you too, Kyron. Of course I'll come over tonight. I can't wait," Torri whispered back.

She squeezed Kyron's hand gently, smiled sweetly, turned, and walked back to her workstation, leaving that enticing familiar scent of jasmine perfume.

Kyron headed off to the internal transporters to catch one to the penthouse, pausing uncomfortably when he saw a bright red sign, 'OUT OF ORDER' draped across one of them. It was obviously the fatal transporter that had ended Samuel Jensen's life. Kyron's mind raced into overdrive. There were so many questions he needed to ask Miss Blake.

Kyron entered the other transporter and touched the illuminated bar for the 30th floor. It was a rapid express ride, luckily without interruptions. He stepped out of the transporter before the doors had fully opened and walked quickly along the passageway, arriving within seconds at Miss Blake's desk.

Miss Blake was obviously caught by surprise to see Kyron. But before Kyron could say a word, she raised a straight index finger to her lips, signalling him to remain silent.

"Follow me," she whispered, and led Kyron by the hand to an empty conference room several paces along the passageway.

As soon as they were in the room, Miss Blake closed the door and activated the controls to blacken the glass walls, preventing passers-by from seeing in. Again, before Kyron could speak, Miss Blake started the conversation.

"This is the only room that doesn't have security monitors, so we can talk freely. Before you start asking me questions, and I know you have many, let me do the talking. I may be able to give you most of the answers you are seeking."

Kyron stood with an intense look on his face and nodded his

head in agreement. Miss Blake invited him to sit down and, as they arranged their chairs, she started to relate, in a very serious voice, the events that had taken place over the last two weeks. She finished by explaining that Mr Jensen's life had come to a sudden end.

"Sadly he was prevented from fulfilling all of his plans. He was killed less than twenty-four hours after these arrangements were made and soon after receiving the copies of all last month's transmissions to and from Terra Iota. The Chief Surgeon was ordered to perform an autopsy because of the suspicious circumstances of his death. An investigation was also requested to ascertain why the internal transporter's emergency braking system had failed. You'll have to talk to the Chief Surgeon if you need information on the results of the autopsy. But they may not release them to you as the case is still under investigation.

"Jackson has deemed himself Head of the Company and now resides in his father's office, which is why we needed to talk away from my work station. He has also dismissed half of the Board members who were not in favour of his future plans. Jackson has ordered production to commence on the new sonar excavators and the first one is to be ready for field operations in three weeks time on Terra Iota. Jackson Jensen now has full control of the security officers. He is currently out of the office but should be returning within the next hour. He doesn't yet know that you have returned Kyron, but it will not be long before he finds out. I suggest you …"

Kyron cut into Miss Blake's dialogue, his mind spinning with all the things he needed to do.

"I need to see the Chief Surgeon for those autopsy results and the Head of Operations to see if they have found the reason for the brake failure. I also need to see our Liaison Officer to organise a meeting for me to address the World Assembly on behalf of Samuel Jensen about the discovery of the blue crystal rock. Can you arrange these meetings for me Miss Blake, without getting yourself into serious trouble with your new boss?"

"Yes, Kyron, I can do that. Samuel Jensen would have wanted me to help you. I miss him very much. He was such a very nice man and a wonderful boss and I want to help as much as I can."

Miss Blake became tearful before she spoke again.

"There is something else you need to know about Mr Jensen's Last Will and Testament."

Kyron interrupted abruptly with some reassurance.

"I'm sure that can wait," he said, and although Miss Blake wanted to protest, Kyron continued. "It's best that we focus our attention on the urgent matters at hand to stop this new tyrant from ruining what Mr Jensen spent a lifetime creating. I'll be off now, but thanks for telling me all this. I'll see you at Mr Jensen's funeral tomorrow. Be careful, Miss Blake."

"I will Kyron, but you need to take extra care, as Jackson will probably be coming after you next to ensure that there is no evidence to expose his conspiracy. He wants no threats to prevent his future plans being carried out."

"Yes, you're right Miss Blake. Jackson has already ordered a couple of failed attempts on my life. But he won't try anything while I am in public view. Besides, I have someone who is watching over me, someone you will most likely meet in due course."

Kyron opened the door cautiously and peered out of the room down the corridor. When he saw it was clear of security officers and there was no sign of Jackson, he quickly headed for the internal transporter.

But just as he was about to enter the half-opened door, two burly security officers stepped out of the transporter. The first officer reached for the handle of his truncheon while eyeing Kyron off and started to address him in an assertive manner while the second security officer reached for the hand restraints from the side of his black leather belt.

"Mr Shield, we've been looking for you since your ID recognition activated on entry to the building today. JB wants to see you so you had better come with us and don't try anything that you might regret!"

Before the second officer could retrieve the hand restraints from his belt, Kyron grabbed him by the arm and tossed him against the wall on the other side of the passageway. The first officer retrieved his truncheon ready to strike, but Kyron turned, and in one sweeping motion, blocked the downward strike with his left arm. Simultaneously he struck at lightning speed with a right knife-hand to the side of the officer's neck, totally disabling him. The officer slumped to the floor.

The second officer, still partially dazed from the heavy collision with the wall and Kyron's unusual strength, attempted to draw his truncheon. But Kyron was too fast. Kyron took a flying leap with an outstretched straight leg, landing on the second officer's chest, forcing him to crash heavily into the wall and rendering the officer unconscious.

While there was still no-one in sight, Kyron quickly dragged the two men into a cleaner's storage room near the transporter. He tied their wrists behind their backs using their own wrist restraints and strapped their legs together with their own leather belts. *By the time they wake up I'll be well clear of the security in the building.* Luckily, this area of the passageway on the 30th floor was not under close security surveillance. But Kyron knew that he had to move fast before the alarms were sounded. Jackson's men would most likely shoot on sight.

Kyron looked around the room for some clothes that might disguise his appearance. He grabbed a cleaner's pair of dark green overalls, which were slightly oversized but fitted well over his own clothes. He placed a matching green peaked cap on his head so that it tilted low on his forehead, shading half his face, turned his collar up, and loosely fastened a red patterned neckerchief around his collar. To add the final touch to his disguise he shoved a worn-out red cleaning rag in the back pocket of his overalls, leaving it hanging out and picked up a squeeze mop and empty bucket. Dressed like this he felt more confident to make his escape unnoticed and was ready to catch the internal transporter.

Kyron opened the storage room door and, in a nonchalant manner, strolled casually to the transporter. He swiped his hand across the illuminated bar for the ground floor and kept his fingers crossed that the transporter would continue uninterrupted. Unfortunately, the lift stopped on the 20th floor and who should enter but the young Communications Officer that Kyron had encountered before his trip to Terra Iota.

Kyron pulled the peak of his cap even lower over his face as the young officer stepped in. Thankfully the officer was absorbed in the paperwork he had in his hand and didn't acknowledge the "cleaner" when leaving the transporter on the 15th floor. Kyron breathed a huge sigh of relief.

There were no more surprises on the way to the ground floor. Kyron dumped the mop and bucket in the transporter, swiped his ID card at the exit and passed without notice to the shuttle station where he quickly discarded his disguise. He was soon on board the next shuttle.

Kyron focused on a plan of action. He had to avoid capture and notify the World Assembly. Realising that Jackson would soon be sending MERIC security officers after him, Kyron's first thought was to collect his father's metal case and some essentials and then find a safe haven.

Arriving at the Central Reception Control Centre, Kyron eyed the giant digital clock which displayed the time as 17.00 hours. He was aware that Torri would soon be arriving at his apartment if she wasn't already there. As he passed by the main reception desk at the Company apartments, one of the staff called out to him.

"Mr Shield!"

Kyron turned to him apprehensively.

"Yes?"

"You have someone waiting for you in your room. They said you were expecting them."

"Thank you for letting me know."

For a moment Kyron relaxed thinking that his visitor was most likely Torri. But then he experienced a sudden sense of fear, realising that the security officers might be a step ahead of him and Torri.

Arriving on his floor, he approached his apartment with extreme caution. Standing to one side of the locked door, he swiped his coded card and slid the door wide open. He stood back for a moment while surveying the perimeters of the room. His body began to tingle as it had done when he encountered the tiny specks of the blue crystal rock on Terra Iota. Not sighting anyone, Kyron slowly entered. Then a familiar voice sounded on the far side of the room from a corner initially obscured by the opening door.

"Greetings my friend." The tone was comforting to Kyron's ears. "I said I would see you in two day's time."

The mild pounding in Kyron's heart instantly subsided and he sighed with relief as he returned the welcome.

"Hello Captain Dakhar, I'm happy to see you again and this time in the flesh. I must tell you though that I'm in kind of a hurry."

Before another word was uttered, Kyron raised his right hand to his mouth and placed a finger across his lips as a signal for Captain Dakhar to be silent. He fetched a large cloth from one of the chairs near the table, unfolded it and placed it over the hologram screen on the wall. Finally, he activated the music system and turned up the volume.

"We can talk safely now. I suspect this room has eyes and ears linked to the communications network at MERIC. The MERIC security officers are probably searching for me since I disarmed two of them a short while ago back at the MERIC Building. They were about to take me back to Jackson. It appears that Samuel Jensen may have been murdered to prevent him from reporting to the World Assembly about the new discovery on Terra Iota and I think Jackson is planning the same misadventure for me. It's not safe in these quarters, but I had asked my fiancée, Torri, to meet me here before my unexpected altercation with the security officers."

The Captain spoke softly, but with a confident authority. He appeared taller and broader than in the hologram. The hood from the robe he was wearing was now pulled back, giving a clear view of his strong facial features. He had straight shiny fair hair, pulled back into a short ponytail. His face was chiselled with high cheek bones, a square jaw and a straight nose. His crystal clear, blue eyes, like polished sapphires set in a clasp, had a powerful interrogating gaze.

"Kyron, let me tell you who you really are and why I'm here. This may take some explaining, so you need to sit down and listen. Do not fear the security officers, or worry about your safety. These issues will be dealt with in time."

They sat and faced each other as Dakhar commenced his fascinating tale of the past leading up to the present.

"You are the son of a Sentinel…," he began.

Kyron listened intently to Dakhar as the story unfolded, resolving the mysteries to the many unanswered questions Kyron had been carrying in his head since he first opened his father's metal case: How and by whom Kyron's father was framed and why his father had to leave Tzurac; the purpose behind Kyron's martial art training; the strange powers he had inherited; the universal importance of the blue crystal rock known as Xytrinium and why it affected his body; and the responsibility that had been thrust upon him as his birthright to become one of the protectors in the Federation of the Planets.

Dakhar told Kyron of the two-hundred year war that almost destroyed Tzurac save for the super-powered army of Sentinels who had been enhanced by this blue crystal; the vow that the Tzuracians had taken to ensure that the universe would never again be under threat of destruction by those who wanted to misuse the power of Xytrinium; and the pledge of the Sentinels to keep that vow and protect those planets that discovered the substance.

Kyron absorbed the words that Dakhar spoke and the role that the Sentinels played as protectors of the Universe and felt a stirring within himself. Emotionally he felt a natural yearning like a rekindling of smouldering coals starting to ignite into flames. Although he had lived his life as a human he instinctively knew deep down there was always this suppressed feeling that there was something else. Kyron could never pinpoint exactly what it was but now that Dakhar had explained things, it was so obvious. Now he was faced with conflicting loyalties. He was torn between a responsibility to Torri and his work with MERIC here on Earth, and his newly discovered commitment as a Sentinel on the planet Tzurac.

Dakhar continued.

"As a representative for the Federation, I've been charged to arrange an audience with your World Assembly to negotiate an alliance and invite the people of your planet to join the Federation of Planets. The explosion on Terra Iota sent shockwaves through the universe and alerted the Tzuracians of this new discovery. Since then we have been monitoring your transmissions from Terra Iota to Terra Major, Earth.

"We also wanted to locate the owner of your father's pledge ring, which was coincidentally activated soon after the explosion. The Tzuracians know of the plot that your Company has in mind for Xytrinium and the man behind it. I am here to neutralise this plot with your help. I am also aware of the danger that you are in and I'm here to prevent any harm coming to you. I want to show you more about the weapon and the robe that your father left you. Can you recover these items now? We have little time left before we are discovered."

Kyron, still overwhelmed and reeling from all that he had heard, walked across the room to the wall panel, pressed the control, and the bed slid out. He retrieved the case from the wall cavity behind the bed and placed it on the bed. Kyron pressed the correct sequence of symbols on his ring and the harmonics resonating from the ring again caused the triangular panel on the lid of the case to illuminate. He pressed the panel and the case instantly sprung open. He took out the short-staff with his right hand and turned to Captain Dakhar. The same feeling he experienced when he held the staff back at his mother's house started to take effect.

Dakhar spoke in a soft tone.

"Kyron, I want you to open the staff to its full length."

Kyron flicked the short stick and extended it to its full length similar to his other staff.

"Now, depress that small dark button on top of the staff."

Kyron again followed the Captain's instructions. What happened next was totally unexpected. Kyron watched the staff open down the middle, starting about seven inches from the end being held and fold outward until the edges of the two halves met directly opposite where they had started unfolding, forming a circular hilt for the handle and revealing a razor-sharp, double-edged metal blade.

Kyron started to wield the sword in the forms that his father had taught him, circling, lunging, parrying and striking, while performing a sort of dancing routine. The sword was so light and so easy to manoeuvre. On closer inspection, Kyron recognised the same symbols as on his father's ring etched into the metal blade. He pressed the dark button again on the top of the handle and the blade retracted instantly to the size of the small eighteen inch short-staff.

"I see your father taught you well in blade technique," said Dakhar with admiration.

"Yes, he was very good, a master in the use of the blade, but he didn't tell me about the hidden secret within the staff."

"Nor the robe either," said the Captain. "Fetch the robe from the case and I'll tell you of its special qualities."

Kyron retrieved the robe, which still felt very unusual to the touch. Dakhar continued to explain.

"This robe is the Sentinel's shield and a part of the regimental dress uniform. Put it on Kyron and I will demonstrate why it is a shield."

As soon as Kyron donned the robe, the Captain pulled out his laser pistol and fired a beam to the back of the robe.

"What are you doing?" shouted Kyron in surprise. "You could have seriously wounded me."

"Take the robe off Kyron and take a look at it."

Kyron did so and was very surprised that there was not a mark to be seen.

Dakhar proceeded to explain.

"The robe is made of a Xytrinium micro mesh, with a similar woven technique used in the chain mail worn by your ancient warriors. When worn by a Sentinel the Xytrinium robe is very lightweight, but worn by anyone else it is extremely heavy. The robe can repel laser beams and blade attacks, is resistant against extreme heat and cold, and can be used as a shield for close range blasts. However, you may still encounter bruising if the blow is quite heavy or administered point-blank."

Captain Dakhar then spoke in a more serious tone.

"You may well need these skills and armaments if we encounter resistance from Jackson and his henchmen and they refuse to abide by the universal code of preservation."

Kyron responded with a note of futility in his voice.

"How can just the two of us, in spite of our unique qualities, prevent Jackson from carrying out his plan?"

"Oh, Kyron," sighed Dakhar in dismay, "Ye of little faith. You don't think that I came across the Universe unprepared do you? I have brought with me to Earth one hundred Sentinels and I have dispatched one hundred more to Terra Iota."

Kyron was speechless.

"You can no longer stay here though," counselled Dakhar. "You must accompany me to my craft. Tomorrow, with the support of my army, we will seal Jackson's fate!"

THE BATTLE CONTINUES

CAPTAIN Dakhar's speech was interrupted by a knocking at the door. An instant reflex transformed Dakhar's staff into a blade and automatically he set himself into a defensive stance. As Kyron moved to open the door, Dakhar grabbed his shoulder and provided a word of caution.

"Careful Kyron, it could be Jackson's henchmen."

Kyron nodded, activating the security surveillance in anticipation. Both relaxed when the screen image projected on the back of the door showed that it was Torri.

As Kyron opened the door, Torri sprang forward without warning wrapping her arms around him, not noticing Dakhar just out of sight behind her.

"Hello Kyron, mmm, it's so good to see you...," she exclaimed emotionally, "But what's that cape you're wearing?"

"Oh, it's great to hold you too sweetheart, but I would like to introduce you to Captain Dakhar," said Kyron.

He turned Torri around to face their guest, Dakhar, who had silently retracted the blade into a small staff and placed it back in his belt hiding it under his robe.

"Captain Dakhar, this is Torri, my fiancée. She is also our computer engineer in my team at MERIC."

Torri felt slightly embarrassed on finding Kyron with a distinguished-looking uniformed stranger in his room. She tried to regain her composure without blushing unduly.

"Hello Captain. Has Kyron done something wrong?"

Kyron spoke before Dakhar could respond to the question.

"No Torri, I need to explain everything to you. Please sit down, darling. Can I get you a drink first? And what about you Captain, what would you like?"

"Water will be fine, thank you, Kyron," Torri replied, with a very puzzled expression on her face.

"Same for me, thank you, Kyron," responded Dakhar.

"VALERI, three glasses of water!" ordered Kyron while heading to the servery.

Within seconds Kyron returned with the drinks, ready to explain everything. But just as he finished handing out the drinks, there was a loud explosion which blew the door open, enveloping the room with thick white smoke. As the smoke subsided, they were confronted by four MERIC security officers with laser pistols drawn and pointed in their direction. One of the security officers in the lead shouted:

"Nobody move! Kyron Shield, you are under arrest for the assault of two security officers. You are to be escorted to the MERIC Building immediately."

With lightning speed, Kyron pushed Torri over to the bed and dived in a forward roll towards the armed unit, knocking them over before they had a chance to fire their weapons. Almost in unison, Captain Dakhar dived over them, disarming two of the officers with his short-staff while Kyron hastily collected the other two security officers' weapons. Standing up and pointing one of the officer's pistols at the group, Kyron nodded his thanks to Dakhar.

"Thank you for your assistance, Captain. What shall we do with them now?"

Dakhar was already contemplating a plan.

"I suggest we restrain these thugs in cuffs and escort them to my craft for interrogation to find out what Jackson has devised. We have methods of extracting information painlessly, Kyron. You can explain everything to Torri on the way."

"Yes, Kyron," came Torri's startled voice from across the room. "Please explain to me what on Earth is going on. Why are you wearing that unusual robe? Who is this Captain fellow? And where are we going?"

"Alright, Torri, calm down," Kyron replied in a concerned voice. "Sorry for pushing you. Are you alright?"

"Yes Kyron, I'm okay."

"I'll explain everything to you Torri just as soon as we're out of here."

After restraining the attackers, Kyron quickly gathered the few things he needed into his father's metal case and they hurriedly left the building, commandeering the security officers' shuttle vehicle to travel to the Tzuracian spacecraft. As they travelled, Kyron reassured Torri that Captain Dakhar was a friend from another planet who was here to help them.

Dakhar's spacecraft, invisible to the human eye through the use of cloaking, had landed about three miles outside the city limits in a vacant uninhabited area that had been levelled for future development. Kyron manoeuvred the security shuttle inside the craft under guidance from Dakhar. They had entered what appeared to be a very large hangar that stored several unusual looking vehicles. Once inside the craft, Captain Dakhar immediately started firing orders to his regiment.

They were approached by ten marching Sentinels wearing full battle dress, which included robes, breastplates and gauntlets all made of a similar blue material. They also wore bluish metallic helmets that were a cross between an American gridiron skull cap, and a medieval Saxon headpiece, shielding both sides of their faces. The Sentinels all carried full-length staffs in their left arms, rigidly positioned at their sides, and laser firearms strapped to their thighs. Kyron thought the Sentinels looked very daunting as they came to a sudden halt, slamming their black leather knee-high boots down in unison and standing to full attention. The leader saluted Captain Dakhar sharply. Dakhar returned the salute.

"Lieutenant Kruzak! This is Captain Tyros's son, Kyron, and his fiancée and colleague, Torri."

The Lieutenant saluted to Kyron in the same manner and spoke respectfully.

"It is an honour to meet you and serve you, sir. Welcome to the battalion."

He tipped his helmet to Torri.

"Pleased to meet you, my lady."

"Lieutenant," snapped Dakhar, "Take these security officers to the interrogation booth. We need information about Jackson Jensen's intentions in order to formulate our strategy. We need this information by morning. Guard them well, for they are the key to our success."

The Lieutenant saluted once more, performed an 'about face', and ordered his men to secure the four security officers. Surrounding the captives, they marched off to one of the passageways leading from the large hangar. Captain Dakhar, turning to Kyron and Torri, spoke in a hurried but friendly manner.

"Come with me my friends, we have much to organise and very little time to prepare."

Kyron and Torri followed Dakhar to a large metallic vertical cylinder in the centre of the hangar, extending from the floor to the level above them. He stepped inside the cylinder with Kyron and Torri following. Briskly waving his hand across one of the illuminated circles to the left of the cylinder wall, the floor they were standing on suddenly pushed upward gaining speed. Within seconds, they were transported to another level that had a rounded passageway about fifteen feet wide with slightly curved walls either side. The walls on the right side had distinct panels about the size of a doorway spaced at intervals approximately ten feet apart. Dakhar led Kyron and Torri to one of these panels and brushed his right hand across an illuminated circle, sliding the panel open to reveal a room containing a large oval table with a transparent top.

"Please sit down and I'll order some refreshments as you both must be quite famished. I have a feeling that you'll like Tzuracian cuisine."

In front of Captain Dakhar on the table top where he had seated himself, was a faint outline of a pattern. When Dakhar touched the pattern with his fingertip, it suddenly illuminated. Tapping it several times, a panel on the wall behind him opened, presenting a tray with three plates of food and three small vessels containing a purple fluid. The Captain swivelled his chair to retrieve the tray, then swivelled back to the table, handing the plates and drinks to Kyron and Torri while continuing to talk.

"Now while we are eating we can discuss a plan of how to capture Jackson, and later on Kyron, you can tell Torri who you are and what this is all about. Let me assure you Torri, you are in safe hands and out of danger."

Kyron lent across to Torri and placed a comforting arm around her shoulders. She gave a faint smile while nodding an acknowledgement, but she was still in partial shock and feeling a little anxious. She hoped this was all a bad dream and she would soon awaken. Questions were buzzing in her head. *Who was Kyron, really? Who was Captain Dakhar? And why was he here to capture Jackson?* While Torri was mulling over this confusion, Kyron was keen to inform Dakhar about the event that would be taking place tomorrow.

"Captain," Kyron began.

"Please call me Ehrane," interrupted Dakhar. "I feel I know you as a friend. And besides, you saved my life back there from those trigger-happy henchmen."

"Alright, Ehrane," Kyron said in a more friendly voice. "There is something you need to know that may assist in our plans and hopefully prevent anyone from getting hurt."

Dakhar leaned forward in anticipation as Kyron continued.

"Samuel Jensen's funeral service is being held at the Crematorium tomorrow. I assume Jackson will be there. If he is, we should be able to apprehend him quite easily because he will be less protected. But if he remains at the MERIC Building, it will be almost empty because the staff will be attending the funeral. So we could avoid any harm to the MERIC staff if we encounter resistance from Jackson."

After a brief thought, Dakhar responded.

"Then Kyron, we have a plan. We will attempt to apprehend Jackson at the funeral as you suggest. That way you can both attend the funeral and pay your respects to Samuel Jensen, as I am sure you would like to. Jackson has no quarrel with you Torri, so being unobserved can you pre-set the security system first thing in the morning to disarm itself at a time when most of the staff will have left the building for the funeral service?"

Torri nodded in agreement.

"Yes Captain, I can arrange that. It should be relatively easy seeing as I was involved in the design and implementation of the security system when it was first installed. I still have my access codes on 'permanent active status' because they still call on me for troubleshooting."

"Perfect," said Dakhar. "This will allow my Sentinels to enter the building without alerting the security officers, taking them by surprise and avoiding unnecessary bloodshed. I will accompany you to the funeral Kyron, and bring some of my soldiers for your protection. They will be disguised as Terranians so as not to draw attention. Once we have Jackson in custody, I will keep him here in the craft and later we can present him to the World Assembly for them to deliberate on his punishment. How does this sound to you, my friend?"

"Sounds good," said Kyron, "But if Jackson's not at the funeral and we change to 'Plan B' how will your Sentinels know where to go once they are in the building?"

Dakhar acknowledged Kyron's question by touching the pattern on the table again. Instantaneously, in the centre of the table, a three-dimensional hologram image of the MERIC Building appeared, showing the internal layout.

"How did you get hold of these?" exclaimed Kyron in surprise. Torri was also amazed at the intricate detail of the image.

"Our technology is quite advanced," replied Dakhar. "We have scanned many of your establishments in the past. This is not the first time we have visited your planet. We visit many planets that have been colonised to monitor their activities and their progress. We are guardians of the universe entrusted to maintain universal equilibrium and to ensure that no harm is done to the planets. We would like to show your Terranians how to restore Terra Major back to a healthy environment by eradicating the pollution and removing the toxins that are poisoning your planet. The objective is for all to live in harmony and peace with nature, with all beings evolving to a higher quality of life."

Dakhar was interrupted by Lieutenant Kruzak entering the room. Kruzak saluted and Dakhar rose from his seated position, returning the salute.

"Sir, I have some vital information for you. We have interrogated all the captives and they have revealed the plan that Jackson Jensen has in store for Kyron tomorrow, as well as what Jackson intends to do with the Xytrinium once it is transported and stockpiled on Earth.

"Jackson knows that Kyron will be at the funeral service tomorrow and will attempt to capture and escort him under guard to the MERIC Building, forcing him to sign some sort of agreement under threat of death. Jackson has given orders to station his security officers in strategic locations throughout the building in case Kyron has supporters who may try to interfere. Jackson and his security forces are currently not aware of our presence. However, he is aware of you Captain. You were being monitored when you first entered Kyron's apartment. He does not know of your origin or your intentions but he knows that you are in allegiance with Kyron. Jackson's future plan is to use the Xytrinium as a weapon to extort the World Assembly for control of the world economy."

"Thank you Lieutenant, you have done well. Induce the prisoners into hibernation state and secure them in the cells. Assemble your soldiers in full battle dress at 06.00 hours tomorrow in readiness. Choose six of your best and have them dress in formal civilian Terranian attire with concealed weapons and report here at 07.00 hours tomorrow. They will accompany Kyron and me to the funeral service. If we are unsuccessful in apprehending Jackson Jensen at the funeral, I will signal you Lieutenant to make your way with the unit to the MERIC Building ready for a confrontation with Jensen's henchmen.

"Lieutenant, you and your unit need to study the hologram of the MERIC Building in detail to familiarise yourselves with the layout. Try to avoid injury to the security officers, but not at the expense of harm coming to you. I will communicate to you as soon as I know of Jackson Jensen's location and movements. That will be all for now, Lieutenant. Good luck and may the spirits of the Ancients protect you all."

"Thank you sir and may the spirits also protect all of you," said the Lieutenant as he saluted his captain. Dakhar reciprocated as the Lieutenant departed, and then he turned and faced Kyron and Torri.

"Both of you need to get a good night's sleep to be up early in the morning so that Torri can be at the MERIC Building before the rest of the staff arrive. I'll show you to your quarters and then, Kyron, you will have time to tell Torri the whole story. Torri, we have already sent to your room new MERIC Company dress uniforms as well as informal attire, so you don't have to return to your apartment. In the morning after you have preset the deactivation timing on the MERIC security system, you should join the other staff as they make their way to the funeral service. Once at the Crematorium, you can meet up with Kyron. Will you be able to manage this Torri, without placing yourself in danger?"

"Yes, of course Captain," Torri replied.

"Very good. Now both of you follow me."

Dakhar led them back along the passageway to the cylindrical transporter to travel to a higher level. They disembarked at a passageway that looked similar to the previous one, but coloured differently with subdued blue illumination emanating from the floor panels. Sentinels as well as other aliens dressed in different coloured uniforms were travelling in both directions along the walkway. Some uniforms were green with silver bands on the sleeves and others were maroon with silver piping around the neck and waistline. The aliens all had similar fair hair and facial features with distinct blue eyes.

Shortly Kyron and Torri arrived at a door panel that slid open when Dakhar passed his hand over an illuminated circle on the wall beside the panel.

"Well this is where I leave you," said Dakhar. "I hope the room is to your liking as it has been decorated in the Terranian style to make you feel more comfortable. There is an automated servery in the room for your breakfast and drinks. All you need to do is verbally command what you would like to eat and the servery will supply your request. Sleep well until the automatic alert wakes you in the morning. I will be here at 07.00 hours to collect you. Good night, my friends."

Kyron reached out his right hand to shake Dakhar's and as he did so Dakhar also reached out his arm. But instead of shaking Kyron's hand, the Captain clasped Kyron's arm near the elbow and Kyron responded with the same motion.

"This is the Tzuracian way of greeting," said Dakhar.

"Thank you for everything, Ehrane," responded Kyron sincerely.

"Yes, thank you Captain Dakhar," said Torri.

"You are very welcome," he said with a warm smile. Dakhar released his grip, turned and marched off in the direction they had come from, the door automatically sliding back into place after him.

Torri was eager to find out all about this mystery and as soon as Dakhar was out of sight she started firing questions at Kyron, one after the other.

"Who is Captain Dakhar and where does he come from? Why are

you trying to capture Jackson? Who are you really Kyron, and why haven't you told me before all this was happening? What is this strange robe you're wearing?"

"Slow down, Torri! All will be revealed just as soon as you give me a kiss."

Torri smiled as Kyron took her in his arms, saying, "I love you Torri."

"I love you too Kyron and I don't want anything to harm you."

"Don't worry. I am well protected with the help of Captain Dakhar and his army of Sentinels. Sit down and I'll tell you everything."

For quite some time Torri sat speechless while Kyron related everything he had been told by Dakhar. It was a fantastic tale that Torri found difficult to accept.

Eventually Kyron dimmed the lights giving their sleeping quarters an ambient glow and creating a soft atmosphere. Although they were both tired from all that had happened, they were also emotionally hyped with a mixture of anxiety and adrenalin. They feared what the near future might bring and what these alien beings were planning. They were excited by the danger of what was going to happen or what could go wrong and the threat to their lives. Most of all they were uncertain of how long they would be together and how the world might be changed forever. All they knew at this moment was that they had each other and that their love was so strong that they could take comfort in each other's arms.

Without a word, Kyron took Torri in his arms again. Gazing into her deep green eyes, he gently stroked her pale, soft cheeks. He brushed his face against her inviting moist lips and soon they were lost in a long, passionate kiss. Torri unconsciously sighed with pleasure. A rush ran through their bodies that ignited their passion for each other. Whether it was the thrill of the events of that day or the thought of being totally out of their comfort zone in an alien world, something had brought Kyron and Torri to a deeper level of commitment for each other.

Caught in the moment, they undressed each other and lay their entangled naked torsos on the crisp white sheets, so absorbed in each other that time and place did not exist. Every kiss, every caress, every touch was charged with emotion and the muffled sounds of carnal pleasure. Torri's kisses were intoxicating and sweet to the taste. Her skin was so soft and smooth and she responded sensuously to Kyron's touch. Torri was transformed into a state of ecstasy as Kyron gently fondled her with his hands while kissing her body.

They became so engrossed in their sexual arousal that they abandoned all boundaries and their senses – physically, emotionally and spiritually – became as one. It was the most passionate night they had ever experienced. Kyron and Torri knew they would be united for the rest of their lives, however long that may be.

THE GATHERING

KYRON and Torri were awoken from a deep sleep when the craft's alarm system sounded at 06.00 hours. The alarm started with a low pulsing frequency and increased in volume until it reached a level that was tolerable but annoying, and then it suddenly switched off.

Kyron was first to rise and step into what he thought was a steam cleansing bath. Instead, when he waved his hand over the illuminated control, a bluish ultraviolet light beam from above the alcove covered his naked body. It felt very warm on the skin and had a slight perfumed citrus fragrance. After three minutes the beam automatically switched off. Although there were clean white towels on the shelving, no towelling was required as his body remained totally dry. Surprisingly, Kyron felt clean, refreshed and alive, with a glowing sensation all over. *Far superior to the steam cleansing bath.*

To shave, Kyron used a small device resembling a conventional electric shaver that was hanging on the wall of the cleansing room. When he switched it on, a small flat bar across the top of the device illuminated with a pale red light accompanied by a low humming vibration. There appeared to be no blade, but when Kyron moved the device across the stubble on his face, his skin was left smooth, supple and invigorated. Kyron was quite taken with it all. *I like the Tzuracian technology!*

By the time Kyron was beginning to dress, Torri had also risen and slipped into the cleansing cubicle, unnoticed. While Torri was experiencing the wonderful Tzuracian cleansing ritual, Kyron pulled his white dress-uniform from his metal case and dressed, placing a black armband on his left sleeve and tucking his father's short blade staff under his jacket in his trouser belt.

Torri stepped from the cleansing cubicle with only a towel wrapped around her and began searching for the clothes that Captain Dakhar had arranged for her.

"Good morning my love," said Kyron beaming affectionately with a satisfied smile. "Did you eventually get some sleep?"

With a cheeky smile on her glowing face, Torri let her towel slip and walked seductively over to Kyron. She pressed her slender body tightly against his and kissed him passionately. They held each other for a long time until Torri broke the silence.

"I love you Kyron. I want to be with you forever," she said in a soft affectionate voice.

"I love you very much too Torri," responded Kyron, "And I feel the same about our future."

Separating for a moment, Kyron looked intensely into Torri's eyes and spoke with conviction.

"When this is over, we'll start our life together as a family. But until then, we'd best prepare ourselves and focus on the day ahead."

Torri nodded in agreement and then went in search of her clothes.

As she waved her hand over one of the illuminated circles on the wall panel, the panel silently slid open and there, hanging up, sharply pressed, was a MERIC formal dress uniform with matching leather boots. Surprisingly she found the uniform and boots to be a perfect fit.

"You look fantastic, Torri," said Kyron, admiring the way her slender figure was accentuated by the perfectly tailored suit. This was the first time they had seen each other in dress uniform.

"So do you Kyron. You look very handsome, quite dashing in fact."

"Thank you my love. Now, let's have some breakfast before Captain Dakhar arrives and prepare ourselves for what the day may bring."

"Yes, I'm famished," replied Torri with a smile on her face, while heading for the automated servery.

Over breakfast, Torri was deep in thought. She was still coming to terms with the reality of what Kyron had told her the night before. How the engineer from the country, who she had fallen in love with, was in fact a Sentinel, related by blood to a race from another planet, born to live four hundred years and sworn to protect the Alliance and the other planets in the universe. Torri thought it was like something out of a science fiction movie and she found it hard to believe that it was real. Despite her love for Kyron, the situation raised some questions in Torri's mind about her future with him. *Would Kyron stay on Earth? Or would he ask her to return to Tzurac with him? Would their children be Sentinels like their father?*

Torri's thoughts were suddenly interrupted by a strong knock on the door that jolted her back to reality. The intercom system came alive with the recognisable mellow voice of Captain Dakhar.

"Good morning, Kyron and Torri, I've come to accompany you to the conference room to make our final plans. Are you ready? Or do you need a few minutes?"

"Good morning, Captain," replied Torri.

"Good morning Ehrane," responded Kyron at the same time. "We're ready."

Kyron opened the sliding door and both he and Torri stepped into the passageway and followed Dakhar down the passageway heading for the cylindrical transporter.

"How is the outfit Torri? And did you both find your quarters comfortable enough to have a good night's rest?" enquired Dakhar sincerely.

Torri couldn't help giving a coy smile.

"Yes, thank you Captain, the dress uniform is a perfect fit and we both slept well. Kyron and I were quite taken with the ultraviolet beam shower."

Dakhar chuckled knowingly.

"We have learnt many ways of conserving our precious water and have found that this is a far superior way of cleansing the body. It would be very difficult to return to the antiquated ways."

By now they had reached the conference room where six Sentinels were waiting, clothed in Terranian contemporary attire and looking very much like humans. Lieutenant Kruzak was also in attendance with another six Sentinels in their battle dress. They were already studying a hologram of the MERIC Building suspended over the table. They all greeted each other and then Dakhar spoke.

"Kyron, could you show us on the hologram where Jensen's office is located and what we are likely to encounter should we have to enter the building?"

"Yes, of course." Kyron pointed to the locations on the 30th floor. "Here is the office where Jackson has taken over from his late father. There are manned security stations on each floor, located in the same place, here and here. All the security officers are armed with laser pistols and heavy truncheons. Knowing Jackson, he will most likely have them wearing laser protection vests. Usually there are two security officers stationed on each floor, but Jackson will probably have doubled the numbers today."

Dakhar nodded in agreement as Kyron continued.

"Their intercom communication system is on their wrist with an earpiece located just behind their ear. They will probably be focussed on the internal transporter and waiting for the doors to open. Although Jackson doesn't know the size of your forces, he may think that I have gathered a few loyal supporters to assist in my confrontation with him. Then again, he may anticipate that you have other soldiers with you, Captain.

"When Torri disarms the security system it will also shut down the camera surveillance in emergency stairwells. So the stairs would perhaps be a more appropriate access that would not alert them. If you entered from the top of the building and simultaneously had some of your Sentinels enter from the ground level, we might be able to take them by surprise and avoid an all-out war. Of course, everything will depend on the timing."

Dakhar seemed impressed.

"That's a very good plan, Kyron. Our craft has the stealth and cloaking ability to deploy the troops at the right time. What do you think, Lieutenant?"

"Sir, I think this is an excellent strategy," replied Kruzak, without hesitation.

Dakhar reinforced the decision.

"Then it's agreed. This will be our modus operandi. Now we all need to synchronise our times. What time does the funeral service take place today, Torri?"

"It's arranged for two hours from 10.00 to 12.00 hours, Captain," replied Torri.

"Very good, Torri. Kyron and I will escort you to the MERIC Building in the security shuttle. We'll leave in ten minutes to allow you enough time to complete your task. We will then rendezvous with you at the crematorium just before 10.00 hours. I'll give you this communication device to wear in case you need to contact us."

Dakhar produced a piece of gold jewellery, a brooch shaped like a small star containing a central blue gemstone surrounded with tiny blue stones. He explained to Torri how to activate it.

"If you attach this to your collar in a similar place to where I am wearing my communication device, it will be easy for you to talk and to listen. Just press on the large blue stone to activate and deactivate the device. It has a long range signal that far exceeds our needs, so it will work wherever you are located. It also acts as a tracking system with pinpoint accuracy, telling us where you are at any given moment. No-one will suspect this being a communication device."

Kyron strolled over to help Torri attach the brooch to her collar.

"We'll be with you all the way," he said to reassure her.

The Lieutenant and his soldiers were setting their timing devices on their wrists when Dakhar gave another order.

"Lieutenant, go and brief your soldiers on the strategy. All going well, we may not need to storm the MERIC Building, however, be prepared in case we need a change in plan. I will contact you to keep you informed of what is happening."

The Lieutenant and the Captain exchanged salutes and the Lieutenant with his Sentinels marched out of the room.

"Okay, Kyron and Torri," said Dakhar. "Follow me. You soldiers also come with me."

Kyron, Torri and the six plain-clothed Sentinels followed Dakhar out of the room to the security shuttle.

After a fond and lingering exchange between Kyron and Torri, Dakhar and Kyron dropped Torri off at the MERIC Building and continued on to the crematorium. Concealing the shuttle behind the building, Dakhar placed his soldiers in various locations in the grounds of the crematorium while the area was still deserted. Then, finding a bench seat in an elevated strategic position in the gardens, Kyron and Dakhar sat and waited for the other guests to arrive.

"Ehrane," said Kyron, "I haven't had the opportunity to investigate the report on Samuel Jensen's autopsy and I fear that the evidence and the answers I need may be destroyed with Samuel Jensen's cremation."

Dakhar responded with a wry smile.

"Don't be too concerned, Kyron. I will be able to interrogate Jackson's memory when we have him in custody. Our scientists have developed advanced methods of mind probing, and can read in picture form the thoughts and actions stored in a person's memory. It is painless and the subject has no resistance to block the process. We will uncover the truth of this in time and Jackson will be held accountable for his actions."

Kyron had another concern.

"And I haven't contacted Miss Blake to reschedule my flight to the World Assembly. I want to present the information that Samuel Jensen was intending to deliver before his untimely death."

Dakhar reassured him.

"Kyron, we'll be travelling there together on my craft after the ceremony to inform the World Assembly of everything including the discovery of the blue crystal. You'll be able to discuss these matters with Miss Blake when she arrives at the service. But there is a question I have for you that requires some serious thought, and you should take some time to consider your answer. It will be a difficult choice that you have to make, and I want to offer my help and counsel in any way I can to assist."

Kyron had been anticipating this conversation but knew he could not commit to an answer until all the pressing matters had been resolved and under control.

"Yes, Ehrane, what is the question?" asked Kyron, feigning ignorance.

"My question, Kyron, is what do you intend doing about your life here on Earth given your Sentinel pledge as a protector of the universe? How will you honour your father's name in the ranks of the Tzuracian army?"

"Ehrane, you appreciate that this is a difficult decision to make at the moment. As you mentioned, I'll need some time to think and I appreciate your offer of wise counsel based on your knowledge and wisdom. I also need to discuss this in detail with Torri as she is a major part of my life. I want to honour my father but at the same time make a future with Torri, whether here or on Tzurac."

"I understand what you are going through, Kyron," Dakhar said, nodding in agreement. "I know you have some serious issues to resolve and need time to discuss this with Torri. I will be patient. I'm sure you will make the right choices."

Before Kyron could continue, the first guests started to appear for the funeral, walking through the gardens and into the crematorium building. From their vantage point, Dakhar and Kyron could clearly see the guests as they arrived.

Miss Blake was next on the scene. Before entering the building she spotted Kyron on the rise and hurriedly walked over to him and Captain Dakhar. They stood up to greet her with a smile.

"Hello, Kyron," she said with a warm smile. "I'm happy to see you safe and to be here for the service."

"Hello Miss Blake, it's good to see you," replied Kyron. "I would like to introduce you to Captain Dakhar. He is a friend who is helping me resolve our problems."

"Pleased to meet you, sir," said Miss Blake as she raised her right hand to make the acquaintance.

"Likewise," responded Captain Dakhar whilst slowly shaking Miss Blake's hand.

Turning to Kyron with an expression of urgency on her face, she again spoke.

"Kyron, there is something important I was trying to tell you before you left the other day." She quickened her speech while surveying the gardens for any signs of Jackson.

"When Jackson took over his father's office, he found a copy of Mr Samuel Jensen's last Will and Testament which I had helped prepare for his legal advisor. The Will had been finalised just before Mr Jensen's fatal accident. But when Jackson read what was in the Will he became infuriated. He went into a rage and made several threats concerning you."

"What was in the document to make him so angry Miss Blake?" enquired Kyron with a more attentive ear.

"Well, although the contents are confidential and no-one is permitted to know of them until the official reading, I believe it is in your best interests, under the circumstances, to know." She paused and took a deep breath.

"Kyron, Mr Samuel Jensen has bequeathed his whole Company and all his assets to *you*. He felt you were like the son he would have wanted and he decided that he could not entrust the future of the Company in the hands of his own son, Jackson. He knew that you would follow in his footsteps and make decisions in the best interests of the Company and its employees."

Kyron was speechless and a little shaken. He raised his hands to cover his face and, steadied by Dakhar, sat back down on the bench seat. After a long silent pause, Kyron spoke slowly.

"I can't believe this. I am only a Company employee and haven't done anything to deserve this. *Now* I know why Jackson is so desperate to dispose of me. Thank you, Miss Blake, for telling me. It's hard to fully comprehend. It's all a bit of a shock."

"Yes, I can understand how you feel," said Miss Blake, as she seated herself beside Kyron and took his hand, gently stroking it to offer support.

Dakhar prodded Kyron's arm with his elbow and leaned over, whispering quietly:

"Here comes Torri."

Miss Blake rose from the bench where she was seated.

"Well, I'd best be attending the service. Let me know if you need anything, Kyron."

"Yes, thank you, Miss Blake," said Kyron. "There is something that I need you to do for me now. Could you please cancel that flight to the World Assembly and I will get back to you with a new time?"

"Alright Kyron, I will." Miss Blake hurried off towards the building's entrance.

"Hello Torri. How did it go?" enquired Dakhar as Torri came within earshot.

Torri replied in a low tone.

"Hi Captain. The security is set to be switched off at 11.00 hours and needs to be reset to activate it again. They won't be able to track how it was done as I have erased my electronic footprint."

"Well done Torri," said Dakhar, satisfied that the first phase of the operation had been actioned successfully.

"Thank you, Captain," she replied before turning to Kyron. "Kyron are you alright, you look a little pale?"

"Yes, I'm alright, or at least I will be in a minute. Miss Blake just told me something that came as a bit of a shock. I'll tell you about it later. We need to focus on what's at hand right now. I saw the project team arrive with you, but there's been no sign of Jackson yet. Oh, there's General Blake from ASPECT with some of his colleagues."

Just as Kyron said that, Jackson walked into the entrance of the crematorium accompanied by five security officers. Dakhar also spotted them, but before he could say anything, Kyron started.

"Are you ready, Ehrane?"

"Yes, let's join the gathering shall we?" responded Dakhar while adjusting his attire.

As Kyron, Torri and Captain Dakhar headed towards the entrance of the building the other six Sentinels came from their stationed positions in the garden, closing ranks behind them as they reached the doorway. Dakhar turned and motioned to the Sentinels to position themselves inside on either side of the doorway. Kyron and Dakhar stood in the back stalls close to the doorway and right behind Torri. The atmosphere inside the hall was sombre. Samuel Jensen had been a well liked and respected figure.

The service was conducted by a Chaplain of Samuel Jensen's denomination and following his sermon, General Blake was called upon to address the group. He gave a very emotional and moving account of his friendship of many years with Samuel Jensen and spoke of his good character and generous nature. Most of those assembled were tearful by the time General Blake had finished his speech, except for Jackson, who remained stone-faced throughout the entire proceeding.

When Jackson gave his eulogy, his words were cold and unemotional and offered without any sign of remorse. It was sadly obvious to the bereaved congregation that there was no love lost between father and son. Jackson spoke more about himself than about his father. Sadly, Jackson's mother had passed away early in his life and Jackson had been sent to boarding school to fend for himself, and that's the way it came across.

Jackson quickly finished his oration and left the podium before the ceremony had finished, deliberately avoiding those wanting to offer their condolences. Jackson strode straight down the aisle towards the exit, not bothering to turn his head to acknowledge those in attendance, with his five security henchmen falling in behind him.

As he approached the back stalls where Captain Dakhar was standing, the Sentinels either side of the aisle lunged out to grab his henchmen, while Dakhar reached for Jackson. But Jackson was too quick. He clutched his hand onto Torri's arm and pulled her towards him. Torri screamed for Kyron, but Kyron wasn't close enough to react. In an instant, Jackson produced a laser pistol and pointed it at Torri's temple.

"Back off, Kyron!" he shouted angrily. "You and Captain America, and your other comic characters will not stop us from leaving! If you want to see Torri alive again, you will come to the MERIC Building alone, today, to discuss some pressing issues that need finalising."

"Hold back soldiers!" cried out Dakhar. "Let them pass. We don't want harm to come to anyone."

"Very sensible, Captain," scowled Jackson. "I don't want to see you or your soldiers again, if you want Torri safely returned."

On that note Jackson and his henchmen stormed out of the complex with Torri to board Jensen's private shuttle. Before Torri was pushed into the shuttle, she turned anxiously in Kyron's direction and Kyron nodded reassuringly, trying to communicate to her that all would be okay.

By this time the crowd was in an uproar, shouting and muttering and questioning what was happening. Thinking on his feet, Kyron strode up to the podium and began an announcement on the personal address system.

"Ladies and gentlemen, may I have your attention, please. Please calm down and I will explain to you what has happened. Please be seated."

The noise subsided and the members of the audience were eventually all seated.

"I apologise for disturbing the service on a day when we have all come here to show how much we cared for Samuel Jensen and to pay him our last respects. I, for one, am going to miss him deeply as he was my mentor and made me feel part of his working family from my first day in the Company."

Kyron paused for a moment before continuing.

"Out of respect for him, I was trying, with the help of Captain Dakhar, to arrest Mr Jensen's son, Jackson, and bring him to justice for arranging … the murder of his father."

The crowd gasped in disbelief.

"Jackson also arranged for several attempts on my life to stop me from exposing his conspiracy to use MERIC for illegal profiteering. He has now kidnapped my fiancée, Torri, and wants to lure me to the MERIC Building to arrange something that I can only imagine is some diabolical scheme. It is not safe to return to the MERIC Building today. So, continue with the service in honour of Samuel Jensen. I have the support of loyal friends who will help me rescue Torri," Kyron said, pointing to Dakhar and his colleagues.

"I ask you all to trust me. Tomorrow I'll be able to tell you more about the future of the Company but, in the meantime, don't worry as I guarantee that your positions will not be affected. I'll now leave you in the hands of the Chaplain. Thank you everyone. Thank you Chaplain."

There were mumblings from the crowd as Kyron left the podium and headed for the exit, with Dakhar and his unit following Kyron out of the building. Dakhar spoke with urgency in his voice,

"Good work Kyron, but in one hour's time the MERIC security system will be deactivated. I think it's time to execute our contingency plan. Don't worry about Torri. Jackson will not harm her while he is waiting for you to appear."

"Yes, I sure hope you're right," said Kyron nodding with concern. "Give the order Ehrane!"

"Before I do Kyron, I want you to return to the craft with me and change into a Sentinel battle-dress uniform. That way you will be one of us in battle. You will be protected from any stray fire and you'll be camouflaged so that you don't stand out in that white uniform."

Kyron acknowledged the suggestion.

"Very well Ehrane, I agree."

"Lieutenant Kruzak, are you there?" Dakhar was now talking into his communicator.

"Yes sir," came the echoed response from the communicator, "I am awaiting your orders Captain."

"We were unable to apprehend Jackson and he has taken Torri

captive. We are returning to the craft and then we'll revert to our contingency plan. See you shortly Lieutenant. Out."

They were soon back at the craft, where Kyron changed into a full battle-dress uniform complete with breast plate and helmet with his father's blue robe. He tucked his father's blade staff into a holster strapped onto the left hand side of his black leather belt. He had also been issued a laser pistol that he attached to the right side of his belt, and a regulation standard boot dagger.

Dakhar and his regiment were assembled in the hangar when Kyron arrived at the scene.

"Do I look the part?" he said, half smiling to Dakhar despite the seriousness of the situation.

"You'll pass, Cadet Shield. Welcome aboard soldier."

The regiment chuckled at the Captain's comment. Then Dakhar turned to the regiment and addressed them in a more serious tone.

"Remember, all of you, we are trying to save the life of Kyron's future wife, as well as apprehend Jackson Jensen. Be prepared for anything. Use your hand command signals with restricted voice communication and, if necessary, use your blades rather than your laser pistols. This is a stealth operation. We do not want to attract attention with unnecessary noise.

"Half of the regiment will be entering through the basement of the building and making their way through the emergency exit stairwell led by Lieutenant Kruzak. The others will be with me and we will be entering from the top of the building through the exit stairwell. Hopefully, with the distraction happening on the lower levels of the building and with the security surveillance out of action, we will have a successful outcome."

"May I say something Captain?" Kyron asked.

"Yes, by all means, Kyron."

"First, I need to warn all of you that you will be dealing with security officers that have been recruited from other armed forces. They include freelance mercenaries and other militia. They are trained and experienced in armed and unarmed combat and all forms of weaponry. They are dangerous, so never underestimate their ability. Second, if by chance you happen to encounter Jackson himself, he is an expert swordsman and has very fast reflexes. He is also well versed in hand-to-hand combat. Last of all, thank you for your support in helping me in my quest."

Dakhar let out a war cry with a Sentinel salute.

"To the Regiment!"

The unit responded automatically:

"To the Regiment!"

They all saluted in unison, including Kyron.

BATTLE FOR TERRA IOTA

A S previously arranged by Jackson, the first unauthorised modified excavator had arrived at Terra Iota with an escort of fifty security officers. Engineer Don Carson was at the transport bay to greet the new arrivals and to organise the offloading of the new equipment as well as arrange where it was to be installed in the mine. Carson, the junior engineer on Terra Iota, was a much younger man than his boss, Grant Thompson, and was taller in stature and of slimmer build. His dark short-cropped gelled hair matched the colour of his eyes, which accentuated his arrogant look.

The leader of the security officers approached Carson while his unit was still disembarking from the craft and lining up in their ranks. He saluted Carson sharply and introduced himself in a guttural accent.

"Mr Carson, I am Senior Constable Dirk Vandel. I have been charged by Jackson Jensen to oversee the security of the mining operations and to ensure the protection of the blue crystal rock during its transportation to Earth. Here are my orders."

He took a mini disc from a zipped pocket on the sleeve of his black leather jacket and handed it to Carson.

"Hello Constable," Carson acknowledged, accepting the disc, "I have been expecting you. Jackson has kept me informed of your intended arrival since you left Earth three weeks ago. I have arranged quarters where your unit will be housed as well as the program for the mining schedules with the amounts we plan to extract in each load. If you'd like to follow me, I'll show you and your men to your quarters and then we can review the schedules in my office."

Just as he finished speaking, Thompson appeared on the scene with four ASPECT security officers. Thompson approached Carson directly, questioning him abruptly.

"What's goin' on Don?"

"Well Grant," replied Carson using a more authoritative voice. "The new excavator for mining the blue crystal rock has arrived with a company of security officers who will be overseeing the security arrangements while the rock is being mined and transported to Earth."

Thompson was now quite agitated and replied assertively.

"First of all Don, there's been no communication from General Blake regardin' new arrangements for the security of the proposed transport of this newly mined blue crystal rock. Secondly, the last direction given by Samuel Jensen was to cease mining operations until further notice. And that is what we'll be doin'!"

Carson was unfazed.

"I'm sorry to say this Grant, but your authority has been revoked by Jackson Jensen, who now runs the Company. Jackson has placed *me* in charge of the operations and *you* in confinement."

"What!" exclaimed Thompson, responding defiantly. "We'll see about that, Don!"

As Thompson went to walk away, Carson gave a command.

"Arrest that man, Senior Constable, and place him in the holding cell."

Vandel instantly signalled to two of his men, who immediately grabbed Thompson. They quickly placed restraints on his wrists and a gag on his mouth. Carson then removed Thompson's transceiver from his pocket.

At that moment, the four ASPECT security officers standing behind Thompson raised their weapons and aimed at Carson. But instantly, the MERIC security officers with Carson drew their lasers in response. Carson, with a casual attitude, and not making any sudden movements, confronted the ASPECT security officers in a confident manner.

"Come, come officers, don't be foolish; you won't stand a chance against Vandel's men. It would only be a futile waste of lives. I suggest you drop your weapons. Now!"

There was a momentary pause and, realising their hopeless situation, the ASPECT security officers did as they were ordered.

"Constable Vandel, place these ASPECT security officers under arrest and throw them in the holding cell with Thompson until I decide their fate."

Vandel signalled his men to cuff the ASPECT security officers and gave orders to four of his men to stand guard at their posts while the excavator was offloaded. Finally, Carson ordered everyone else to follow him out of the loading dock.

A hive of activity ensued for the next two days. While Vandel's security officers were busily setting up guard posts and strategic lookouts, the excavator was lowered into position in the crater in readiness to commence mining operations on the seam of blue crystal rock two thousand feet below the surface. Carson was eager to start the drilling to see if this innovative new machine was capable of mining the volatile substance without causing further explosions.

Carson had been keeping in contact with Jackson Jensen on a regular basis through the whole operation, alerting Jackson of the security officers' arrival with the excavator and the capture and confinement of Thompson and the ASPECT security officers. However, Carson was shocked by a transmission he received from Jackson on the second day of operations. The message read:

DATE: 10 AUGUST
TO: ENGINEER DON CARSON – TERRA IOTA
FROM: JACKSON JENSEN
TEXT: 100 TZURACIAN SENTINEL SOLDIERS
BEING DISPATCHED TO TERRA IOTA AND WILL
POSSIBLY ARRIVE WITHIN THE NEXT TWO
DAYS TO PREVENT MINING OPERATIONS. BE
PREPARED FOR SERIOUS ENCOUNTER WITH
THESE SENTINELS. KEEP ME POSTED OF
DEVELOPMENTS.
-END

Carson checked the date. It was already August 11. He hadn't heard of these Tzuracian Sentinels and his mind was full of questions as well as some fear. *Who were they and where were they from? What sort of weapons did they possess and what did they look like? And how did Jackson know about these Sentinels and their plan to arrive on Terra Iota?*

Carson wasted no time informing Constable Vandel and asking him to make arrangements to defend the mine. Vandel reassured Carson that work on the strategic lookouts had been completed and that his men were well trained with plenty of field experience and capable of dealing with any military encounter.

"Carson, you just focus on the mining operations and leave the battle tactics to the experienced," Vandel said self-confidently.

Vandel briefed his men about the impending arrival of Sentinels. He organised shifts to guard and patrol the mine day and night, arranged for laser cannons to be placed in the sentry lookouts, and land mines to be placed strategically around the base camp and the mining area. The miners and other staff were restricted to safe areas. Terra Iota was taking on the semblance of a prison camp rather than a mining colony.

***

On board their craft heading for Terra Iota the Sentinels were preparing for an encounter with Jensen's security officers. They knew that they could not negotiate surrender. Captain Dakhar had explained to the regiment that Jackson Jensen was obsessed with having total power and control of the Xytrinium and that he would not give up his quest at any cost.

It was nightfall as they approached the orbit on the eastern side of Terra Iota and the Tzuracian craft activated stealth and cloaking modes to avoid detection. The craft's lasers could not be used for fear of exploding the deposits of Xytrinium, so the Sentinels prepared for hand-to-hand combat. Second Lieutenant Kal Zawkon, the unit leader, gathered his troops in the conference room to brief them on the plan of attack.

The Second Lieutenant was a force to be reckoned with. He was a veteran warrior and survivor of many battles and the untreated scars on his hardened one-hundred-and-fifty year old body were reminders of his fearlessness and bravery. His broad chest dominated his six-foot muscular frame. His rugged handsomeness was partly obscured by a well-kept full beard and his long thick, fair hair was pulled back into a tightly plaited pony tail that trailed down the length of his neck like the groomed mane of a dressaged Andalusian stallion. A unique strategist, accomplished in all forms of weaponry, he was a formidable enemy. His troops admired and respected him, not only as a dedicated soldier, but also as a strong and just leader who protected them in life-threatening battles.

Zawkon's plan was to take the whole compound by surprise without harming innocent civilians. Because of their superior night vision, the unit would be attacking at night and Zawkon intended to be extra careful by landing the craft a mile away from the mining site.

The craft's heat sensing scanners identified small ground patrols around the mine as well as ten battlements on its perimeter, each manned by at least two or three security officers. The main residential complex some distance from the mine was also well fortified. It had been designed to protect and shelter the miners and their families from the weather and the wild beasts that inhabited the planet.

A ten-foot-high electrified, solid-metal fence completely surrounded the perimeter of the one acre square block of land on which it was built. There were towers reaching ten feet above the walls at each corner of the block as well as halfway along each wall and each was manned by one guard. The three towers on the wall facing the mine also housed large floodlights that continuously swept the area in a semi-circle near the wall outside throughout the night. The scanners detected additional security officers for the day shift who were off duty in their sleeping quarters and small illuminations scattered around the mine area and complex indicated land mines.

The Sentinels outnumbered the security officers two to one. So the Second Lieutenant organised ten groups of six Sentinels to disable the lookout posts or battlements at the mine, while the other forty Sentinels were ordered to neutralise the patrols around the mining area and secure the main building in the residential complex where the remaining security officers were housed.

Zawkon reminded the Sentinels heading to the mine to refrain from using their laser pistols because of the volatile Xytrinium and to try and capture the security officers alive using their laser swords. Given their plan for a surprise attack, he did not anticipate any major encounters. Zawkon continued his briefing.

"The scanners have also detected land mines scattered around the mining area and the base camp, so activate your wrist trackers to alert you to these explosive devices, and disarm them silently as you find them. Good luck, soldiers."

It was now midnight and, as planned, the craft landed on the surface of the planet in the chosen location. Lieutenant Zawkon gave the order to advance. Silently the Sentinels disembarked and, with amazing speed, arrived approximately one hundred yards from the mining compound within minutes. Raising his hand, Lieutenant Zawkon signalled to the regiment to form into their pre-arranged groups and commence the attack. Blades drawn, forty Sentinels headed in the direction of the residential complex, while ten units commenced stalking the lookouts at the mine.

But suddenly, without warning, laser blasts from several of the battlements around the mine fired at the intruders wounding a few of the Sentinels. Zawkon and his troops were stunned at the rapid response, realising that the security officers would now have to be taken by force. It was evident to Zawkon that Jackson's men on Terra Iota had been forewarned. *How? Could he have an informant within his ranks?* He knew his soldiers well and all had pledged to live by a code of loyalty, but Zawkon was suspicious that one of them had betrayed the regiment.

Zawkon gave the order for the ten units to surround the mine and, on a given command, they simultaneously charged the towers. With speed and the cover of darkness working to their advantage, the Sentinels were soon face-to-face with the security officers.

Before the other forty Sentinels could reach the main complex, the commotion at the mine stirred the day-shift crew from their sleep and the Sentinels came under heavy attack as they arrived. Laser cannons from the ten-foot towers fired relentlessly, showering the Sentinels with high-speed gravel pellets as laser blasts hit the ground around them.

The unit leader of these forty Sentinels was Sergeant Montark, another veteran. With his unit pinned down five hundred yards from the front complex gates, he hastily devised a plan. The Sergeant quickly briefed his soldiers.

"We have to kill the spotlights. Once the spotlights are knocked out, I want ten Sentinels on each perimeter wall to surround the complex. When I give the order, simultaneously laser blast a hole in each wall, enter the complex and take out the security officers in the towers, using two Sentinels for each tower. The other Sentinels will deal with those security officers on ground level and inside the buildings within the complex. This should throw them into confusion as we hit them from all sides. Stay in communication to synchronise the blasts. Are we all clear on our mission?"

They all silently nodded in agreement.

"As soon as those spotlights on that front wall are out of commission, we make our move. Private Nardikz, you are our best targeter. I want you to kill those three spotlights now."

"Yes sir!" whispered Nardikz.

Nardikz reached for the long barrelled laser pistol strapped to his back and hidden underneath his robe. Zap! Zap! Zap! Within a minute, all three spotlights had been decommissioned with pinpoint accuracy.

"Good work soldier," Montark praised. "Now let's move out soldiers!"

All went according to plan but it was a gruelling battle and the Sentinels had to fight hard as the security officers were skilled opponents experienced in close combat warfare. Laser blasts were flashing. Swords and staffs were striking. Sentinels and security officers fought blow for blow. Cries of pain were heard and bodies lay scattered on the ground. In a savage encounter between the two leaders, Senior Constable Vandel was shot at point blank range by Second Lieutenant Zawkon and the battle turned in the Sentinels' favour.

After almost two hours of continuous exchanges, the security officers were eventually overpowered by the superior strength and agility of the Sentinels. Gradually the fighting subsided and the Sentinels regrouped to assess the damage and count the casualties. Many of the security officers had been seriously wounded and others killed. The Sentinels too had not survived unscathed. In his encounter with Vandel, Zawkon had sustained a partial laser burn to his left shoulder, but he shrugged this off to his troops as a minor inconvenience.

"Oh well, another memento. So much for our best laid plans. But I knew I could rely on you soldiers to pull it off. Well done and thanks to the Gods."

In their locked-down quarters, Thompson and his four ASPECT security officers had been listening in amazement to the raging battle outside and were relieved and surprised to be found and freed by an army of alien soldiers.

"Jesus, Mary and Joseph, what the bloody hell's going on?"

Zawkon settled Thompson by explaining who his Sentinels were and where they came from and reassured him that they had been sent to prevent Jackson Jensen from exploiting the blue crystal from Terra Iota.

"But what about Carson, Jackson's right hand man here on Terra Iota?" Thompson asked, "Did he survive?"

After searching the complex with Zawkon, Thompson soon found Carson cowering under his bed. Carson had hidden away from the battle leaving his security officers to face the danger.

As the Sentinels secured him, Carson lashed out desperately, making wild threats.

"This isn't the last of it, Thompson! Jackson will see to it that you and these invaders are thrown in prison along with anyone else who opposes his master plan. Once Jackson gets his hands on the blue crystal, you'll all be in trouble."

"Shut up ya cowardly traitor," yelled Thompson, as he landed a heavy blow on Carson's jaw. "You're the one who'll be put behind bars along with the other turncoats!"

Clutching his bloodied jaw, Carson was dragged away by the Sentinels and thrown into confinement on board the Tzuracian craft with the other conspirators. The Sentinels had thwarted Jackson's plan for Terra Iota. Thompson was relieved that Carson was out of the picture, but Zawkon was left wondering how Carson and Vandel had anticipated the Sentinels' arrival. *If Jackson had warned them, then who had informed Jackson? Obviously, Carson was not the only traitor.*

THE RESCUE

IN a small parkland area a short distance from the MERIC Building, Dakhar's craft had rendezvoused, still cloaked in stealth mode. Just before the Sentinels were about to disembark from the craft, Dakhar received a distress hologram transmission from Terra Iota. It was Second Lieutenant Zawkon.

"Yes Lieutenant, what's the situation?" Dakhar enquired.

"Well sir, we came under attack from the security officers who appeared to be expecting us in spite of our craft's stealth and cloaking. We have secured the mine with a few minor injuries to the unit and have taken the surviving security officers as prisoners. Their commander, Senior Constable Vandel, was killed and some other officers wounded. On interrogation, the surviving officers revealed that they had been warned by Vandel that one hundred Sentinels were on their way to Terra Iota and told to prepare for a battle. Sir, I mean no disrespect to the regiment, but our security has been breached. I think we have an informer siding with Jackson Jensen in our ranks."

Dakhar was stunned by the suggestion that a Sentinel might have betrayed their plan.

"I find that hard to believe Lieutenant, but I'm sure all will be revealed when we capture Samuel Jensen's son," Dakhar replied. "Thank you, Lieutenant, for informing me. I appreciate your concerns and I'll be on the alert. But don't discuss this matter with anyone else. We don't want to raise unnecessary suspicion amongst the troops. You have done well to win the battle with only limited casualties to your unit. I want you to remain there on Terra Iota for the time being to protect the mine. I'll contact you in the next two days. Over and out!"

The trees made a perfect cover to disperse fifty of the Sentinels who made their way to the basement of the MERIC Building. The craft then proceeded to the top of the building and the other fifty Sentinels, as well as Dakhar and Kyron, disembarked on the roof. It was now just after 13.00 hours and, thanks to Torri, the security surveillance system had been deactivated. Heat sensors on the craft identified the locations of the security officers stationed throughout the building. They were not in pairs on each floor as Kyron had expected, but instead there were four to a floor, with two security officers strategically placed at either end of all the floors in the building.

Through his communicator Dakhar notified his troops of these changes, instructing them to be on extreme alert and to use laser pistols if required. It was obvious that Jackson knew of the increased army of Sentinels supporting Kyron and Dakhar. Dakhar was now sure that there was an informer within his ranks. However, Dakhar chose not to inform his unit of his suspicions, knowing it would lead to distrust at a time when they needed to be working together. He needed his soldiers to focus on the task at hand and to be on full alert.

Once inside the building Dakhar, Kyron and their unit of Sentinels descended the emergency stairwells. Those Sentinels who entered from the basement had already started to ascend to each floor. It was a two-pronged attack. At every level, groups of Sentinels broke off in threes. Accessing each floor by the stairwell, the Sentinels were potentially exposed to the security officers guarding that end of the building. But the Sentinels had come prepared with small grenades containing a form of gas similar to, but more potent than, the humans' tear gas—a gas that would temporarily incapacitate humans, but not Sentinels.

Prying the Fire Exit doors slightly open, the Sentinels threw several of the charged gas containers along each floor, releasing a smoke screen which disoriented the security officers. Caught off guard and unable to see through the smoke and tears, the security officers fired their weapons wildly in all directions.

Diving through the doors and using their shield robes to fend off the laser shots, the Sentinels manoeuvred their way to the confused security officers. The Sentinels could easily have killed Jackson's henchmen but their orders were to take them alive.

The security officers were no match for the Sentinels and one by one the floors were secured and Jackson's henchmen bound and gagged. However, one of the security officers on the 17th floor managed to evade the Sentinel attack for a time and, before he was captured, made radio contact with Jackson, alerting him of the attack.

While the rest of their unit descended to the floors below, Dakhar and Kyron headed for Jackson's office. Dakhar stopped suddenly in his tracks.

"Listen, Kyron, something is being transmitted."

Dakhar and Kyron could hear voices on their collar communicators.

"We're under attack men and they are already on the 17th floor. You ten men start heading them off. You others stay here with me, and you two, take Kyron's girlfriend to the conference room and tie her up. I'll deal with her later when this is all over."

"That's Jackson's voice," whispered Kyron, relieved to hear that Torri was still alive. "Torri must have activated the brooch, hoping we'd be listening. I'm going to get her! I'll take the air duct that leads into the conference room."

Dakhar grabbed Kyron by the arm.

"Alright, Kyron," he whispered. "But be very careful! I'll take my soldiers and intercept the henchmen who are on their way to the 17th floor. I'll leave two of my soldiers on this floor to deal with the security officers accompanying Jackson."

Captain Dakhar gave specific hand signals without uttering a word, and the group immediately divided. As Dakhar and his group sped off, Kyron gave a hand signal to the remaining two Sentinels, directing them to the exit door.

Silently removing the vent cover, Kyron quietly climbed into the ceiling vent. As he made his way carefully along the narrow ducts in the direction of the conference room, he could hear muffled voices in the rooms over which he passed. He deliberately moved slowly and cautiously to avoid making unnecessary noise, trying to work out who was speaking and where they were.

Hearing Jackson's voice coming from Samuel Jensen's office, Kyron finally got his bearings. Through the micro-slits in the vent, he could see Jackson leaning over a desk pointing to something on a blueprint and talking with one of the security officers. He decided not to confront Jackson until Torri was safe from harm.

Continuing further along the duct Kyron reached the ceiling vent in the conference room. Though the vent slits, he could see Torri tied up in one of the chairs, struggling to free herself. He surveyed the room and noticed the drapes were drawn. No-one else appeared to be present. He whispered to Torri through the vent.

"Torri, don't be alarmed. It's Kyron."

Torri looked up in the direction of the voice.

"Kyron, is that really you?" she exclaimed in a whisper of relief. "I'm so happy to hear your voice."

"Don't move, Torri, I'll be down in a minute."

Kyron removed the vent cover, again being very careful not to make any sound. He swung down onto the table and then leaped to the floor. Placing his finger to his pursed lips, he signalled silence. He reached down into his right leather boot and withdrew his dagger. Slicing easily through the ropes, he released Torri from her hold and replaced the dagger in his boot. Torri sprang to her feet and wrapped her arms around Kyron giving him a warm tight hug. After several precious moments Kyron stepped back before speaking with urgency.

"It's good to see you unharmed sweetheart, but we don't have much time. I want you to climb up on the table and into that vent. Make your way along the duct until you come to the vent in the exit stairwell. Then take the stairs to the rooftop. There'll be someone there to meet you to take you to safety on board the Tzuracian craft."

Torri kissed Kyron quickly on the cheek and then turned away and began climbing into the vent.

"But what about you, Kyron?" she whispered. "Aren't you coming?"

"Not yet my love, I need to help Captain Dakhar apprehend Jackson."

Kyron had no sooner finished speaking when the door burst open and there stood Jackson, smiling smugly with raised sword in hand. Four henchmen were flanking him, two on either side, their laser pistols drawn and aimed directly at Kyron.

Jackson spoke, sarcastically.

"So, you have joined forces with Captain America and tried to play the hero in an attempt to rescue the love of your pathetic life."

Torri quickly disappeared into the vent and started to scramble along the duct as fast as she could. One of Jackson's henchmen standing closest to his left side aimed at the vent and was about to let fire. Kyron's heart suddenly skipped a beat thinking Torri would be shot. But Jackson grabbed the officer's arm, forcing the weapon to the floor.

"Not yet, but don't let her escape," shouted Jackson to the two accomplices on his left flank. "Both of you head to the other end of that duct, but do not harm her in any way. I want her alive! Bring her back here to me. I'll take care of Mr Shield so that he never interferes with my plans again."

The two security officers immediately bolted out the door and raced off down the passageway.

"Just like you dealt with your father eh, Jackson?" sneered Kyron, checking discreetly that the communicator on his collar was activated while pretending to adjust his robe.

"Yes, but this time I'm not bothering to make it look like an accident," retorted Jackson arrogantly. "I'll just say that you broke in here and attempted to kill me and that I acted in self defence."

Jackson narrowed his eyes as his smile turned to a snarl. He clenched and raised his left hand, pointing his rigid index finger towards Kyron. Then he spoke in a threatening manner.

"You could have saved your life and Torri's if you had just come to my office as I requested earlier at the crematorium. All I wanted was for you to sign an agreement stating that you could not accept being my father's beneficiary and bequeathing the Company with all its assets to me, his deserving son and rightful heir."

Kyron, unable to contain himself, laughed out loud.

"Deserving son? The only thing you deserve, Jackson, is a life sentence for murdering your own father, for instigating attempts on my life, for kidnapping Torri, and for breaching international law by not declaring the discovery of a new natural energy resource. Why don't you just give up and plead forgiveness for making a serious mistake and perhaps the court will show leniency?"

The anger raged on Jackson's face and he clenched the hilt of his sword even tighter. He was losing his patience with this smart kid from the farm.

"Sorry to disappoint you, Kyron, but that is not what I've planned and I'll soon have the power to choose my own destiny once I rid the world of you and your soldier friends."

With a swift movement Kyron pulled the staff from his belt, activating the blade.

Jackson spoke again in a condescending voice.

"Quite an impressive weapon you have there farm boy, but do you know how to use that blade against lasers?"

Then Jackson cried out to the two security officers.

"Shoot him!"

Kyron, acting on reflexes, ducked down and swivelled around on his heels, swapped his sword to his left hand, and with his right hand grasped the dagger from his boot. To the surprise of both Jackson and the security officers, the laser shots ricocheted off Kyron's robe. With lightning speed Kyron dived and somersaulted onto the conference table, landing on his feet, and threw the dagger forcefully at one of Jackson's henchmen. The dagger's sharp pointed blade quickly found its mark, piercing the carotid artery in the neck. The security officer slumped dead to the ground, blood gushing from the wound.

Jackson and the other security officer were momentarily distracted. This gave Kyron enough time to leap over their heads, striking the other security officer across his back with his blade; and landing back on his feet just behind Jackson. The security officer fell to the ground, lifeless, blood seeping from the fatal gash.

Jackson swung around and made a sweeping blow at Kyron's head with his sword. Kyron ducked and then flipped backwards, again landing on his feet with his sword raised in a defensive threatening position. Jackson wrenched his laser pistol from his belt and fired several shots at Kyron. This time Kyron waved his sword at rapid speed blocking the approaching laser shots with his double-edged blade. With anguish on his now contorted face, Jackson hastily holstered his laser pistol and charged at Kyron, waving his sword in a downward thrust intending to slice Kyron's shoulder.

Kyron's quick reflexes allowed him to step to the side, just in time, and deflect Jackson's blade with his own. Jackson spun around and rapidly slashed sideways at Kyron's torso, but Kyron reacted too quickly and he again intercepted the strike, blocking Jackson's blade and producing a snap front kick to his opponent's stomach. Jackson reeled back onto the table, doubling over in pain. Kyron was trying not to kill Jackson, only to disarm him so that he could bring him before the Assembly. But Jackson was not going to give up easily.

Partially winded and now enraged, Jackson retaliated by picking up one of the padded conference chairs and heaving it with his full might towards Kyron. Kyron raised his sword and in a quick downward thrust slashed at the missile, shearing it in half, the pieces landing on the floor either side of him.

Jackson reverted to his classical 'en garde' stance ready to perform a killer lunge at Kyron's chest. This move had never failed him as a winning move in his past tournaments. But this was not a game to determine who would be awarded the trophy. This was a real life-and-death struggle. The beads of sweat were dripping from Jackson's red-faced brow. He realised now that his opponent had superior skill. This was a last-ditch attempt to finish Kyron for good.

Kyron braced himself, standing side on with his left side towards Jackson and raising his two arms, his hands clasping the handle of the upward pointing blade. Jackson stepped forward two rapid paces, leading with his right leg, and thrust. Again, Kyron blocked the attack with amazing speed, stepped in and elbowed Jackson to the face, almost breaking Jackson's nose and jerking back his head, forcing Jackson to back-pedal several paces.

Jackson slowly raised his left hand to feel his injured nose, which was now bleeding profusely. He was furious. He had never lost a fencing match before and was in shock, still wondering how a farm boy could be so skilled in martial arts. In a burst of fury Jackson ran at Kyron, thrashing wildly and lunging forward. But Kyron blocked and counter-blocked every attack with relative ease. Kyron was merely defending and almost playing with his opponent. Jackson was becoming even more infuriated as the harder he tried, the less he was succeeding in his attempt to defeat his foe.

By now Jackson had sustained several gashes to his left arm and right leg from Kyron's defensive moves. In a final attempt, Jackson made a powerful swing at Kyron's head. Kyron counter-swung to block, deliberately snapping Jackson's cutlass blade in half. Jackson staggered back, half in shock that his tempered Toledo steel sword, crafted by the best, had actually been broken without making any impression on Kyron's blade.

Realising that he was no match for Kyron, Jackson threw the rest of his damaged sword at Kyron's head and reached for the pistol at his side. But before Jackson could fully draw it from its holster, Kyron crouched on his haunches to avoid the missile and sprang at Jackson, like a leopard pouncing on its prey. He somersaulted in mid-air and landed right in front of Jackson. Kyron placed the edge of his blade on Jackson's throat and at the same time grabbed Jackson's arm, forcing him to release his grip on the handle of the pistol. Using his left hand, Kyron wrenched the pistol out of its holster and thrust the weapon under Jackson's rib cage.

"Turn around with your back to me!" ordered Kyron in an authoritative tone.

"So you can't look me in the eye to kill me? You would rather shoot me in the back, you coward," mocked Jackson.

Kyron was not perturbed.

"Jackson, we're not all like you, and besides, I would not let you take the easy way out. I want you to answer to a higher authority for your crimes. Now, turn around."

Shoving Jackson to face the wall away from him, Kyron deactivated his blade, returning it to its shortened staff size and placed it in his belt holster. He reached for the cord which had been used to restrain Torri and started to bind Jackson's hands behind his back.

Jackson could not contain himself, still amazed at what had just transpired. Although furious at being defeated he also felt fear mixed with admiration. He had to know.

"Where did you learn to fight like that? And where did you get that fancy weapon? Who or what are you?"

Kyron just smiled to himself.

"Never underestimate your opponent, Jackson, and never assume your superiority. You may learn in the near future but, for now, just be thankful that I let you live."

"What do you intend doing with me?" asked Jackson with a slight tremble in his voice, his wrists now tightly bound behind his back.

"You will be dealt with as the law sees fit. Now, come with me. I need to find Torri and you had better pray that no harm has come to her or your life won't be worth saving."

Suddenly from behind them came an aggressive female voice.

"Hold it right there, son of Ahrmon!"

Kyron swung his head around to see a female Sentinel standing at the doorway, blade drawn. Forcing Jackson to sit in a nearby chair, he turned to face the demanding figure. From the outline of her tight-fitting uniform, Kyron could see that she had the taut and muscular body of an athlete.

"Perfect timing, Khaneera," exclaimed Jackson. "Dispose of this guy and cut me loose."

Kyron was bewildered that Jackson knew the Sentinel.

"Who are you and why are you giving orders?" Kyron asked. "This man is my prisoner and I am bringing him to justice for the crimes that he has committed against humanity!"

The stranger responded quickly as she removed her helmet and shook her long fair hair loose, letting it fall over her shoulders. She had piercing steel blue eyes and a very determined look on her beautiful, yet harsh face. She spoke coldly.

"You talk about justice! Your father is the one who should have been brought to justice for the crime that he committed against my father, and for the humiliation my father suffered for being expelled from the Academy. I cannot kill Ahrmon Tyros but I can kill *you* to take my revenge. I have waited a very long time for this and I will take great pleasure in eradicating the name of Tyros forever. I am Khaneera Zarkwin, daughter of the late Khane Zarkwin, Chief of Security. Now, prepare to die!"

Kyron was shocked to hear this stranger talking about his father, Ahrmon, and the Chief of Security, Zarkwin, who had framed his father in the distant past. Until recently he had never even known about Zarkwin, yet here was Zarkwin's daughter ready to kill him. But Kyron was confused. *What crime had his father committed against Khaneera's father to want her to take revenge? Surely it was Zarkwin who was the villain? Doesn't she know the truth about what happened?*

"Wait Khaneera, you're making a mistake!" shouted Kyron.

"Quiet, Tyros, you've said enough!" exclaimed Khaneera, making a sudden leap towards Kyron, her blade aimed at his upper torso.

Kyron dived sideways, turning a cartwheel and drawing his blade simultaneously. Jackson seized the opportunity, dashing out of the room, his hands still tied behind his back.

Khaneera was on the attack and again leapt towards Kyron, who stood his ground in a rigid pose. Swords clashed again and again with Kyron using defensive moves, trying not to harm Khaneera, but to disarm her. She was an expert martial artist with strength equal to Kyron but he had also mastered the art and could counter her every move. While Khaneera was using her pent-up hate and aggression to attack her opponent, Kyron remained mentally focussed and was able to plan his strategies with better precision. He knew that to disarm Khaneera he would have to force her to drop her weapon by wounding her right arm.

The chance came when Khaneera made a killing lunge at Kyron. In that split second, Kyron somersaulted over Khaneera's head, at the same time slicing at her right arm. The razor-sharp edge cut deeply and cleanly into Khaneera's bicep. She cried out in pain, dropping her sword and grabbing the wound with her left hand. But she was not to be beaten. With quick reflexes, she crouched down, reached for the dagger in her boot with her left hand, sprung up and swung around full circle, lashing out at Kyron.

This time she was too quick for Kyron's reflexes and the dagger penetrated the left upper radial muscle of his forearm, just missing his main artery. Khaneera withdrew the dagger and Kyron staggered back two paces, wincing in pain. But Kyron quickly regained his focus, just in time to counter Khaneera's second lunge, this time aimed at his chest just above his heart. Kyron's blade intercepted Khaneera's dagger, wrenching it from her grasp. On his return strike, he placed the edge of his sword blade to the jugular vein on her soft throat. She was now in no position to attack without fatally cutting her neck on the blade.

"Kill me now. You have won," cried out Khaneera, without any sense of fear. "I am finished anyway, whether dead or alive."

"No Khaneera, I won't kill you. I want you to live and realise that you have been living a lie all these years. You are misguided in your quest. It was *your* father who framed mine for murder. Your anger and passion should be spent on saving lives, not destroying them."

"You don't know the full story. It was your father who ruined my father's career as a Sentinel. My father was expelled from the Academy when Ahrmon Tyros severed my father's hand in a duel and humiliated the family name. You will regret not killing me Kyron, for I will be back to finish what I started!" threatened Khaneera.

"I don't think so, Khaneera. Well done, Kyron," came a familiar voice from the doorway of the conference room.

It was Dakhar who had returned, marching Jackson in front of him, a laser pistol pointing at Jackson's back. Kyron's struggle to piece together his father's story was temporarily interrupted.

Dakhar spoke again, looking directly at Khaneera with contempt.

"I see you found our informer. Jackson has just admitted that Khaneera is the one who helped him in this conspiracy and the one who warned him of our coming."

"Ehrane," said Kyron, relieved to see his friend, "I've got to find Torri! Jackson sent two of his thugs to capture her!"

"Don't worry Kyron, she is safe and unharmed," replied Dakhar. "She's waiting in Jackson's office with some of my soldiers."

Kyron breathed a sigh of relief. Now he could calm himself. He had been anxious throughout this entire mission, harbouring a deep fear for Torri's safety. If any harm had come to her he would never have forgiven himself. He hid his human emotions well in the presence of others, portraying a tough exterior with a strong sense of mental control. But underneath this veneer was a very soft heart.

Dakhar passed Jackson to another of his Sentinels and gave the order for some of his soldiers to cuff Khaneera, allowing Kyron to release his hold and pick up her blade and dagger from the floor. Kyron retracted Khaneera's staff blade and handed both weapons to Dakhar. Dakhar spoke with a voice of authority.

"You won't need these where you're going. You are a fool Khaneera, blinded by your obsession for revenge. Sentinels, don't let these traitors out of your sight."

Kyron and Dakhar followed the Sentinels out of the room and headed for the door to the exit stairs near Jensen's office that led up to the rooftop. Two of Jackson's henchmen appeared out of Jensen's office door with their hands secured behind them. They were followed by one of the Sentinels holding a sword to their backs. Behind him was Torri with several other Sentinels.

"Kyron, you're alive," Torri cried out, as she rushed towards him, her words mixed with joy and relief. But, as she went to embrace him she noticed the blood stain on his uniform.

"You've been wounded," she exclaimed, stepping back with a worried expression in her eyes.

"Yes," replied Kyron, holding his injured arm. "But it's not as bad as it looks and I've stopped the bleeding. I'm so happy to see you safe and unharmed Torri. I was worried that Jackson's thugs would catch up with you."

"No," said Torri still anxious about Kyron's wound, "I managed to contact Captain Dakhar on my collar communicator and he was able to intercept the two henchmen before they reached me."

"Thank you Ehrane, I owe you a debt of gratitude," said Kyron sincerely.

"No, I thank *you*, Kyron," said Ehrane. "I owe you much more for apprehending Jackson and his accomplice, Khaneera, and for putting an end to this conspiracy. You have saved the planet and the Sentinels from possible destruction."

Dakhar tapped the communicator on his collar.

"Report your status, soldiers!"

The same message came through, floor by floor.

"All clear and secured sir!"

"Return to the spacecraft with your captives, secure them in the holding cells and reassemble in the main hall at 17.00 hours. We will meet you there. Over and out," commanded Dakhar.

"Lance Corporal," Dakhar ordered, pointing his outstretched hand at Jackson, "Escort Jensen junior and his henchmen to the craft."

Eyeing Khaneera sharply, he gave another direct order in a more harsh tone.

"And as for this traitor, place her in the high security cell."

Just before they marched off, Dakhar raised his hand for them to wait.

"Just a minute, Lance Corporal!"

Dakhar strode up to Khaneera and stood facing her.

"You have breached the Code of Honour, disgraced your uniform and the regiment, and brought shame on your mother's family. You will be brought before the Senate to answer to the charges of treason and the attempted murder of Cadet Shield. I'll take your robe as well as your pledge ring for you will not need them again."

There was a look of hatred on Khaneera's face as she stared Dakhar in the eye.

"I will return to finish what I started!" she burst out, looking in Kyron's direction. "And you, Tyros, will pay for your father's crime against mine!"

She turned to face Dakhar again.

"This is not the end for me, but it will be the beginning of the end for the Sentinels." Without warning, she spat in Dakhar's face.

"Gag her Corporal, so she doesn't try that again on anyone else," said Dakhar wiping his face with a small maroon cloth he retrieved from his sleeve pocket. He then proceeded to detach Khaneera's robe.

She was still struggling while Dakhar slid the pledge ring from her finger. He placed all her belongings into the black leather satchel that the Lance Corporal was carrying and sealed the cover.

"I cannot bear you in my presence any longer," Dakhar said with disgust. "Take her away soldier!"

"Yes, Captain!" The Lance Corporal saluted Dakhar, who reciprocated. The Corporal then ordered the captives to start marching.

Kyron could sense that Dakhar had mixed feelings about the events that had just taken place. The Captain was embarrassed that one of his trusted soldiers had shamed the visitors to Earth, and worried that this could jeopardise the proposed future peace treaty with the Federation of Planets. He was also concerned that he had placed his new-found friend in grave danger from one of his own Sentinels.

Before Dakhar could say anything, Kyron placed a hand on his shoulder and spoke his mind.

"Do not be too concerned about what has happened, my friend. You and your regiment have shown that you are sincere in saving Earth and becoming close allies. And I will support you in your efforts to secure the Assembly's trust in an alliance that will see Earth join the Federation of Planets."

Dakhar placed his hand on Kyron's as it rested on his shoulder.

"Thank you my friend for your words of comfort. You are worthy of your heritage both in valour and honour. You are a true Sentinel. Your father would be proud of you."

"And your father of you also," replied Kyron.

Feeling more relieved, Dakhar turned to Torri and Kyron.

"Shall we join the others and make plans for our next move?" he asked, smiling warmly.

THE DECISION

O N board the spacecraft, Kyron contacted Miss Blake to advise that Jackson and his men were in custody and secured in the holding cells. In the Great Hall, the regiment of Sentinels assembled and Captain Dakhar began to address them, commencing with the traditional Sentinel salute.

"Soldiers, you have done well today and I am again proud of you all. You have managed to destroy a conspiracy that could have destroyed this planet with universal repercussions. You have also managed to remain anonymous throughout to the citizens of this planet, avoiding alarm and panic. Our brothers-in-arms on Terra Iota have also been successful in quelling the threat.

"Tomorrow we are to visit the Terranians' World Assembly and prepare the way for our Tzuracian Council of Elders to negotiate a treaty and invite the planet, Terra Major, into the Federation of the Planets. Thank you again for your loyalty, dedication and commitment."

"To the Regiment!" Dakhar saluted again.

The soldiers returned the war cry, saluting in unison. Lieutenant Kruzak then gave the dismissal command and the unit disbanded.

Dakhar turned to Kyron and, noticing his wound, raised an eyebrow in concern.

"Come with me, Kyron. I want our healers to look at that wound and treat it before you two turn in for the night."

Kyron and Torri were taken by Dakhar to the medic bay which was on another level of the craft. Kyron surveyed the room, subconsciously comparing it with the medical facilities on Earth. The room was approximately twice the size of the conference room where Dakhar had taken them when they first boarded the craft. It was illuminated with white light emanating from the whole floor, the walls and the ceiling, yet it was not harsh on the eyes. Several flat, sheeted tables were positioned along two of the walls with control panels on overhead canopies above each table. Two more tables, with the control panels affixed to one end, stood in the middle of the floor.

On the other walls there were strange looking machines of different shapes and sizes, some positioned on the floor and others on shelves. They were constructed of a white material with no cables or tubes in sight. A subtle fragrance, like a mixture of orange blossom and fresh summer rain, had been noticeable when they first entered the room. This was accompanied by unusual, but pleasant, soft musical sounds. Kyron was starting to feel better already and had almost forgotten about his flesh wound.

"Come this way, Cadet Shield, and we will have a look at you."

Kyron, being too pre-occupied with all the new things, was somewhat surprised by the synthesised tones of a strange, alien voice somewhere close behind him. He quickly turned his head to the right to identify the figure standing close by.

"I am Jarkor, from Armonus, the healing planet. I will be your attending healer or in your world, physician."

Jarkor had a striking appearance, unlike the Tzuracians. He was devoid of hair on his entire bulb-shaped head. His skin was smooth with a pink tinge and his eyes were emerald green. His ears were also a strange shape, more like the small gills of a fish sculpted into the side of his head. He appeared to be exceptionally healthy and spoke with an articulate, mellow tone. His dark-green tunic fitted loosely over flared trousers and his matching boots were made of a soft suede-like material that made no sound when he walked.

As Jarkor led Kyron to one of the tables in the centre of the room with Torri close by his side, Dakhar excused himself.

"I will be back shortly. I leave you in good hands," he said confidently.

"Please lie on the table Kyron, while I perform a diagnostic," requested Jarkor, waving his hand in the direction of the table.

Kyron removed his blue cape and handed it to Torri, who gave him a faint, reassuring smile as she folded the cape over her arm.

No sooner had Kyron made himself comfortable on the table, than Jarkor waved his right hand over the controls at the end of the table. Much to Kyron's surprise, several luminous, wide red bands of light encompassed the table, sweeping inches from his still body. These bands of light were accompanied by a soft low hum. A green tinged hologram of Kyron's musculoskeletal system instantly appeared above the rings and rotated slowly clockwise. The wound was clearly visible on the hologram, showing up as a dark red mark on the left arm. Text appeared beside the hologram, written in alien symbols and strange pictures. The whole experience lasted several seconds and then the machine instantly switched off.

"The diagnosis is complete, Kyron," Jarkor announced in a confident tone. "The image confirms that you have a superficial injury to the kordin zentay, or in your Terranian terms, the brachioradialis muscle. There is no injury to the artery or vein, no damage to any nerves and no infection. You may sit up and remove your tunic above your waist and we will commence the surgical regeneration."

As Kyron sat upright on the table, following the directions of the physician, Torri moved closer to help him out of his jacket.

"Are you alright?" she said quietly, sounding concerned.

"Yes, fine," responded Kyron, now struggling with Torri's help to slide his injured arm out of the partially bloodied sleeve of his regimental jacket. "But how are *you* coping, sweetheart?"

"I'm okay," she whispered, while slightly nodding her head.

"Torri, can I please ask you to stand back from the table while I perform this operation?" Jarkor asked politely.

"Yes, of course," she replied, quickly moving away.

The instrument Jarkor had retrieved from above the table, connected by white tubing to the ceiling, resembled a slim torch.

"Don't worry, Kyron," Jarkor said, reassuringly. "You will feel no pain, only a tingling sensation. Just sit still and this will only take a moment."

The instrument targeted the wound with a mauve laser beam, and the physician was right. Kyron felt no pain. In a matter of minutes the operation was completed without anaesthetic or loss of blood. Where there had been a reasonable-sized gash on Kyron's upper arm, there was now no mark or scar. Kyron was astounded at the remarkable healing power of this instrument. He started to test out his rapidly recovered arm by twisting and weaving it as if wielding an invisible sword. His arm felt normal, as if there had been no injury.

Before Kyron could utter a word, Jarkor explained the mystery behind this technology.

"This surgical equipment uses laser technology powered by Xytrinium. When the Xytrinium laser fuses with the same substance in your DNA, it sets off a regeneration process by exciting the cells containing the blue crystal. Wounds, whether to bones or muscle tissue, heal one hundred times faster in Sentinels. Added to this is an anaesthetic, antiseptic light and high-pitched sound frequency that numbs and cleans the wound."

"Thank you Jarkor," said Kyron. "I'm very impressed and amazed at this advanced technology."

Dakhar, who had just returned, interjected.

"Well Kyron, we have much to teach you Terranians if you join the Federation. We can talk more on this matter later. It's time to get you two back to your quarters."

They departed from the medic bay and on the way to their quarters, Kyron asked Dakhar to explain how Khaneera had gone undetected amongst the Sentinels and how she became part of the conspiracy.

"Kyron, I was just as surprised as you were when she revealed her true bloodline, but I now understand how she became a trusted soldier in our ranks. Information has been passed to me through those that knew my father and it relates to the story of Zarkwin and Khaneera's mother, Syrina.

"Syrina was a Sentinel in the regiment at the time your father was serving and she was betrothed to Khane Zarkwin. When Zarkwin was exposed as a traitor, Syrina could not endure the shame so she resigned and went to live on the planet Urgellan. There, after a very short courtship, she met and married an Urgellan citizen of nobility and together they raised a child. The child, Khaneera, carried her mother's Sentinel DNA and, when she came of age, she was recruited to the Academy on Tzurac to become a Sentinel.

"It was assumed that Khaneera was the daughter of Syrina and her new husband. But it now appears that Syrina was with child before she left Tzurac, Zarkwin being the child's real father. Syrina must have told Khaneera about Zarkwin, how he lost his hand in a fight with your father, and how he was relegated from the Sentinels. Khaneera was inducted into the regiment in her mother's maiden name of Penzark and no-one suspected her true bloodline. But she was full of resentment and she secretly vowed to destroy the Sentinels and avenge those who had mistreated her father.

"Khaneera volunteered for this mission the moment she found out that Captain Ahrmon Tyros had a son who was living on Earth. And she learned this after I informed the regiment of your existence following our hologram communication. While travelling to Earth, she secretly intercepted transmissions between Jackson Jensen and Terra Iota. Immediately, she realised she had an ally and made a pact with Jackson. If she helped him in his quest for power, then in return, he would supply her with the Xytrinium needed to destroy the Sentinels. It turns out that they both had reasons for disposing of you, Kyron, because you were getting in Jackson's way."

As the pieces of Khaneera's puzzle fell into place, the trio arrived back at Kyron and Torri's quarters.

"Remember," said Dakhar. "Ask the servery in your quarters for anything you desire to eat or drink and it will supply your needs. I have also arranged for a new regimental uniform to be brought to your quarters in the morning Kyron."

"Thank you for everything Ehrane. So, until the morning then, I will bid you good night."

Kyron signed off with the respectful salute which Dakhar returned before stepping forward to offer Kyron the Tzuracian handshake of friendship.

"Good night, Captain," said Torri. "Thank you again for coming to my rescue in time."

"You are welcome, my lady," responded Dakhar with a warm smile. "Sleep well. I will see you both in the conference room tomorrow morning at 07.00 hours."

As soon as they were inside their quarters, Torri began firing questions at Kyron.

"What's this about you being the owner of MERIC? And what decision is Captain Dakhar talking about that he wants you to tell him tomorrow? I have so much to ask, Kyron."

"Whoa, slow down Torri," responded Kyron raising his arms in protest and reeling back. "Give me a chance and I'll explain everything. But first I want you to sit down and I'll get us both some dinner and a drink."

Kyron headed for the servery and soon returned with a tray with two plates of food and two crystal glasses filled with a purple liquid.

"Here, taste this, Torri," he said handing her a glass. "This is one of the Tzuracian herbal mixtures used for a calming effect and for rejuvenation. After what we have just experienced it should have just the right effect."

"Mmm! That tastes delicious Kyron. Thank you," Torri replied. She ruffled the cushions of her chair to find a more comfortable position, just as a cat does when it circles and gently pummels a couch with its paws.

"You have my undivided attention," said Torri staring at Kyron with a serious expression, while devouring a morsel of food taken from her plate. Now that he had the time, Kyron began to tell Torri the events that had taken place over the last two days.

"Torri, I was told by Miss Blake at the funeral service that Samuel Jensen had bequeathed the Company and all his assets to me in his last legal Will and Testament. Samuel Jensen believed that he couldn't trust Jackson and felt that I was the son he wished he had, who followed in his moral footsteps for the good of mankind."

Kyron paused and took a sip of his drink, allowing Torri a moment to digest what she was hearing.

"I was just as surprised as you, Torri, and I'm finding the news hard to accept. According to Miss Blake, when Jackson found this out, he became angry and obsessed to dispose of what stood between him and total power."

Kyron paused again, placing his face in both his cupped hands.

"I feel torn between different loyalties, Torri, and I'm finding it hard to make a decision that would have a happy ending to please everyone with whom I'm close. I love you Torri and want to stay with you for the rest of my life, to raise a family and stay on Earth. I want to fulfil the wishes of Samuel Jensen for the sake of the Company. I know that I was born a Sentinel and pledged to help protect Earth and the other planets of the universe and I want to uphold my father's reputation to reinstate his name in the ranks of the regiment."

Torri responded in a gentle voice.

"I have a suggestion Kyron that may help you resolve this problem and satisfy all your loyalties."

Kyron raised his head to listen with keen interest as Torri continued.

"You know that I love you and feel the same way about you staying with me. Well, why not stay here on Earth as both the Head of MERIC and as a Sentinel to ensure that the blue crystal is used for the betterment of mankind as well as to protect it from being used for any destructive purpose? If our children inherit the Sentinel DNA you will be able to instruct them in the ways of a Sentinel warrior while they are growing up here on Earth. And when they are old enough you can then return to your true home and continue serving in the regiment. I am only human, Kyron, and I have accepted that you will outlive me. I think that we should make the most of our time together and enjoy our family."

"Torri, that sounds very sensible and practical," Kyron responded after a moment of contemplation. Then, becoming more emotional, he added, "But I never want to lose you."

"Well, you never know, Kyron, what they may discover in another fifty years. Maybe they'll find a way of prolonging human life with the blue crystal."

Kyron pondered for a short time before responding.

"Yes, I very much hope this will happen. Another good reason for staying here is that we would have more time to spend with my mother and for her to see the grandchildren. You know, she deserves to learn about my father's past, where he came from and the legacy that he's passed on to me. She needs to know after all these years the truth that my father kept from her for her own safety."

Without saying anything more and both being deep in thought, contemplating what the future might hold for them, Kyron and Torri rose from their chairs and prepared for bed.

As they lay close to each other, Kyron turned to face Torri and whispered, "Thank you, Torri, for being so understanding and suggesting a compromise. I will tell Dakhar in the morning about your suggestion."

They embraced like they never wanted to let go and kissed passionately. Neither needed to say another word and, eventually, they fell asleep in each other's arms.

***

The next morning Kyron and Torri rendezvoused with Captain Dakhar in the conference room as planned. Kyron was dressed in his MERIC day uniform, which made for a dramatic change in appearance from his regimental battle dress.

"Good morning Kyron, good morning Torri," said Dakhar with an optimistic greeting. "I hope you both slept well."

"Yes, Captain," replied Torri in a similar tone. "We slept very well after resolving a few concerns about Kyron's future."

Dakhar responded quickly to Torri's statement.

"Does that mean you have something to tell me Kyron?"

"Yes Ehrane, I do have a proposal which I think will satisfy both our needs."

Dakhar focussed on Kyron's eyes.

"Go on my friend, I'm listening."

After Kyron explained their proposal, Dakhar thought for some time before answering. He leaned back in his chair, looked up to the ceiling with his eyes wide open and ran the fingers of both hands through his untamed blonde hair several times, as if brushing it back. His hands came to rest under his chin with his elbows leaning on the table for support and eventually he spoke in a somewhat sad tone.

"Actually, I think that this is a very wise decision and I support it. But I would like some day to have Torri come to Tzurac to see your other world Kyron. In the meantime you will be given the official title as the Tzuracian Ambassador for Terra Major and act as the formal host for Tzurac's visiting dignitaries. How does that sound for you both?"

Kyron was elated and looking at Torri's expression; she was also very happy with the decision.

"I humbly accept the role and responsibility, Ehrane, and will be honoured to fulfil the position. Thank you my friend," replied Kyron, while holding out his arm to Dakhar.

The agreement was sealed with a Sentinel handshake. Then Dakhar patted Kyron on the shoulder.

"Now, you both must go to the MERIC Building and make your arrangements," he said. "And take the security officer's private shuttle."

"Yes, alright," agreed Kyron. "We'll meet back here at 11.00 hours. I'll ask Miss Blake to contact our Liaison Officer at the World Assembly and have them make the formal arrangements for our visit."

"Very well, Kyron, good luck and take care," said Dakhar sincerely. "I'll see you soon and may the Ancients' spirits be with you."

When Kyron and Torri returned to the MERIC Building they parted, Torri going off to the project team and Kyron to see Miss Blake.

"Kyron, you're alright!" exclaimed Miss Blake with a big reassuring grin on her face and outstretched arms. She hugged Kyron like he was one of the family and asked if he would like some tea.

"Yes, I'm alright, thank you Miss Blake and, yes, some tea would be nice. Make a cup for yourself as well and come into Mr Jensen's office. Bring your transcorder. We need to sit down and discuss a few things and sort out future arrangements."

Miss Blake departed and soon returned with a tray of refreshments, setting it down on the desk and taking a seat. Kyron spoke in an articulate manner as he started to list his immediate requirements.

"Now Miss Blake, here is what I need you to arrange very quickly."

She raised the transcorder in her hands and started to rapidly tap the illuminated buttons in a short-hand code.

"First of all, I want you to assemble all the staff in the Main Hall at 10.00 hours so that I may address them personally to tell them about my informal appointment in the new position as Head of the Company. Please contact the legal firm to make an appointment in one week's time to read the Will of Samuel Jensen. That should allow you time, Miss Blake, to contact those concerned to be at this meeting as you already know the beneficiaries of Mr Jensen's estate. It probably sounds very presumptuous of me to start acting as if I am the new Head of MERIC, but I think that someone has to take control to keep things running. We can worry about anyone contesting the Will later, but I'm sure that Mr Jensen would approve of the current arrangements until things have been formalised. What do you think, Miss Blake?"

"I agree most definitely Kyron, or should I address you now as Mr Shield?"

"You'll do no such thing, Miss Blake. I am still the same person, Kyron, as you have always known and this does not change our status in the least. I would feel most alienated if you started addressing me formally. Alright, Miss Blake?"

"Yes, Kyron, but please call me Lauren."

"Done! Now, Lauren, I also want you to arrange for me to talk to our World Assembly liaison officer this afternoon so he can arrange for Captain Dakhar, myself, and our captives to approach the Assembly. After that I need you to reinstate the Committee members that Jackson fired and send my apologies for Jackson's irresponsible actions. Can you also please sort out the new security officers when they arrive and inform them of their responsibilities? Then set up a meeting with your father for next week to discuss our future requirements for transporting the mined minerals and metals from Terra Iota."

Miss Blake was busy operating the transcorder when Kyron spoke again.

"Now for you, Lauren."

Miss Blake was concerned; her face momentarily turning pale as if she thought her future with the Company may come to an end. Kyron patted her on the hand before he spoke.

"Relax Lauren, no need to look so worried. Put down the transcorder and have a sip of tea."

Her hand was shaking as she slowly raised the cup to her lips and hesitantly sipped a small amount of the tea, before returning her cup to the saucer still with an unsteady hand.

"I have a proposition for you." Kyron paused a moment to allow Miss Blake to compose herself and settle her anxiety.

"Would you be my Assistant Manager to run things in my absence? You know more than anyone else about how Samuel Jensen ran this Company. You will be well compensated for this responsibility."

The look on Miss Blake's face was one of complete surprise and shock. For a little time she was speechless. Then, she began to respond in a slightly trembling voice.

"I, ah," she stammered and slowly, but humbly spoke after containing her composure, "I'm very flattered Kyron that you have so much trust and faith in my abilities. I would be most happy to accept your kind offer and do all in my power to protect the Company."

"Thank you Lauren. I knew I could rely on you. You will need to have a personal assistant of course to do all the administrative duties and I will leave it up to you to choose someone. I'll be away for a couple of days and there will be many other times in the near future that you'll need to mind the Company, but I have every confidence in you. Now let's get cracking shall we, first with that assembly for the staff."

"One question if I may, Kyron," she said timidly.

"Yes, sorry, Lauren, I forgot to ask if you had any questions."

"Who is that military person, Captain Dakhar? And where does he come from?"

"You will find out soon, but I cannot tell you just yet."

An hour later, Kyron was standing on the raised platform addressing the staff in the Main Hall through the PA system.

"Thank you all for being here. As you are aware, the Company has unfortunately lost a great man with a great vision, a man we came to love as our boss and who I felt was more like a father to me. His son, Jackson, has been taken into custody and is being brought to trial for contributing to his father's death, and conspiring to breach international law by not declaring a new mineral the Company had recently discovered on Terra Iota. You will hear more about this extraordinary mineral in the very near future. Jackson is also being charged with other criminal offences. I need to attend the World Assembly to testify in this matter as well as report to them about the new mineral discovery.

"I have also been informed, much to my surprise, that Samuel Jensen's Will places me in ownership of the Company. In the meantime, in my absence, I have asked Miss Blake, and she has humbly accepted, to be my Assistant Manager because of her knowledge and long-term dedication. So, I hope all of you will still stay with the Company and help me to continue the legacy of Samuel Jensen. Thank you for your time and I wish you well in the Company."

The crowd, with pleased expressions on their faces, all applauded Kyron as he climbed down from the dais. As they slowly dispersed back to their workstations, Kyron made his way to Torri in the crowd and together they returned to the project unit. On arrival, both Whitey and Guy Simmons came over and couldn't wait to talk to Kyron.

"Man," said Whitey, "you have turned out to be a real hero. Saved Torri, captured the villain and put in charge of the Company. "

"Yes, I'm also very impressed Kyron," chipped in Simmons.

"Now hang on you guys, you would have done the same if you happened to be in the wrong place at the wrong time, wouldn't you?"

"Oh yes, of course we would have," said Whitey half-joking, while Simmons nodded his head in agreement.

"Besides, I had a helping hand from Captain Dakhar and his soldiers," Kyron humbly replied.

"What soldiers and who's Captain Dakhar?" asked Whitey seriously. "Was he that caped crusader who was with you at the Crematorium?"

"Trust me, Whitey, there were soldiers, and yes that was Captain Dakhar," stressed Kyron. "And you may get to see them from time to time in the near future."

Whitey raised his eyebrows with an expression of half disbelief on his face when Torri chipped in.

"Yes Whitey, there were soldiers; in fact the Captain of these soldiers saved my life."

Whitey clearly didn't believe this.

"No, come on Torri, is that true, or are you joking?"

"Whitey, have I ever lied to you before?"

"No, Torri, you're the most honest person I know. I do believe you. It's just that something like this has never happened before."

Kyron interjected.

"Well enough said about this, you will learn more Whitey, and so will you, Guy, as the time progresses. I have to go now, so I'll leave

Torri to manage the project team while I'm away. Please give her as much support as you can. After all, she has been through quite a lot in the past two days."

"Yes, Kyron you can depend on us," said Whitey looking sternly at Simmons for reassurance. "We'll look after her, right Simmo?"

Simmons just nodded again, letting Whitey do the talking.

"Thank you men," responded Kyron as he grabbed Torri by the hand and led her to his office to say his goodbyes.

"I should return within the week, Torri, all going well. Think you can manage this time without me, without getting into trouble?" said Kyron in good humour.

Torri smiled, "Yes, I'll be alright, now that I know I have my very own hero to get me out of trouble when I need him."

They laughed and embraced.

"Oh," said Torri, holding out her hand to Kyron, "Here's the star brooch that Captain Dakhar lent me. Can you please return it to him and thank him again for me?"

Kyron took the brooch, grinning warmly. They embraced again for a fleeting moment, before Kyron headed for the door.

THE ASSEMBLY

THE following morning Captain Dakhar, Kyron, and ten Sentinels escorted Jackson and his thugs to the World Assembly building, a magnificent domed building that had served as a centre of law and order for decades. They were greeted by Harper and led immediately into a huge assembly hall that was filled with three hundred members from all nations. The sight of the Sentinels leading the restrained security officers caused quite a stir amongst the members.

At precisely 10.00 hours, Kyron and Dakhar were called to the podium to speak to the assembled crowd while the restrained prisoners remained standing at the side of the room, under close guard. Kyron took his seat behind the dais and Dakhar stood facing the members. A hush fell over the gallery, all members now focussed keenly on this strangely dressed figure. Dakhar spoke first.

"Members of the Assembly, thank you for allowing me to talk to you this morning. This is an historic moment that you will all remember. It will be recorded in your history for future generations to reflect on and appreciate."

The members were now even more intrigued and mumblings of speculation were bandied in low tones throughout the ranks. Dakhar continued.

"I stand here before you in this unusual attire and you are most likely wondering who I am and why I am here. I am not from your planet, but from the planet Tzurac, one of six planets in the Grekadian Domain, three hundred light years from your planet. I am a Captain in the Tzuracian army of Sentinels and the Sentinels are the protectors of planets that contain a valuable resource known as Xytrinium. Let me explain to put your minds at rest.

"While mining for your much-needed ores and minerals, the people of your planet recently discovered a new energy source on Terra Iota. If it is controlled and properly administered, this new substance will revolutionise the way you currently apply your technology and services. However, if this resource is not controlled, it will most assuredly destroy your planet as well as other planets in the universe. The Mining Engineering Resource Industry Company, MERIC, the company that discovered this powerful resource, is now officially reporting this find under your International Law.

"Negotiations with the Assembly will need to be arranged with the new head of the company, Mr Kyron Shield, who is seated behind me."

Dakhar turned and with a friendly gesture of his hand indicated MERIC's new CEO.

"If it were not for this gentleman, your planet would have been held to ransom by that conspirator standing over there under guard, Mr Jackson Bartholomew Jensen, son of the late Samuel Jensen."

With outstretched arm, Dakhar pointed directly at Jackson.

Captain Dakhar's address was interrupted by a deafening outburst from the members, shocked by the news. Jackson's jaw was also agape with disbelief. He was astounded to hear of the Sentinels' role in the Universe, realising all too late the magnitude of what he was up against. Kyron's words, "Never underestimate your opponent," resounded in his mind.

Jackson was now beginning to wonder whether Kyron was also a Tzuracian Sentinel. His mind replayed the events that had occurred in the MERIC Building on the day of his father's funeral. *Kyron had been dressed in a similar uniform to Dakhar. Kyron had also wielded the same weapon as the other Sentinels. And he had fought in a superior style. But how could this be?* Jackson was intrigued by the possibility.

It was almost five minutes before the members composed themselves and the noise subsided, allowing Captain Dakhar to continue.

"Two thousand five hundred years ago in your Earth time, the Tzuracians discovered this valuable resource on Tzurac. A two-hundred-year interplanetary war over possession of the Xytrinium ensued. Finally, after much suffering and loss of lives, a peace treaty was signed that established the Federation of Planets. It was agreed that Tzurac would share their resource with the other planets, under strict conditions as part of a trade arrangement and that this energy source would never be used as a weapon. What I am proposing is for Terra Major to join the Federation of Planets and avoid the struggle that my people suffered in the past.

"Through trade arrangements with your planet, we can show you how to use this substance, not just as a new source of energy, but for medicines and other industrial applications which will eventually eradicate your diseases and pollution, leading to a clean, healthy, habitable planet with advanced technology.

"I ask the Assembly, in the very near future, to welcome ambassadors from the Tzuracian Council of Elders to discuss an alliance with the Federation of Planets. I will let you debate this offer and when you are ready to contact me, please let Mr Shield know and he will communicate your decision. Be advised that Tzuracians will be monitoring your planet in the meantime to ensure that this new found Xytrinium is not used for destructive purposes.

"I should mention that there are still marauders out there in the galaxies hunting for this valuable material. And when they hear that Terra Major has access to it they will not hesitate to attack your transport ships and murder your crews. I am not attempting to threaten or frighten you in any way, merely to warn you of the potential seriousness and very real danger. I think that I have said enough for now for all of you to think about your future and that of Terra Major. I will now let Mr Kyron Shield address the members. Mr Shield's father was also a Tzuracian Sentinel, a fact that Mr Shield has only recently become aware of. Raised as an Earthling, he has allegiances to both of our planets, Terra Major and Tzurac and has proved himself worthy to hold the position as an ambassador to liaise between our races."

The members of the Assembly as well as Jensen were in a mild fluster after Dakhar finished. It was so much to digest. The speaker of the Assembly struck his electronic hammer several times and the ear-piercing sound resonated throughout the hall. Both Kyron and

Dakhar had to cup their highly sensitive ears to prevent their eardrums from being perforated.

"Silence in the hall! Silence, members of the Assembly!" shouted an elderly silver-haired figure clothed in a white robe and seated overlooking the dais.

The excitement subsided once more.

"You may proceed, Mr Shield," said the Speaker of the Assembly while motioning with a wave of his hand for Kyron to come forth.

Kyron began.

"Members of the Assembly, before I present my case, I would like you all to thank Captain Dakhar and his regiment for his much-needed help in capturing the culprit behind this conspiracy and for his kind offer to welcome Earth into the Federation of Planets. I have personally witnessed the sincerity of the Tzuracians and the wondrous gift that they have to offer and I urge you all to accept the hand of friendship that they extend to our planet."

His comments drew a spontaneous and lengthy outburst of applause and acknowledgement from the members of the Assembly. Finally, the clapping ceased and the members settled themselves.

"I am presenting before you today the conspirator and his followers for you to decide what punishment is warranted for their crimes. I have brought with me evidence which clearly exposes this man, Jackson Jensen, for treason in his attempts to use this new-found powerful resource, Xytrinium, to wield power over Earth for his own selfish gains. I also have evidence of his attempts on my life, the murder of his father, Samuel Jensen, and the kidnapping of one of his father's employees, my fiancée, Torri Madison."

In turn, Kyron submitted the communication transcripts between Jackson Jensen and the engineer Don Carson on Terra Iota; the transcripts of the confessions of Jackson's security officers, recorded transcripts of the security officer who had attempted to kill Kyron on board the spacecraft travelling to Terra Iota, the visual security recording of the second attempt on Kyron's life on the ore transporter on his return voyage to Earth; the recording of Jackson's boastings about his father's death; and the names of the staff who witnessed the kidnapping of Torri at the crematorium.

By the time Kyron had finished presenting all the evidence,

Jackson's facial expression had turned cold. He glared at Kyron with dark piercing eyes and struggled to escape the hand restraints, desperate to take revenge.

The Speaker of the Assembly spoke out.

"Members of the Assembly, you have heard and seen evidence relating to crimes that have been committed by Jackson Jensen. He has voluntarily, and unknowingly, confessed to the murder of his father and to the conspiracy that breaches our international laws. He is a dangerous liability and I propose to take a vote on the appropriate punishment for these crimes. I am in favour of life imprisonment for Jackson Jensen, as this will give him years to reflect on his misconduct and his disrespect for human life. Executing him would be too kind. As for the security officers, they also should be incarcerated, but for a lesser time, since they were following direct orders from their employer, Jackson Jensen. Does anyone oppose this sentence?"

No-one stirred, except Jackson.

"You are all fools!" he yelled out, "and not worthy of the powers bestowed upon you!"

"Silence Jensen!" ordered the Speaker of the Assembly, "or we'll silence you!"

The Speaker continued his announcement.

"Then record these deliberations in the transcripts and take the prisoners to their cells."

As the prisoners were being taken away by the Sentinels and Marshals, Jackson suddenly turned in the direction of Kyron and cried out in a hateful tone.

"This is not the end, Kyron! I swear we will cross swords again!"

Captain Dakhar spoke again to the members of the Assembly.

"Members, I thank you for welcoming us to your citadel and for listening to what I had to say. I look forward to working with you in the near future and I hope that we will be friends with the citizens of your planet. I will leave in peace and return to my planet bearing good news. Farewell, and may the spirits of the Ancients bring you good fortune and health in restoring your planet with the new-found resource."

Dakhar saluted the members, turned, gave an order to the Sentinels who had returned to the hall, and strode briskly towards the exit with Kyron following. As Captain Dakhar and Kyron departed, there was feverish excitement in the Assembly. The crowd marvelled at the presence of aliens on Earth and the discovery of the new substance, Xytrinium, that could change the future of Terra Major.

As soon as Dakhar and Kyron were back on board the cloaked craft, the thrusters were activated in stealth mode and the craft was soon travelling to the MERIC Building. Dakhar suggested to Kyron that he replace the Sentinels on Terra Iota with newly-recruited security officers to continue guarding the mine and overseeing the security of the transportation of the precious resource. Kyron agreed.

Dakhar also explained to Kyron what the symbols on his father's ring represented and instructed him on how to use the different functions, of which there were many, including how to send hologram transmissions. One of the symbols, when depressed, gave access in the form of a hologram to the Library of Tzurac, including all the history and literature since civilisation began on the planet. It also projected images of Kyron's father, Ahrmon, at different stages of his life. Kyron was fascinated as well as overwhelmed and vowed to Dakhar that he would study everything there was to learn about his heritage and his family.

"Remember, Kyron," said Dakhar, "I will always be your friend and you can contact me at any time if you need me. I respect your decision to remain for a while on this planet, but I also look forward to you coming to Tzurac. There are so many things I need to show and tell you about your father, Captain Tyros. My father told me much about him, and you are so much like your father. I hope you and Torri have a happy life together. With any luck, I may soon return to Terra Major as an escort for the dignitaries from the Council of Elders. In the meantime, you must continue your training in the disciplines of martial arts for you will always need them."

With nothing more to say, Dakhar fell silent with sadness in his eyes.

"Thank you Ehrane," responded Kyron. "You have become a very good friend and I thank you for coming to my aid and that of Earth's. I will miss you, but I will stay in touch and, when it is time, I will return to the home of my forefathers."

Kyron and Dakhar clasped their right arms together in the way of the Tzuracian warrior, the gesture acting as a farewell, a thank-you and a confirmation of their friendship.

The craft arrived back at the MERIC Building and Kyron, after collecting his luggage, was soon ready to disembark.

"Wait a moment Kyron, I have something for you," said Dakhar handing Kyron a new Sentinel regimental dress uniform along with his father's robe which he had worn with pride on the day they captured Jackson.

"Now that you are formally a cadet in the regiment and our official Ambassador you will need this to receive our representatives on their visits to Earth. Your father would be very proud of you, Kyron Tyros."

"I have something for you too, Ehrane." Kyron reached into his jacket pocket and produced the star brooch. "Torri asked me to return this to you and to thank you again for saving her from Jackson's thugs."

Dakhar raised his right arm and gestured with his hand to stop the offer.

"Thank you, Kyron, but you may tell Torri that she can keep and wear the star brooch to remind her of the Tzuracian Sentinels."

Kyron saluted Captain Dakhar as a thank-you for all that the Sentinels had done and as a mark of respect and, with a final Sentinel hand shake, Kyron departed from the craft.

www.ingramcontent.com/pod-product-compliance
Lightning Source LLC
Chambersburg PA
CBHW030422120726
47903CB00003B/761

9 780987 124357